# PE[...]

"A capable pro who has been there."
*Cleveland Plain Dealer*

"[Has] a crime-writer's sharp eye
and a novelist's warm heart."
Nicholas Pileggi, author of *Casino*

"Peg Tyre knows her cops, perps
and plenty more about life."
*New York Newsday*

# IN THE MIDNIGHT HOUR

"Gritty . . . Engrossing . . . Fast-paced . . .
Darkly humorous . . .
A well-written story about tough lives"
*West Coast Review of Books*

"Tyre hasn't lost her unerring eye for the
kind of characters that populate
a cop reporter's world."
*Detroit Free Press*

"Realistic settings, likable main characters
and fast action . . . A rousing climax."
*Publishers Weekly*

"This book has it all."
Sharon K. Penman, author of *The Reckoning*

*Other Avon Books by*
**Peg Tyre**

STRANGERS IN THE NIGHT

Avon Books are available at special quantity discounts for bulk purchases for sales promotions, premiums, fund raising or educational use. Special books, or book excerpts, can also be created to fit specific needs.

For details write or telephone the office of the Director of Special Markets, Avon Books, Dept. FP, 1350 Avenue of the Americas, New York, New York 10019, 1-800-238-0658.

# IN THE MIDNIGHT HOUR

## PEG TYRE

AVON BOOKS  NEW YORK

VISIT OUR WEBSITE AT
http://AvonBooks.com

AVON BOOKS
A division of
The Hearst Corporation
1350 Avenue of the Americas
New York, New York 10019

Copyright © 1995 by Peg Tyre
Published by arrangement with Crown Publishers, Inc.
Library of Congress Catalog Card Number: 95-2001
ISBN: 0-380-72811-7

All rights reserved, which includes the right to reproduce this book or
portions thereof in any form whatsoever except as provided by the U.S.
Copyright Law. For information address Crown Publishers, Inc., 201 East
50th Street, New York, New York 10022.

First Avon Books Printing: November 1996

AVON TRADEMARK REG. U.S. PAT. OFF. AND IN OTHER COUNTRIES, MARCA
REGISTRADA, HECHO EN U.S.A.

Printed in the U.S.A.

RA  10  9  8  7  6  5  4  3  2  1

If you purchased this book without a cover, you should be aware that
this book is stolen property. It was reported as "unsold and destroyed"
to the publisher, and neither the author nor the publisher has received
any payment for this "stripped book."

*To my sister Pat, who stands by me,
and to Peter, who won't let me fall.*

# ACKNOWLEDGMENT

I'm deeply grateful to Jane Cavolina, my editor, and the fine team at Crown—including Michelle Sidrane, Ann Patty, Joan De Mayo, and Julie Lovrinic—for their support and enthusiasm.

Also, Richard Pine, my agent, one of the very best.

Thanks go out to John Clifford, Brian Carroll, Joe Gallagher, Rose Arce, Mike Taibbi, and Mike Race, who helped me research this book.

A handful of people have earned a mention in ways too various and personal to list here. They are Fran Tyre, Cathy Woodard, David Kocieniewski, William Rashbaum, Deidre Murphy, Christian Wright, Liz McGrory, K. Tracy Barnes, Val Bishop, Cynthia Crossen, and Sheila Ellis.

# IN THE
# MIDNIGHT
# HOUR

# Prologue

Despite the sumptuous piles of produce, Kate Murray always thought the Vietnamese grocery store near her apartment in Park Slope had the bright, cheerless lights and antiseptic feel of a hospital ward. Of course, it could be that the store's proprietor, Kim Sou, made her think of hospitals. He'd been a radiologist in Vietnam and had been waiting for four years to be certified in his adopted country. While the American Medical Association tried to translate his diplomas, he ran a grocery store in Brooklyn. His wife, Sonya Sou, gave the store a certain tragic air. Back home, she was a well-known country-western singer. In a land where Johnny Cash and Tammy Wynette songs dominated the radio, Sonya had been a sought-after celebrity. In Brooklyn, no one gave her a second look as she sat on a barrel in front of the store snapping green beans. Sonya didn't know enough English to work the cash register, but Kate had once overheard her mournfully belting out a Loretta Lynn song whose words she knew by heart as she unpacked a crate of pineapples.

Kate nodded to Kim and Sonya and selected a large plastic box for her salad. She stared at the salad bar offerings with a critical eye, trying to remember which trays looked untouched from last night. Through the Plexiglas sneeze protector she could see three other customers—two lonely looking women about her age and a thin guy with a bony neck and a sallow complexion.

She watched one of the women load her tray with romaine and then drown it in some goopy-looking blue cheese dressing. Kate smiled, selecting some broccoli. Salad bar dinners were probably more fattening than a steak and fries. It just seemed more virtuous.

She grabbed another set of stainless steel tongs and loaded her tray with tofu and some carrot salad. She wished she had lingered a little longer at the *Daily Herald*. She wished she didn't have to go back to her empty apartment. She wrestled a rubber band around her tray and straightened. Everyone had sadness in their life, she thought, looking around at the groceries neatly stowed on the floor-to-ceiling shelves. But at least Kim and Sonya were together, she thought sadly. Even her personal idol Katharine Hepburn had Spencer Tracey, if not as a husband at least as a mate. As her eyes traveled toward the register where Kim Sou stood, Kate heard her breath break like a wave in her ears. Standing in front of the counter, nonchalantly holding a bottle of Snapple, she recognized the broad back of her old lover, John Finn. She took a quick step forward and stopped. What would she say to him? I've been trying to call you for two years? Maybe she should just kiss him firmly on the lips like the vamp in a soap opera. That might keep him from walking away. On the other hand, she reconsidered, he was a cop. He might think he was getting mugged and reach for his gun. She took a few steps forward and raised her hand to touch him lightly on the back. She shivered slightly and hesitated. The man with the soda reached into his pocket and asked for a package of razors Kim Sou kept behind the counter. Kate's hand hung in the air a few inches from his back as she felt her heart plunge to her knees and stay there, unwilling to rebound. It wasn't John Finn at all. Finn spoke with a quiet, steady voice. This impostor had a high nasal whine. For maybe the one hundredth time, Kate felt a cold finger dig into her heart. She was always catching glimpses of Finn. She had mistakenly spotted him inside her local coffee shop, at her favorite bookstore, and on the street near her office at the *Herald*. She would be standing alone in a crowd and his face would leap out at her like a reflection in a room full of mirrors. She felt the pain in her chest lessen and she forced herself to exhale. This was just another soldier in the squadrons of John Finn look-alikes that seemed to follow her everywhere. She let her hand fall to her side and dropped her chin so Kim Sou wouldn't see her tears.

The bodega looked like it had survived an explosion. The front window was cracked and repaired with black electrical tape. The OPEN 24 HOURS sign hung at an angle. The door looked as if it had been dented by a burly shoulder, and the webs of shattered glass were reinforced with a metal plate. Det. John Finn barely noticed. He was hoping to get this detail over with before the summer sun had set. The quicker he joined his boss, Doug Bigelow, in their dark Narcotics Division sedan, the quicker the two men would be drinking beer together at O'Brien's.

He pushed through the door and almost fell flat on his face as the toe of his cheap wing tips wedged between two uneven floor slats.

Mom-and-pop businesses didn't do well in this section of Bushwick. Ravaged by a double plague of drug dealers and stickup men, the stores got more decrepit as customers began avoiding them and the owners tried frantically to salvage a remnant of their savings. This store was hit harder than most. Finn hoped that the owners would be desperate enough for money to agree to let a Brooklyn Narcotics unit use their back room for surveillance. The room would provide a nearly unobstructed view of the Group C undercovers making drug buys. Of course, the drug dealers would torch the store if they found out the owners had leased it to the cops. Finn sighed. He wouldn't know until he asked.

He pulled a package of Ring-Dings off the display stand, opened it, then tried to find his way up the dim aisle.

As he approached the counter, he could see an old Puerto Rican man, probably the owner, having an animated discussion with two young men near the ancient cash register.

Finn sighed, this time loud enough to make everyone in the store aware that he was waiting. He could hear O'Brien's calling his name.

"Excuse me, ah, pardon," he began, hoping the young customers would fade when they saw he was a cop.

"We ain't finished here yet," said the largest of the young men, who wore the hood of his jacket pulled up despite the warm weather. The other boy sniggered.

Finn frowned, not understanding the frantic look on the owner's face.

"No need to hurry, gentlemen," Finn began, biting into his Ring-Ding impatiently.

He didn't look into their faces until he felt a cold metal cylinder poke against his throat.

"You the Man?" the tall, heavyset kid asked. His ally laughed nervously.

Out of the corner of his eye, Finn saw that the tall boy was holding a shotgun under his chin. The skinny boy with a complexion like a rough patch of sidewalk was smiling, but Finn could see that his teeth were chattering with fear.

Finn opened his mouth and a chunk of Ring-Ding fell onto his tie. The tall boy made a disgusted *tsk.*

"You in the wrong place at the wrong time," he said.

"You sell lottery tickets?" Dougie Bigelow's voice came booming down the dusty canned-goods aisle. "You know, Pick 5, Empire State, anything." Finn tried to make a warning noise, but felt metal press into his throat.

Unmindful, Bigelow kept advancing. He barged into the tall boy like he needed a Seeing Eye dog.

"Oh, what have we here? Boys pretending that weapons make them into men?" Finn couldn't believe his ears. Bigelow was doing a tough-guy routine with an idiot kid who had his finger wrapped around a trigger. The boys were plainly unnerved.

"This got nothing to do with you. Why are you getting involved?" said the tall boy.

Bigelow cupped his ear. "I can't hear you. Finn, can you hear him?" boomed Bigelow, taking every advantage of his wide chest and bulked-up arms.

Finn made a gargling sound.

"And communication is very important," Bigelow continued, leaning so close to the pimply kid that the boy took a step backward. He looked at his tall friend in panic.

Bigelow picked up on his fear. "Take this youngster here. There's something he needs to know. Something to keep him from making a very large mistake."

Everyone in the bodega was watching Bigelow in amazement, as if a superhero had stepped off a movie screen and begun throwing theater chairs around.

"Don't get closer," warned the tall boy.

Bigelow reared back.

"See, he doesn't want to hear it, so I'll tell you the news. But I don't want to shout it. I'll whisper it to you." Bigelow almost chest-butted the smaller boy. "It's something you'll need to know if you want to grow up to be a man." Bigelow was close enough to grab the tall boy's shotgun. But instead, Bigelow reached out with a muscular arm that looked like melons in a stocking and pulled the smaller boy's head to his own.

"You fuck with me," Bigelow began, his voice silky and seductive—Finn heard a collective intake of breath as their brows touched—"I'll bite your fucking head off!"

Finn saw Bigelow's teeth close over the boy's oily cheek and felt a warm spray.

The boy let loose an unearthly scream and clutched his bleeding face. The shotgun clattered to the floor.

Finn grabbed the gun. The owner dived under the counter. Bigelow, blood dripping from his mouth, whipped a set of cuffs from his back pocket.

"Don't fuck with Dougie Bigelow!" roared Bigelow, wiping his lips.

Then he turned to Finn, who was sagging against the counter in a stupor. "Let's process these guys and go to O'Brien's."

# 1

Kate was halfway through her feature story on the new breed of yuppie mobsters when she began to contemplate a new career. Not that the story itself was a problem. Every FBI agent Kate talked to had an anecdote about a young capo who refused to eat red meat, another who wore only Armani, and another who went on hits in a late-model Saab with a Graco baby seat in the back. No, the story was going fine. It was the newspaper that was crumbling around her.

This morning, Marvin Sugarman had announced that he had sold the *Daily Herald.* The buyer was an eccentric parking-lot tycoon named Solomon Randall, who everyone suspected was senile. Ten years ago, Randall had run for city comptroller. He had two planks to his campaign. The first was a "return New York to New Yorkers" movement, a thinly veiled attempt to further polarize an already racially divided city. The second was a well-publicized vow to hand a $1,000 bill to any girl in New York City who remained a virgin until she was seventeen. He'd been savaged by pundits and received less than 5 percent of the vote. But his brief stab at public life had left him with an obsessive craving for the limelight.

Thirty minutes after the sale was announced, the *Herald's* newsroom was in an uproar. Union leaders began issuing complaints. Managers who hadn't written a word in years sat at computer terminals typing out their résumés.

Two hours later, Randall, a sweaty man with pig eyes, huffed through the double glass doors marked *THE DAILY HERALD*—NEW YORK'S HOMETOWN PAPER. A few low-level managers cheered and quietly staked out the offices they would inhabit when their bosses were fired wholesale.

"I want you to know what I want you to know," began Randall. Okay, Kate thought, mentally forgiving the non sequitur. He's nervous. Not everyone is Dale Carnegie.

"This paper will continue in its great and historical tradition." Kate was cautiously hopeful. "Except now there will be something for everyone."

He paused for a few moments to survey his newly purchased domain. Kate thought of slave auctions and wondered if he'd ask to check anyone's teeth.

Instead he extended his chubby arm toward the *Herald's* longtime editor, Steven Ridgeway. Randall slowly unfurled his finger.

"You, Ridgeway," he barked. "Clean out your desk. You're fired."

Randall continued, insensitive to the waves of dismay radiating around him. "Something for everyone," he repeated. "More scandal. More shocks. More movie stars. More gossip. More Elvis. More Marilyn. More Lotto."

He extended his arm again, this time pointing to the metropolitan editor, Mark Hartman, who had come to the *Herald* with three Pulitzers on his résumé.

"You, Hartman. You're the new editor."

Hartman looked straight at Randall. "I'm not working for a jackass like you. I quit."

A smattering of applause broke out behind the pillars.

Randall raised his caterpillarlike eyebrows, walked over to the business desk, and grabbed Mickey Banes, who had been put out to pasture after his second heart attack.

"You. What's your name?" Randall barked in the tone he might use on a clumsy busboy.

"Ah, Banes, sir . . . Mr. Randall. Mickey Banes."

"Well, Banes. You're the new editor of the *Herald*."

Banes's hand flew to his left shoulder. "I can't do it. I've got a bad heart. You got to believe me. I can't take stress."

"That's a lot of crap," growled Randall. "I'll expect you in my office in thirty minutes."

Kate's head bobbed as if she had been hit. All around the newsroom, career reporters looked at Banes, then at Randall.

"Now, let's put out the best paper we know how."

The staff remained silent until Randall closed the glass doors to his new office and sank back into Sugarman's custom-designed leather easy chair.

Then the floor erupted.

"I'm out of here."

"I just got a mortgage."

"We can't live on my wife's salary with my kids in private school."

"California here I come."

Kate quietly dialed an editor she knew at the *New York Times*.

"You hiring?" she asked him without preamble.

"I'm on hold with two of your colleagues," he said apologetically. No news traveled faster than bad news. "Send your clips."

Kate hung up, put her notebook in her black leather bag, and took an elevator to the ground floor.

# 2

It was the middle part of the afternoon at O'Brien's, slightly closer to dinner than lunch, and John Finn knew exactly where the day was headed. It was the hour when he realized that he wasn't going to even start the things he had set out to do. The most pressing chore he was ignoring was to pay off his building manager. Three weeks ago, he had fallen asleep while broiling a hamburger and set his oven on fire. The flames destroyed his kitchen, and the fire hoses sent a deluge of filthy water into the apartment below. Since then, his neighbors were giving him the silent treatment, and the building manager had been slipping urgent messages under his door. Five crisp twenties would smooth over any hard feelings. But it seemed that every time he found himself at home during the daylight hours, all he had in his pocket was lint.

The second most important thing he'd failed to do was find someone who had read *The Tools of Surveillance,* a textbook on undercover work that he was supposed to have memorized by training class on Tuesday.

Finn squinted at the gold beer in front of him and then at the ribbons of sun streaking through the bar window.

"Yo, Bigelow, did you read the surveillance book?" Finn asked his group supervisor, who was pushing quarters into the jukebox. You could choose between bad songs and terrible songs on O'Brien's jukebox—a

*11*

breathtaking array of pop hits from the seventies that burrowed into you like a tick so you found yourself slapping handcuffs on street dealers while you were humming "Muskrat Love."

"Police work is instinctual, it's not something you learn in a book," answered Bigelow, pouring a Tanqueray and tonic into his mouth and turning on his smile like a lightbulb. "You gotta be willing to bring the street scum to their knees any way that you can. That's the core of police work. It's not something in a textbook, it's something in the blood."

As Bigelow was talking, Finn was running his hands inside his jacket, getting ready for a long night of partying. He pulled out his gun. He knew better than to carry a weapon when he was getting drunk. He pulled four twenties out of his wallet and stuck them in his back pocket. Then he placed his wallet, shield, and service revolver on the bar and pushed it toward Bigelow like winnings at a casino. He'd lost his wallet once after a long day like this. He had to wait on line for two hours to get another driver's license. Another time, he had misplaced his shield and had to fill out four forms in triplicate to get another one. Finn watched Bigelow push his valuables deep into his jacket pocket and smiled. It was a familiar ritual, one that left him feeling naked, expectant, and ready to face his destiny.

At first, Finn didn't like his supervisor. For one thing, Bigelow blustered like an army recruiter, always gung ho and ready for action. And Finn had heard the stories about that messy business in College Point where Bigelow had been a detective in the robbery squad. A young prostitute was found raped and strangled on the roof of a warehouse. It didn't raise any eyebrows. Prostitutes were killed all the time. But this one had the key to an apartment near the precinct where Bigelow paid the rent. The homicide was never solved and Bigelow was quietly transferred to Brooklyn Narcotics.

After Bigelow busted up the bodega stickup and saved his life, Finn started to look at Bigelow a little differently. He figured his boss had a reason to swagger. The more he got to know him, the more he was sure that Bigelow was hard-wired differently from most men. He lived with a kind of reckless bravado, an assurance that nothing bad could ever happen to men who were bold and true. When it really sunk in that Finn had lost the only woman he ever loved and his hold on his job began to drift like silt in a rushing river, Bigelow was there for him. In a funny way, his boss gave him the threads to bind his life together. He made sure Finn had good assignments on the job—keeping him safely behind a camera during the undercover part of the operation and closest to the front door during the raids. After work, he was always ready to hang out, buy him a drink, or drive him home after a long night at O'Brien's. Until Finn could pull himself together, it was almost enough. His boss was also generous to a fault. At least once a week, Bigelow shoved a few twenties in Finn's pocket. Walking-around-money is what Bigelow called it.

Finn tried one last time. "Yeah, but say it's not in my blood. Just say I want to read about it."

"Alcohol is what's in your blood. A rarefied mixture of alcohol and dumb luck," said Roy Johnson, laughing. A stiff-backed black man, he'd been transferred into the C team of Brooklyn Narcotics around the same time as Finn and Bigelow.

Bigelow looked at him in mock surprise, then pushed his drink toward the bartender for a refill. "Are you implying that we are merely drinking? Why, Detective, we are conducting a surveillance."

"O'Brien's being a well-known drug location for the Medellín cartel," said Alfonse Versos, picking up on the joke.

Dark-haired and handsome, Versos was the second youngest member of the C team and an enormously talented trumpet player. Untutored, he passed the admission auditions for Juilliard after graduating from Erasmus Hall High School. Unfortunately, Versos was stricken with a brutal temper. He was thrown out of music school after one semester for beating a

cellist senseless, and he enrolled in the Police
Academy.

"Not that an Internal Affairs stiff would recognize a
drug location," said Johnson to no one in particular.
Johnson was only fifteen years older than the Hispanic musician, but was several generations removed. He
constantly pined for the old days, a halcyon era after
cops stopped walking the beat but before they were
expressly forbidden to take payoffs.

Mark Money, the youngest member of the group,
nodded. Beneath his longish, dun-colored hair,
Money's gray eyes looked glassy. Finn privately
thought that Money smoked too much marijuana.

George McCoy, a farm boy who'd applied to the
NYPD from his hometown in Mineska, Minnesota,
let loose with his dumb, yuk-yuk laugh. Stephen Lee,
a Chinese American who combed his hair into an
Elvis-style pompadour, showed his teeth in a sem-
blance of a smile.

"I'm on the t-top of the wor-reld, looking down,
down on creation," Bigelow was singing along. For a
long time, Finn thought Bigelow was joking when he
said his favorite group was the Captain and Tenille or
that Karen Carpenter had a voice like an angel. Now
that Finn knew Bigelow better, he realized his hulking
boss, who was canny about police department politics
and street-level dealers, had a blind spot when it came
to music.

Finn tuned out the banter from his partners and
moodily eyed his beer. He hadn't felt on top of the
world in the eight months since he'd been transferred
to Brooklyn Narcotics from homicide, an unwilling
recruit in the police commissioner's personal War on
Drugs. In fact, he thought bitterly, he hadn't felt any
emotions good enough to sing about since Kate
Murray left him, and that was over two years ago. He
scowled at the television above the bartender's head.
It was one of those American Express commercials
where tan lawyers, husband and wife, look pissed off
even though they're sitting in a nice car in an expen-
sive neighborhood. With a quick flick of a green card,

the lawyers ended up mashing jaws in the tropics on a yacht they'd just rented with their plastic.

"Fuck them," Finn said aloud, and gestured to the bartender to pour him a shot of brandy.

American Express never thought of him. They never considered cardholders who had to live in a filthy city where a man can draw his gun and decide in an instant to end another man's life. They didn't make a card tough enough to deflect a stray bullet. Or smart enough to keep a man from interrupting a bodega stickup. They never showed one of their customers getting his soul ripped from his body as the woman he loves walks away laughing. Finn felt like cutting his credit card into small pieces and mailing it to American Express, but all he had in his wallet was a maxed-out Visa.

Finn took a large mouthful of beer, swallowed, and then belched quietly into the back of his hand.

McCoy grabbed him in a headlock from behind.

"I'm on t-top of the w-world," McCoy joined Bigelow in a warbling falsetto. "This woman knew what it felt like to be in love."

"Get off me, asshole. She starved herself to death," said Finn, pulling himself out of McCoy's grasp.

"Figures you'd know something like that, Mr. Sunshine," said McCoy. "I never understood what *black Irish* meant until I met you. Forget Johnson, you're the blackest man in the unit."

It was true and Finn knew it. It wasn't that his day-to-day life was so difficult. The undercovers in Group C had been buying drugs from middle-level Dominican dealers who had recently begun to traffic in almost pure heroin. Because Finn, a detective, had seniority, and looked like a poster boy for the NYPD, Bigelow never assigned him to go undercover. Instead, he sat outside the target location taking surveillance photographs that would be introduced at trial. Aside from the winter after he graduated from high school when he spent the Christmas season filling in at the post office, surveillance was the most monotonous work Finn had ever done. But unlike sorting mail, you couldn't settle into the grind. Sooner or later, Richard Bollini, Bigelow's boss, would decide it was time to apprehend the target. You couldn't just call his lawyer and ask Mr. Montero or Mr. Fernandez to come to the precinct. You had to arrest him during a drug buy. Catch him up to his elbows in heroin.

To Finn, every raid was a living nightmare; running up the stairs, banging down people's doors with a battering ram. All the screaming and chaos and adrenaline pumping so hard your brain felt like it might explode. The worst part was that once you were through the door, you had to run through the apartment like a panther, gun drawn, ready for some cracked-up dealer to jump out of a closet and try to blow you away with a shotgun. Finn knew he took the coward's route—staying out of the target apartments as much as he could. Even still, every time Finn had to do it, he was depressed for a week.

He gestured to the bartender for another beer and watched Versos stagger into the men's room.

No. Finn had been involved in too much gunplay in his sixteen years on the job to enjoy the unexpected. He shuddered.

Bigelow loved drug raids. It gave him a perfect chance to show what a good soldier he really was, kicking down doors with a rebel yell and grabbing dealers as they scurried like roaches when the overhead light gets switched on. Afterward, Bigelow would be lighthearted, his arm around yet another woman with a great body and no expectations.

Finn sipped his beer and squinted at Bigelow. Maybe women were attracted to his looks. From a distance, Bigelow looked like a hybrid between the old Olympic swimmer Mark Spitz and the Marlboro Man. He was always flashing those even white teeth, always giving you a twinkly-eyed smile, like he was sharing a secret that only you could understand. But when Bigelow stopped smiling, his face changed dramatically. His features looked pudgy and pale behind an overgrown mustache that streamed from his nostrils and across the plane of his upper lip. His jawline jutted out like a powerful stave that extended from his chin past his ear and was finally embedded deep in his hairline.

Finn's attention rocketed away from Bigelow when he heard a high-pitched scream from the men's room. Versos walked out, flexing his right hand.

Versos became aware of the silent crowd, then doubled back and opened the men's room door again.

"That'll teach ya, ya fucking degenerate."

Two seconds later, a curly-haired man in a rumpled suit staggered out. The man was a stranger at O'Brien's, a bar whose patrons were either Police Academy graduates or had relatives in the department. His jacket sleeve was ripped at the shoulder, and an angry bruise was rising above his left eye.

No one moved an inch.

"He beat me for no reason," the man sputtered, fingering the bruise. "No reason. He held my hand behind my back. He tried to break my arm."

The patrons remained silent until the man weaved out of the bar.

"You tried to break his arm?" said Bigelow, turning to his warrior friend. "Jesus, Versos, I don't know whether I'm disgusted that you tried it or impressed that you stopped yourself before you broke it."

Versos sniffed.

"I'm impressed," chirped McCoy, smiling his big dumb-cowpoke smile.

"You're a dangerous weapon," said Money solemnly.

"What did he say that made you so nuts?" asked Finn.

Versos looked around at the expectant faces of his friends. "He asked me where I got my shoes."

The members of Group C grew quiet again.

"That's it?" asked Bigelow.

"That's enough," said Versos defensively.

From across the room, Stephen Lee gave Versos an encouraging smile and threw a punch into the air.

Bigelow ordered another round.

*   *   *

Three hours later, Finn was threatening the bartender.

"Just keep 'em coming, goddammit, or I'll shoot ya," he snarled, half-joking and completely drunk. He reached into his jacket toward his empty holster. "I'll shoot ya, I will. Right in the arm."

Versos, Money, and McCoy laughed as the bartender paled.

"Better do as the man says, keep pouring," said Bigelow, but he put a steadying hand on Finn's upper arm.

Finn wasn't planning to shoot anyone. As a matter of fact, he was surprised that his hand had even tried to back up his words. It was a joke, but his hand got to the punch line first.

Suddenly, he felt tears in his eyes, not of sadness, but of deep-running affection for the brave men around him. They were good cops. Men who would risk anything for each other. They had rescued him, after all, when his personal life had nearly pulled him under. They were his buddies.

"Hey, I love you guys," he said to Money, who just smiled and sang "Seasons in the Sun" along with the jukebox.

"I do," said Finn, clapping his hand on Versos's shoulder and grinning at the sight of his nose, which was swelling and purple from the fight.

He was drunk enough to do or say just about anything, which was something new. He used to be a quiet drinker. Had a few and got quieter and quieter until he eventually passed out. Now he was quieter when he was sober and unpredictable when the alcohol kicked in.

The next time Finn looked up, he was settled in the seat of Bigelow's black Lexus. He had no idea how much time had elapsed. He clutched his empty holster and felt panic flatten his lungs like a steamroller. For a few blinding seconds, he sucked in air mixed with cold panic. Then he realized he was staring at Bigelow's profile and remembered he had given his boss his gun for safekeeping. As he got his bearings, his breathing returned to normal. Finn shuddered. It shook him up, these blackouts. He was usually around Group C friends when they happened, but he didn't like the loss of control. It was like missing two scenes in a movie and trying to catch up with the plot.

"How can you afford this on your salary, you fuck?" Finn said thickly. He listened to the motor hum. "You got a nice condo, a great car. You got a boat. I don't even have money to pay off my building manager."

Bigelow navigated a left turn and didn't look up. "I got investments. Good investments. That's all."

"Stocks? Bonds? Krugerrands? Tell me your secret. I figure you're dealing drugs on the side," Finn slurred.

"Fuck you, you're drunk," said Bigelow, cuffing him on the head in fun.

"Yeah. Yeah."

Just as Finn was settling into sleep, Bigelow pulled up to a neat tenement and parked squarely in front of a fire hydrant. Through weighted eyelids, Finn could see some kind of Chinese letters in the windows of a darkened café on the first floor.

"This isn't my house," he mumbled peevishly.

"Wait here, I got someone to see," said Bigelow, pulling the keys out of the ignition and disappearing before Finn could ask him to turn on the radio.

Finn crossed his arms, yawned, and looked down the block. It was the same as all the others in this cookie-cutter neighborhood except it was cleaner. If you looked hard, you could see that most of the people who lived here were Chinese. There were little tip-offs. They piled their garbage too neatly to be Americans, and most of it was tied in small packets with cast-off string like presents for the garbagemen. Finn thought it was as if the Chinese people were saying, "In this new land, we can even make our trash look good."

Finn checked the rearview mirror and his heart sank. It was after nine on a Wednesday night, and probably the only meter maid on duty in all of

Brooklyn was headed for Bigelow's car. It used to be you could show your shield and they'd rip up the ticket on the spot. Now, they'd laugh in your face and tow your car.

"Shit," Finn said, and heaved himself out of the front seat. The alcohol had moved from his stomach to his brain, and he was much drunker than when he'd left the bar. As soon as he took a step, he fell, sprawling on the sidewalk. A small cat ran by him like an apparition.

Eye level with the concrete, he could see the meter maid's slow, steady approach.

Finn pulled himself to his knees and weighed the possibility of crawling into the tenement to find Bigelow. What if his friend was on the fourth floor? He leaned back on one haunch, then stood unsteadily. His feet felt like wooden mallets. He staggered into the building and up the stairs.

"Yo, Bigelow," he called up the stairwell.

Like a mountain climber, Finn used the banister to pull himself up the first flight.

"You wanna spend eighty dollars for this parking space, Detective?" he called again. He was babbling. "Mr. Supervisor, Group C, Brooklyn Narcotics. Man-about-town, premier swordsman Dougie Bigelow. You're about to get tagged. That'll be a sixth of your weekly take-home going back to the city. And investments or no, you don't want to let that happen."

Two men dressed in black grabbed Finn's arms and quickly pinned him to the floor. They were calm and deliberate, and some vestigial street-cop instinct made Finn instantly understand that they were armed. His chest began to throb and he tried to protest as they dragged him up a flight of stairs to the third floor. His body was drugged with alcohol and couldn't respond to the waves of adrenaline blasting through his brain. He felt as if he'd plunged through a hidden trapdoor and was falling, knowing he couldn't possibly survive the drop.

He was so drunk and frightened that at first he couldn't see anything in the dim room.

Then, through the cigarette smoke, he saw Bigelow suddenly stand up from a round table. Still seated at the table were two middle-aged Chinese men in business suits and three young men in leather. Between them was a small mountain of cash. Finn noticed that the young man closest to him didn't wear socks. All five kept their eyes on Finn, and their lips curled in disgust and anger, as if he were a neighbor's mutt howling at the moon. He looked at Bigelow, then at the men. He felt his skin crawl.

He reached into himself, trying to find the old Finn: the sober, self-assured cop smart enough to figure his way out of a bad situation. He couldn't find a trace of the guy.

"Yo, Bigelow. What's going on here?" He was terrified but the alcohol made his voice sound belligerent. "Why you sitting with these gangsters?"

"Get out of here," Bigelow screamed as he gestured for the men to take Finn away. But the men on either side of Finn didn't respond, and Bigelow seemed to reconsider. "Gentlemen, my apologies," Bigelow said, smiling gracefully. Then he reached down and tucked a two-inch packet of money into his breast pocket and loped across the room to take Finn's arm.

Before Finn could react, he felt himself being pulled down the stairs, dragged across the pavement, and shoved roughly into Bigelow's car.

When they'd driven about ten minutes, Bigelow pulled a flask out of his jacket and passed it over. Finn grabbed it eagerly and took a long pull. He saw that Bigelow was shaking.

"What the fuck happened?" asked Finn, his voice still sounding far away.

Bigelow said nothing.

"I'm asking you," Finn insisted.

"Nothing really. A miscalculation."

"Who were those people? They looked like members of the Ghost Brigade."

"Nah, they run a laundry business. They owed me something, money."

Finn tipped back the flask, feeling the whiskey

calming him. He wanted to drink until the empty feeling in his gut was gone. He wanted his bed.

"Yeah, and who were the goons? The laundry guards? Christ, I could have gotten hurt."

"Nah, they just overreacted, that's all." Then Bigelow playfully punched Finn's shoulder.

By the time they got to Finn's apartment in Bay Ridge, Finn had passed out with his head lolling backward and his mouth wide open.

Bigelow carried Finn into his apartment and deposited him on his bed. He threw Finn's wallet and shield on the bed beside him and stowed away Finn's gun in his nightstand. Then he stood for a moment, sniffing the sooty air of the apartment.

"Sweet dreams, Detective Finn," said Bigelow. "Sweet dreams."

# 3

Kate had been hired by the news director, Josh
Bartlett, without setting foot in the Channel 7 studio.
She knew she owed the job to her close friend and
mentor J.J. Perez. A former reporter at the *Daily
Herald,* J.J. had made the jump from newspapers to
local news two years ago and then, after a round of
dramatic plastic surgery, had vaulted to network news
last fall. It was J.J. who had set up the lunch with
Bartlett when the *Herald* changed hands.

"D'ya have any television experience?" asked Bartlett, eyeing her suspiciously over their entrées. J.J.
never bothered to tell Kate that Bartlett was coming
until he took a seat at their table. Bartlett was a bony
red-haired man with an unhealthy skin tone under a
rash of freckles and red-rimmed eyes. He didn't look
happy. J.J. introduced Kate to Bartlett as "the reporter I've been telling you about."

"She knows the news business," said J.J. quickly.
"She knows it as good or better than anyone on your
staff."

Bartlett looked unimpressed. Kate forced herself to
smile, weighing just how angry J.J. would be if Kate
excused herself, walked to the ladies room, and left
through the back entrance of the restaurant.

By dessert, J.J. was unashamedly bribing Bartlett to
give Kate a chance. There might be an opening for
him on a new network news show, she said, enjoying a
chance to flex her muscle. If they understood each
other. Bartlett fixed his pale rabbit eye on Kate. They

needed someone to do the reporting and writing so one of their television legends, Vic Manero, could string a few coherent phrases together for the six- and eleven-o'clock news shows, Bartlett explained. Once in a while, the producer had to do a promo at ten. Kate kept smiling.

"I don't even know if I want to work in television," said Kate, exploding as soon as Bartlett excused himself, leaving them to finish their cappuccino at the table.

"If he offers you the job and if it turns out you're happy at the *Herald*," said J.J., shrugging, "go ahead and turn him down."

A week later, Randall fired a longtime city-politics columnist and hired a well-known fashion model to do a society column in its place. Two hours later, Bartlett offered Kate a job producing for Manero. The salary was a steep increase, but she'd be earning it, Bartlett told her. She'd have to work Tuesday through Saturday and any other days the station needed her— round the clock, if necessary. It hadn't taken much to convince her. The *Herald* was disintegrating around her. Kate accepted.

The offices of Channel 7 contained no natural light. Instead, the newsroom was illuminated by a steady fluorescent glow, like a casino, so the employees couldn't tell day from night.

Kate walked into the newsroom and blinked at a bank of televisions flashing images of a fluffy-haired soap-opera actress.

She stopped a sleepy-looking brunette. "Where can I find Steve Landis?"

Bartlett had told her she would be taking assignments from Landis, the executive director of the evening news.

The brunette frowned and pointed to a young-looking man with prematurely gray hair.

"Steve Landis? Kate Murray." She extended her hand and he smiled at her. Kate took in his well-pressed chinos and the intelligent, neurotic gleam in

his eye. Then he shifted his attention to the Joan
Rivers show on a television to his left as a celebrity
aerobics teacher began working out on a Thighmaster.

He turned back to Kate and stared at her blankly,
as if she were another guest on the Joan Rivers show.
She saw that he was quaking. An almost impercepti-
ble shiver rattled him from his knees to his chin.

"So you're the new producer?" he said with a nasty
edge. "You look too relaxed to work here."

Kate tried to smile but Landis seemed to be working himself up to a tirade. "Look around you." Kate
looked at the open-plan room, not unlike the *Daily
Herald* newsroom except every terminal had a television screen blasting a soap opera. "Unless our Nielsen
jumps up, half the people in this room will be fired."
He let his words sink in for a moment. "Let's go into
the morning meeting. Let Bartlett know that you've
arrived."

Bartlett's office was crammed with producers, and
above their heads, five large-screen TVs were tilted
downward.

"This is Kate Murray, Vic Manero's new producer," announced Landis, then he shrugged as if to say,
"Don't blame me," and took a seat.

Kate smiled stiffly.

"Another victim," said Bartlett. Kate raised an
inquiring eyebrow and took a seat. But the producers
had already begun discussing the headlines from the
day's newspapers.

At lunch with J.J. and Bartlett, she had asked him
what had happened to Manero's last producer. Bartlett had smiled but said nothing.

"Let's have Patty Anne Roebuck do the I Love New
York segment. A voice-over, then a tape of kids
planting flowers in Battery Park," suggested Landis to
Roebuck's producer, a young woman dressed entirely
in black.

"Patty Anne won't be able to find Battery Park,"
thundered Bartlett. The young woman flushed,
clasped her hands, and said nothing. Sensing weak-
ness, Landis seemed to have forgotten he made the

suggestion in the first place. "She couldn't find a story if the newspaper clip was pasted on her forehead," he shouted. Roebuck's young producer regarded the televisions overhead without speaking.

Landis turned to Bartlett. "Six more months on Patty Anne Roebuck's contract, then she's *out!*"

Both men nodded and Bartlett checked off a time slot on his clipboard.

Roebuck's producer scurried away.

They rehashed newspaper headlines, finally assigning Manero to interview a Jersey City father whose twelve-year-old foster child was missing.

"We don't expect Manero to find the child," explained Landis. "We don't really expect Manero to even find the father, much less talk to him. You should do the interview, then set up a few cutaways with Manero and the father. Make it look like Manero knows something about the news business."

Bartlett turned to Landis. "How many more months on Manero's contract?"

"Four, I think."

"Four more months of this man," said Bartlett. "I hope my nerves can take it."

Kate found the famous reporter in front of the studio, sitting inside a mini-van topped with some kind of Star Wars apparatus. Despite the perfectly clear sky, he was dressed in an expensive-looking trench coat.

Kate nodded to her cameraman in the driver's seat. He jerked his head curtly, and his mossy helmet of black curls that extended past his shoulders began to bob. In the back of the van, a pasty, myopic soundman was setting out an elaborate maze of wires. He ignored Kate's faint greeting. There was so much tension in the van, Kate could hardly breathe.

"What are cutaways?" she asked Manero, after offering him her hand.

"Shots of me and the subject talking." He held her hand and, before she could stop him, lifted it to his lips. She pulled it away and wiped it on her skirt. Her cameraman caught her gesture in the rearview mirror and smiled. Manero continued smoothly, "Makes me look like I asked all the questions." He paused. "I bet they said they didn't think I could even find the father. Right? Then they asked how long I had left on my contract? Right?"

Kate nodded her head. Manero smiled nonchalantly, pulled a yachting magazine from under his hinged chair, and began flipping the pages.

She studied him. He had perfected the look of an intelligent, polished middle-aged man. Up close though his face was waxy and his hair was stiff like a Ken doll that had come into an inheritance.

The microwave van began to move slowly through traffic, and Kate took in her surroundings. Every possible space in the vehicle was crammed with some kind of equipment or monitor. She felt a little like Neil Armstrong. "One small step for man, one giant step for Kate Murray's career," she mumbled to herself.

Manero looked up from his magazine. "You married?"

She squinted her eyes. "Why? You think we should get engaged?" She heard the soundman snort in approval.

"How 'bout your friends? Got any friends who might want to date me?"

"I'm your producer, not your pimp."

He went back to his yachting magazine. The cameraman looked up from the traffic and swiveled around in his seat like an airplane pilot. "I'm Manuel. I do camera. That's Bernie. He does sound. Welcome to the show."

Five hours later, Kate's heart began to race as she watched the plastic-looking anchors kick off the news in the minivan's monitors. Their interview was eight minutes into the show. At 6:08 they would go live from the missing girl's bedroom.

Kate had already interviewed the father and written the script while Manero applied his makeup and made small talk with the dad upstairs. Now she was

trying to sort out the noise of the broadcast from
Steve Landis's voice as he barked directions through a
listening device, called an IFB, she had shoved into
her ear.

Bernie, the sound tech, was running electrical wire
down the carpeted stairs and out the front door to the
truck. Manuel, who looked after the visual image and
drove the truck, had elevated the transmitter and was
trying to find a way to bounce signals from the golden
rod—the tall microwave transmitter at the top of the
truck—to an aerial at the top of the World Trade
Center, where the station had a receiver.

"*Cono,* something's blocking it, man. Something's
in the way," he kept muttering.

"Tell him to get the connection," screamed Landis
into Kate's earphone.

"Landis said get the connection," said Kate to
Manuel.

"Tell him to fuck himself."

Landis began screaming in her ear. "Jesus Christ,
lock in the signal. Lock in the signal. You're on the air
in four minutes. Get the fucking signal."

Suddenly a calm, sweet voice overrode Landis's
screech.

"This is Andrew Fink in microwave. Tell Manuel to
pan west to east, I'll try to pick it up." He spoke
carefully, with a cultured private-school accent.

"Manuel, Andrew Fink in microwave said pan west
to east," she called out, mystified. Manuel nodded
and began flipping switches.

Kate could hear the golden rods grinding as they
shifted, and then her head was filled with the sound of
Landis shrieking. "If we go to black at the top of the
show, it'll be my ass. I'll get fired. And I'll take
everyone with me. I will. I swear."

"He says if you don't get the signal, we'll all be
fired," Kate hissed to Manuel.

He shrugged without looking up. "Me and Bernie
are union. He can't touch us."

Andrew Fink broke in again, patiently explaining,
"Sometimes other signals can block ours, so we have

to find a way of bouncing them in, ricocheting them off buildings, hills, any kind of surface. There. I'm getting you. Closer. Got it. You're received in transmission. Lock it down."

Kate signaled to Manuel, who nodded and smiled. Then they lurched for the stairs. Kate ran, taking two at a time, listening to Landis scream.

"Thirty more fucking seconds. Twenty-five. Twenty," he screeched.

She and Manuel reached the door to the girl's room as Vic Manero cleared his throat. Manuel went directly to the camera and turned it on. The dad smiled when he was introduced, looked upset when he was describing the day he discovered his foster daughter was missing, and burst into tears when he held up her picture. Too bad this was supposed to be such a touchy-feely segment, thought Kate. If she were interviewing the dad for the *Herald,* she would have asked him point-blank if he had killed his foster daughter. Kate watched Manero with the uneasy feeling that she was manufacturing news. She had run the foster dad through the questions four times so he could perfect his "spontaneous" answers for Mancro. Standing in the room, it looked to her like bad summer-stock theater. But on the tiny monitor screen attached to the camera, the interview looked sad, heart-warming, and totally spontaneous. But was it journalism?

Andrew Fink spoke into her IFB, sharing the thought. "Welcome to TV."

# 4

At nine A.M., Finn woke for the first time. He felt like a boy again, lighthearted, almost joyous, as if a burden he had been carrying were lifted, as if a slate had been wiped clean.

But as soon as he tried to move his head, he felt the full weight of his thirty-seven years. His stomach seized and he closed his eyes, willing sleep to overtake him.

He woke again about noon. He licked his lips and found that his mouth was full of fur.

*Gah. Gah.* It took him a few seconds to realize that his parched throat was making the sound as his lips opened and closed. He was still in his clothes from the night before, and his hand traveled tenderly to his bruised shin. His heart began to contract, then his fingers found his wallet wedged under him and then his shield. He reached out his arm and yanked open his nightstand, exhaling when he saw that his gun lay safely among the dusty Trojans and his allergy medicine. He swung his legs over the side of the bed, his hand on his stomach as if he were trying to quell an internal riot.

He tried to stand, but swooned and fell back on his bed.

"Once more, with feeling," he commanded himself. He stood up and stumbled to the bathroom. His first piss of the morning felt too hot, as if his insides were being cooked. He had heard that cirrhosis meant you boiled your liver in alcohol, one day at a time. He looked in the mirror and a face of pure misery stared back.

In the last two years, he'd lost his appetite and his body had changed. Once robust and strong, he had become thinner and somehow more taut. His square, regular features, which had remained unchanged since puberty gave way to manhood, now seemed more intense, slightly more fierce, and although he would never acknowledge it, more attractive. Finn blinked, thinking that this morning it was his eyes that betrayed the most. They were red and glassy with a hangover. But it was more than that. It was as if all his life's disappointments had reshaped his retinas so that he now looked out at the world through a prism of pain. He used to think that in another week, another month, the hurt would go away. Now he just didn't know.

He turned on the faucet full blast and put his head under the cold stream. As soon as the water hit his eardrum, he remembered Bigelow and the table full of Chinese gangsters.

"Oh, shit," he said, and bashed his eye on the faucet, knocking himself to his knees.

It was almost nine P.M. by the time Finn met up with Group C in the surveillance apartment. His hangover had settled into mild nausea and a dull ache where his neck met his shoulders.

Not that anyone would notice. The rest of Group C looked as if they'd spent the night rolling on a barroom floor. Money, as usual, looked pale and had beads of sweat on his upper lip. McCoy had a black eye. Lee kept his head down, as if he were lost in prayer. The men of Group C sat in the tattered apartment that consisted of four chipped-plaster walls, half a dozen folding metal chairs, some camera equipment, and a toilet that rattled. On a tiny portable stereo, Terry Jacks warbled out "Seasons in the Sun."

Doug Bigelow sat opposite Finn. Draped in an OPERATION DRUG FREE team jacket, he looked like a big, sallow bear. The two undercovers, Johnson and Versos, were sprawled in the other folding chairs, smoking cigarettes and looking murderous. Finn felt pity for them, especially Versos, knowing he would be standing next to the dirtbag holding a kilo of cocaine when the other armed police officers came crashing through the door. If the supplier was smart, he might shoot Versos, rob him of the buy money, and try to escape in the confusion. If the supplier was stupid, he might shoot Versos out of panic and fear.

Finn tried to wash the stale taste out of his mouth with Diet Coke and nervously pulled at his collar under his heavy Kevlar vest.

Yesterday's joking tone was subsumed in hungover carping.

"What are we doing this for?" asked Johnson. "Public relations. We put one kilo into evidence while tons of it are flooding every port and airport in the country. I tell you, it's public relations."

"Fuck you, Johnson," Versos snarled. "Don't be spreading that negativity around. I only want to hear positive talk. Positive talk or prayers." He paused. "Or anything by Miles Davis."

"Don't worry, I have a good feeling about this one," said Bigelow. "Everyone knows what he has to do, and I think everyone is going to do the right thing."

Finn saw Versos stare bleakly out the window at the target apartment.

Finn had been trying to get a quiet word with Bigelow since the beginning of the shift, but it was impossible in the small room. He had to know what had happened last night. He couldn't remember much. It was as if the alcohol had flooded his memory, crystallizing some images and washing others away altogether. He remembered the meter maid, the henchmen, the feel of ten flinty black eyes looking at him as if he were an antennae-waving cockroach. The steps banging on his shins. Something lurking just beneath the surface of his memory was scaring him.

He tried to catch Bigelow's attention but his supervisor wasn't registering. His eyes were already glassy with anticipation of his adrenaline high. During these raids, Finn tried to hang back, unwilling and unable to go inside. He busied himself at the doorways, arresting the human detritus who scattered when they heard police thumping down the door. He was happy to let the others secure the scene, grab the evidence, and scoop up the guns. Let them be the heroes.

Bigelow's voice filled the room.

"Yeah, everyone will do the right thing."

"Fuck you, Bigelow," said Versos unexpectedly. But Bigelow simply looked at him without expression.

Before Finn could figure out what Bigelow and Versos had between them, the radio began to squawk.

"It's time, Johnson and Versos," said Richard Bollini, the coordinator of the task force groups, who was monitoring the raid from a black van set up half a block north of the target apartment.

"Is that the way you're going to be?" Finn heard Bigelow say to Versos, who dropped his head, grabbed a red duffel bag of buy money, and walked out the pocked door. Johnson fell in behind him.

The rest of the group took their positions behind the high-powered cameras and began filming as Versos, then Johnson, went in. When Johnson walked out of the building, that would be the sign that the deal was going down.

"Keep your eye on the porch," said McCoy. "When he hits the porch, let's go."

"That's not a porch, you hayseed," said Finn. "It's a stoop."

"What kind of word is *stoop*?" said McCoy suspiciously. "Here in America, we call it a porch." Money sniffed in agreement.

"You're not in America, you're in Brooklyn. It's a stoop," said Finn.

"Jesus, I hate this," Bollini muttered into the radio. Finn pinched the bridge of his nose. They'd had a full briefing on the operation so he could easily imagine what was going on. In the foyer of the building, Versos and Johnson would get patted down for weapons. Everyone involved in the deal knew that he was carrying $7,000 in his duffel bag, and they'd be staring at Versos as if he were a dripping ice-cream cone in the Gobi desert. They'd lead Versos upstairs to the third floor into a four-bedroom apartment and into a smaller room in the back where the cocaine was stored in a suitcase, ready for the deal. Johnson, who was supposed to be acting as Versos's street muscle, would stay downstairs in the foyer to protect his "boss" from an ambush. When Johnson heard the apartment door slam behind Versos, he would wait a few minutes and then step out the front door, alerting the squads of police officers watching the building.

Just then Johnson, his face blank with fear, stepped out of the foyer onto the stoop. His appearance triggered a flood of men, who swarmed from the surveillance house across the street. Johnson, still pretending to be a player in the drug deal, ran away. The men crashed through the building foyer. An old woman yanking a laundry cart full of dirty clothes behind her momentarily blocked the stairs. Bigelow grabbed her and pushed her into the open door of a neighboring apartment. Her laundry spilled under their heavy boots. Finn could hear women wailing like cats. From somewhere, he heard a baby's ragged cry. Bigelow bolted up the stairs to the apartment where the drug dealer and Versos were making their deal.

"Slow down," Finn called out to him, but Bigelow was a full stairway ahead of the other cops. Money had finished trying door handles on the first floor. They were all dead-bolted. "Go on, ya rabbit-legged fucker," Money called after Bigelow, who looked down from the third-floor landing and smiled. "You want to dodge bullets all by yourself, good for you."

From a door on the second floor a young Hispanic man stepped onto the landing, drawn by the commotion. Money ran up the stairs and began patting him down. He found a box cutter tucked into the young man's waistband. Money cuffed the man to a stairway spindle and began beating him until Finn puffed up the last few stairs and pulled him away. Despite his

intention to hang back and leave the heroics to the
others, Finn was a single flight away from the target
apartment and the only one covering Bigelow's back.
The raid was unfolding so fast Finn was hardly aware
of the single cold finger of trepidation jabbing him.
He jerked Money up the last flight. They were stumbling together onto the third-floor landing when the
door of the target apartment slammed behind Bigelow.

"Oh my God, they're locked in there," screamed
Finn, and he and Money began pounding helplessly
on the metal door.

"What's going on, boss?" shouted Money frantically. Finn was backing up to charge the door when
the shooting started.

Finn hit the floor one second behind Money, his
face almost buried in Money's rear. He counted three
ringing bullets. Then there was silence.

The two men scrambled up, guns drawn. Bigelow
opened the door and the two men pushed past him.

"Jesus, Mary, and Joseph," screamed Money, frozen in the middle of the room.

McCoy pounded up the stairs behind them and
entered the room. He, too, stood frozen.

"Ohm'god, ohm'god," murmured McCoy, and began shouting into his radio for help.

In the middle of the living room was a table topped
with bricks of shrink-wrapped cocaine. The target of
the raid, a Dominican man, lay dead on the floor, a
red circle widening on his shirt like a bull's eye. To the
left sat Versos, one hand holding his chest and the
other hand over his stomach, holding back a swampy
mess of cloth and entrails. Bigelow walked over to
Versos, crouching over him, not comforting him but
whispering urgently, as if he were administering last
rites.

For a moment Finn felt exhilarated that he was
unhurt. Then he felt ashamed. He couldn't believe
that it was Versos on the floor and not him. Almost
every night Finn had imagined himself wounded and
bleeding to death inside a drug dealer's apartment.

Now, it seemed as if Versos had been felled by Finn's worst nightmare. Finn couldn't shake the feeling that he was responsible.

"Jesus," Finn said, moving closer to Versos, but Bigelow waved him off.

A minute later, EMS arrived and swept Versos out of the apartment on a stretcher. The sidewalk was thick with rescue vehicles, supervisors, IAB investigators in spit-shined shoes, and beat cops drawn to the shooting in horror and fascination. It was past midnight, but no one suggested that the members of Group C go back to the precinct. No one wanted to go back to the surveillance apartment. They stayed, holding a vigil, as if their presence at the scene of the shooting would keep their wounded friend alive.

# 5

Before Manuel had parked the van, Kate knew something had gone terribly wrong. It was 10:35 and according to the all-news radio station, the shot cop, Alfonse Versos, had been rushed to King's County Hospital in Brooklyn. The choice of hospitals was a bad sign. It meant the medics didn't think Versos would survive being air-vacked across the East River to a first-class trauma center like Bellevue in Manhattan.

It wasn't just that a cop had gotten shot. Something else was going on. Instead of swarming together like a big blue mob, the cops stood in small clumps, as if they wanted to be among friends and supporters when the blame got handed down.

A familiar-looking photographer from the *New York Post* was already there.

Kate jumped out of the van and hailed him.

"Who shot the cop?" asked Kate. Print reporters often pooled boilerplate information—who shot whom, who was dead, who was under arrest. But they never handed over one decent scrap of information to their colleagues in television. Not only did television reporters make three times as much money as newspaper reporters for less work, but they could take a lead that a print reporter had sweated to get and broadcast it seven hours before the newspaper hit the street.

"One suspect, a drug dealer, is dead, but smart money says he didn't shoot anyone," said the photographer, sticking a piece of chewing tobacco into his cheek. He was around emergencies so much he was immune to their frantic pace. He looked relaxed, as if he were taking pictures at the dog show. He looked carefully at Kate. "You still work for the *Herald*?"

"Nah, I work for Channel Seven now," said Kate hurriedly.

"Go on then. You're making the big money, now earn it. Stop leeching off your poor brethren in the print business."

Kate was stung. "What do you mean?" she said, but the photographer had turned away.

Rex Miller, the Blow-Dryer King from Channel 4, loped over.

"Got any information? I'm live in ten minutes," Miller said, giving her an empty-headed grin that he probably thought made him look like Clark Kent. If you told Miller the time, he was usually grateful.

She gave him a thin smile, trying to mask her misery. "Not this time, Rex, sorry. I work for Channel Seven now. I'm your competition." His smile dissolved and he looked flustered. For the first time in her life, she was beginning to feel sorry for on-air talent. Television forgives nothing. Screw up on live television in a major market like New York and you look like a jerk in 2 million living rooms throughout the tristate area. Screw up twice, you'll be reading crop forecasts in Abilene, Texas.

She walked slowly up to the police ribbon and ducked under. Another bad sign. If it were a straight cop shooting, the brass would be so frantic about disturbing a crime scene, they would've cordoned off the block. She made her way to the front door of the apartment building and walked up the decrepit stairs.

She was already into the drug dealer's apartment before a patrol cop asked her for identification.

"Sorry, ma'am. You can't go any farther. There'll be a press briefing at eight A.M. tomorrow."

She looked past the cop to where the drug dealer lay dead on the floor. To his right, a scuffed brown stain was littered with dirty gauze, rubber tubing, and surgical gloves, which EMS technicians had used and dropped in their frantic effort to save Versos.

She nodded to the cop and walked downstairs. She'd been about to end her first day in television with a cold Michelob and this guy was getting his chest torn open by a piece of lead.

She nudged past two large-shouldered men who stood whispering on the stairway.

"Excuse me," one of them said. The words made Kate freeze. She looked up fast.

She heard the sound of a locomotive and realized it was her lungs, swelling and shrinking. She felt weightless and bent her knees slightly to reconnect with the earth. This has happened too many times before, she chided herself. She forced herself to blink. But when she opened her eyes, he was still standing there. She knew it was really him because he was about ten times more attractive than she remembered him. He had lost weight and the last vestige of his varsity-football-team physique. He looked older, more sophisticated, and sexier. She felt as if every nerve ending in her body paused and leaned slightly in his direction. She felt a pressure below her stomach. She licked her lips instinctively and the corners of her mouth softened into a smile.

"Finn," she exhaled. The sound of the locomotive stopped. It seemed like such an inadequate way to begin.

For an instant, Kate thought he might lean over and kiss her. But instead, Kate watched a kaleidoscope of emotions swirl across Finn's face. Then he clamped down his jaw and scowled, his blue eyes sunk in a web of lines. He turned away. Kate could see his shave was uneven and his shirt collar was tucked inside his vest. Whatever emotions he was feeling, he was trying to make himself look angry and remote.

She glanced at his companion but didn't recognize him.

"Versos was your friend? I'm sorry," she said.

His face opened slightly to accept the comment, and she met his gaze. But then he looked past her. She felt like a scuba diver whose oxygen line had just been cut. He was slipping away. She couldn't let him go. I've waited so long to see you, she wanted to shout. I've missed you.

"Were you there? What happened?" she asked. She hated herself for sounding professional, but she didn't know what else to say. She could barely stop herself from taking his chin in her palms.

The other detective started to answer, but Finn interrupted.

"Can't make a comment, ma'am," he said, enunciating every word with anger. Each syllable was like a blow. She shook her head quickly, like a wet dog shaking droplets of rain off his fur. "Can't talk to the press." He was sealing a barrier between them, thick, unyielding, and impenetrable.

"No." She held up her hand. "Let me start again. What I meant to say was . . ." But Finn had already moved away. She closed her eyes. When she opened them, he had moved out of earshot. She stared at his broad back, wondering what he would do if she walked over and whispered in his ear. But the image of Kate Hepburn she carried like a mental mascot wouldn't let her do it. She measured the space between them with her eyes. Five feet. She was five feet from the man she loved. She stood still, feeling a tractor trailer running over her heart. Then, without a word, she clumped down another flight of stairs. Out of sight, she sagged against the wall and felt tears in her eyes. She felt like a little flame inside her had been extinguished. She didn't think she could make it to the van.

Blinking rapidly, she recognized the stooped shoulders of Joe Baeder, a duty sergeant from the Eighty-third Precinct, trudging up the stairs. Baeder had always told her she reminded him of his daughter. She was grateful to see a familiar face.

"What's it look like?" she mumbled to him as he grabbed her elbow and steered her to the corner of the landing. She rubbed her eye with her sleeve. She suddenly remembered that she was working. She checked her watch. She had about seven minutes to airtime. She was cutting it fine.

"Bad shooting. And the suspect is dead."

When police officers talked about a bad shooting, it meant the cops had misjudged the situation and when the smoke cleared, fingers were being pointed at the cop who fired the gun. It happened all the time. A housing cop shoots a fourteen-year-old carrying a toy gun believing it is the real thing. Bad shooting. A patrol cop trying to quiet a rampaging husband misfires and shoots his partner, who is trying to protect the wife. Bad shooting. They were tragedies for the victim's family, an embarrassment to the police department, and an endless horror for the surviving police officer.

Kate looked at Baeder, trying to read his face. She had to make him say it. "But the dead guy was a suspect, right? What makes it a bad shooting?"

It wasn't like the C unit stormed into the wrong apartment and shot a priest. Ordinarily, police brass wouldn't be upset about a dead drug dealer when a cop was mortally wounded.

She pushed. "And the apartment was full of drugs. Right?"

"Right."

It isn't a crime for a police officer to kill someone if he feels his life is in danger. A grand jury would surely see how a police officer might feel mortally threatened running through an apartment where the occupants kept bricks of cocaine lying around like cutlery.

Normally paternal and effusive, Baeder looked as if he wanted to leave before anyone saw him talking to her.

She took a step, blocking his retreat with her body. "So?" she prompted.

"The suspect appears to have been unarmed."

Got it, she thought. She checked her watch. Time was running out. Undercover shot by his backup. It had happened before. "Sorry to have to ask you this, Joe, but if the suspect wasn't armed, which police officer shot Versos?"

He looked at her and lowered his chin. "That, my dear, is the sixty-four-thousand-dollar question."

At 10:58, Landis was screaming. Bernie and Manuel were set up to do a live feed from the scene, but Vic Manero still hadn't arrived. At 10:59, Andrew Fink's disembodied voice floated over the IFB and suggested that Kate clip back her wildly curling hair so it didn't cover her brow.

"If there's a breeze, stand facing it so you don't get sideways hair. People want to see your forehead," Fink said soothingly. "It makes you look honest."

"I'm having a bad night here, Andrew," Kate whispered into the camera, thinking how Finn had turned away. She was hoping Landis wouldn't have the volume up on her image as it was beamed into the newsroom. "I don't think I can do this."

"Sure you can," Andrew said. "I've seen a lot of faces on the screen here. You're a natural."

She smiled wanly into the camera and concentrated on not bursting into tears. She tried to imagine what Fink looked like, standing in front of a bank of screens and dials in the microwave booth. She figured him to be a handsome, informal guy who didn't pay attention to fashion. Probably wore crew shirts under a sports jacket to work and looked better than most buttoned-down executives.

"Don't forget to lean into the camera a little, it makes you look trustworthy. And smile. The news is grim enough. Nobody wants to hear it from someone who looks like an undertaker."

Landis's voice broke through on her IFB. "Don't mess this up or we're all fired."

"Yeah, yeah, Landis. Why don't you give the girl a break?" Kate looked around for the unfamiliar voice. It was the first time she had heard Bernie, her soundman, say a word.

"Relax, sister, and put on some lipstick," said Manuel. Kate did as she was told. "That's better."

As Landis counted down the seconds, Kate faced the camera and began.

# 6

The five cops from Group C sat slumped in the small airless office of Brooklyn Narcotics Task Force trying to come up with an official explanation of how Versos had been shot and killed.

"You'll all have your individual interviews with IAB, but as your commanding officer, I am trying to establish, in a preliminary way, what happened," said Capt. Richard Bollini. "I feel foolish doing this, because I think of you all as my sons, but when something like this happens in a family, it's best to clear the air fast."

Finn heard the words but their meaning kept slipping away. This afternoon, Group C had gathered in the locker room of the precinct to console one another and drink. "Versos's dead," Money murmured, handing Finn a flask. "Hell of a guy," Finn answered, taking a long swallow and silently acknowledging his inner torment. He was shattered by the sight of Versos lying bleeding on the floor. And sleep was no escape. Every time he closed his eyes, he saw Kate Murray's face. Seeing her was a moment he had been dreading. Even in the dingy hallway, she looked so breathtakingly beautiful that he almost forgot how angry he was when she walked away from him. Every cell of his body was crying out for a woman he could never have. He took another swallow. When Versos was shot, he had lost a good friend, he thought, feeling the vapors of the whiskey attack his sinuses. When Kate walked away, he had lost everything.

Bollini turned to Bigelow, who was sitting with his back against a dingy file cabinet, still wearing his Operation Drug Free jacket. "Bigelow, no one wants to close this investigation out quicker than me, but you were the ranking officer, so I have to ask you, what happened?"

Bigelow swallowed and looked around the room, then stared at Mark Money before he spoke.

"When Johnson came out of the building, we got your signal." Bigelow nodded at Bollini. "We ran across into the target apartment. Money was the first one up the stairs. I was behind him. When I ran in the room, I saw Mark Money with his gun drawn, and Versos and the dealer were lying on the floor."

Finn's head snapped back and he felt panic flood in. He must have blacked out, missed something crucial. He never should've started drinking this early. Now he was intoxicated on duty and it sounded to him as if Bigelow were about to blame Money for the shooting.

Bigelow continued, "There didn't seem to be anything I could do for Versos at that point. So I held him and . . . ." Bigelow's voice cracked with emotion and then he was silent.

Money looked green and sick as he rested his elbows on his knees and let his head slump forward.

Finn's mouth began to move before he considered what he was going to say. "That's not what happened. Bigelow was first. Money was in front of me. The door slammed behind Bigelow and we tried to get it open. We dropped to the third-floor landing when we heard shots." Finn could hear his words slurring, and a small voice scolded him for making a fool of himself in front of his boss. "It was Bigelow in the room with Versos, not Money."

Bollini turned his large hound eyes to Finn.

"Detective Finn, it is clear to me that you are under the influence of alcohol. To compound matters, you are technically on duty." Finn felt himself flush as all eyes turned on him. "Because this is a difficult time for all of us, I will excuse your behavior, but the next time I see you, I hope you have sobered up."

Bollini directed his next question at Money.

"Listen, son. No one blames you." Finn waited for Money to set Bollini straight, but Money never looked up. Finn looked around, but McCoy and Bigelow were both staring at the gray linoleum floor.

Bollini continued, "But there will be repercussions. As of this moment, you are on modified duty. And I'd imagine that once IAB does its interviews, there'll be a grand jury. You'll need to get yourself a lawyer, so call your union."

After the meeting, McCoy, Money, and Bigelow walked to the parking lot together, a few paces ahead of Finn.

Finn looked around, making sure no cops were loitering around outside the precinct during the change of shift. The pavement was as soft as buttered toast and radiated warmth into the soles of Finn's sneakers.

"Bigelow, Money, McCoy," he called out. "What the fuck's going on?" At first, they pretended not to hear him.

Finn called out again and Bigelow turned slowly, as if he weren't quite sure who was calling.

"What's going on?" repeated Finn. McCoy looked at his shoes. Bigelow put a protective hand around Money and stared at Finn as if he were a stranger.

"Why don't you take a hint from Bollini, John Finn. Sober up," Bigelow said, irritated. "Versos's shooting is a family matter and it's going to stay in the family."

# 7

It was a little after nine and Kate Murray was sitting in her parked car outside the Soldiers and Sailors Social Club in a quiet section of Ozone Park. For the past three days, she and the crew had ripped through segments on traffic and lead poisoning, dropped Manero and Bernie off at the station, and headed out to a mob social club in Queens. For three nights, Kate and Manuel had sat in her car, his small, portable camera aimed at the thin wood door of the social club, waiting for a Brooklyn judge to turn up. If her FBI source was right, and she could get footage of the Honorable Guiseppe Cresia having regular sit-downs here with the Gambino family, she'd have made television history. Even if her source was wrong, she'd still have to cover traffic stories with Vic Manero during the day. Either way, the long stakeout was having a soothing effect on her. It made her feel as if she was earning the generous salary the station gave her. Producing for Manero was frustrating, and doing the showy stand-ups when Manero was too drunk or belligerent to get in front of the camera had pushed her anxiety to a new level. For Kate, the feeling that she was doing the real pick-and-shovel work of investigative journalism made her feel secure.

She was also learning a lot about Manuel. Her cameraman was the only son of the first Puerto Rican ironworker to get hired at the Brooklyn Navy yards. He'd been fired in the economic nosedive of the seventies and returned to Puerto Rico a broken man.

Manuel, who looked like a Hispanic Howard Stern, wanted to make sure the same thing never happened to him. With the help of his uncle, a major Brooklyn numbers runner, Manuel was, at the age of twenty-five, accepted into the union that covered the technical side of television—an organization that guaranteed him a job for life.

She watched another thick-necked goon walk into the social club. No sign of the judge. She looked at her watch, hummed quietly to herself, and thought of her empty apartment. If she were at home, she would be dropping her skirt and garters in a heap, dialing for takeout, pulling on her sweatpants, and sitting down to review the most recent tapes she'd made of her standups. It had almost become an obsession. She was too nervous during the broadcast to know if she was managing to carry it off, and every time the red light on the camera went dark, Kate felt like throwing up. The only way she prevented herself from quitting on the spot was to set her VCR to record every newscast in case she went on camera. Then she would rush home and review her performance frame by frame. She shook her head. Two years ago, in a fit of impatience, Kate had destroyed her chance of adding natural-looking red highlights to her jet-black hair by walking out of a salon with half her scalp wrapped in aluminum foil. Now, she sat in front of the television, mesmerized by her image. With every tape she was able to isolate another mistake in her delivery. She would run to her bathroom mirror and reread her script out loud. She was learning to keep her eyes steady, not to bob her head to emphasize her words, and to smile without crinkling the skin around her eyes.

At nine-thirty, Landis began beeping her at regular three-minute intervals. By nine forty-five, she decided she couldn't ignore him any longer. Maybe a subway train had crashed. Maybe the World Trade Center had been bombed again. She pulled out of her shadowed spot near the social club and drove five blocks until she found a public phone. She held the receiver between her chin and shoulder and shook her head slowly as he talked.

It wouldn't be the biggest story of the year, but it was the kind that brought joy to the tiny black hearts of every television news editor in town.

To Kate, it was an assignment from hell.

"Nah, Landis, lose my beeper, will you? I'm doing two stories a day for you guys. We're working on a big enterprise piece. . . . Yeah. Big. . . . No, bigger. . . . Bigger than a voodoo killing? I don't know." She rubbed her brow. "How many were ritually slaughtered?"

When Landis was trying to be persuasive, he had an infectious habit of talking as if he were already listening to promos of the broadcast. Two minutes on the telephone with him and Kate always found herself referring to a witness as "the innocent bystander" or a female student as a "coed."

"What if we leave and the judge shows up? I'll have missed him and ruined my social life for nothing and blown the station's budget on Manuel's overtime," Kate groused.

Forty-five minutes later, she stood in a moldering one-bedroom apartment behind a liquor store in Crown Heights watching two laughing assistants from the medical examiner's office trying to fit a headless sheep into a body bag.

They greeted Kate like the visiting dignitary from a leper colony.

"I know you, you're the lady on television," chortled the older ME, who had a walleye and a hearing aid. Kate felt herself blush. Five years writing for a major New York tabloid had left her almost entirely anonymous. After a few stand-ups on local news, her dry cleaner began to call her "Ms. Murray, ma'am," and people on the street had begun to stare.

The older ME's assistant continued, talking to her in an aggressively weird way. "Well, I'd like to see their faces at the morgue when they unzip the vinyl and meet Mary's little lamb."

The deceased man lay glazed-eyed in the bathtub,

flanked by two uniformed police officers drinking coffee. Their sergeant, one of Kate's longtime sources, was talking to the crime-scene detectives. As far as Kate could tell, the dead man was either a voodoo priest who was killed as part of a Santeria mass or a crazy son-of-a-bitch who, in a psychotic frenzy, tried to eat the flesh of a dead animal before settling into the bathtub to cut his own throat.

She needed to hear it from the experts, so she waited until the MEs bagged the sheep.

"Crime scene? Or was this self-inflicted?" She thought of Manuel outside and hoped he had hooked up with the news crew the station had sent out. She checked her watch. She needed to get this story on the air in less than thirty minutes.

The younger ME sniffed as his laughter trailed off.

"Ms. Murray," he said stiffly, "suicides and homicides are both serious crimes in the state of New York."

The older ME started to laugh again. "Yeah, let's bring back the death penalty for suicide."

The younger ME brayed.

"Please, could you help me?" Kate asked.

"You're the television lady. You tell us," said the older assistant.

There was something mean about these two, Kate decided. They thought that being on television made her somebody important. That sharp little crystal of fame was scratching at them, making them cruel and stupid. She couldn't tell them that getting hired at Channel 7 was a lucky break. They didn't want to hear it. They hated her. In a better world, they seemed to say, we would be on television and you'd be stuffing dead bodies in bags.

"I don't know a thing about forensics," she pleaded. "What do you think?"

"Can't tell," said the younger one, stonewalling. "Got to wait for the ME's report."

"Guess."

The young ME said nothing.

"Did it his own self," said the other.

"Why?" Kate asked.

"How bad do you want to know?"

Kate shrugged. A bell was ringing inside her head. There was a charge in the room. The walleyed ME was challenging her. Even his sidekick shut up and watched them, waiting to see what would happen.

"Stick your hand in the bathwater," the older ME directed Kate.

She looked at the dead man's face. The flesh of his face draped over his cheekbones. She was tired, she wanted to go home.

The cops had stopped talking and were watching to see what she would do.

"You've got to be kidding," she started.

"You want answers? Do what I said," the older ME said. "Go on."

She thought about Landis. She thought about a stack of *Daily Heralds* she had at home under her couch with headlines like LIZ TAYLOR HAS AIDS and THE INCREDIBLE SECRET LIFE OF MICHAEL JACKSON. She wanted to get this over with. She stared at the older ME as she stalked over to the bathtub, willing her face to give away nothing. She felt revulsion roiling upward from the pit of her stomach, but she swallowed hard.

She glanced into the bathtub before she dipped her fingers into the bloody water. She didn't want to look, but her pupils were drawn to the gaping wound under the dead man's chin.

The older ME didn't miss a beat. "See, it's still warm. Someone wants to kill you, they don't care if you're in a comfortable bath before you die. A warm bath makes the blood run faster. Says to me he was preparing to enjoy his last brief moment on earth."

"Self-inflicted," Kate and the young ME said together.

Twenty minutes later, Kate stood outside the liquor store while Manuel, his camera on a tripod, pleaded with a pack of weary hookers leaning into waiting cars to stay out of the background of the shot.

"You got it?" Landis's voice came over the IFB. "You got the voodoo angle?"

Kate sighed. Abused from all sides. "Let me talk this one through, Steve. A guy is dead, but I can't say for sure if it was a voodoo killing. It could have been a voodoo suicide."

"What? We air in four minutes. I don't want to hear anything about a voodoo suicide!"

Kate was distracted by a well-muscled pimp who walked too close and drawled, "Hey, baby."

The crazy fear of the crime scene had left her drained. In the light of the streetlamp she thought she saw a faint stain on her fingers. She felt her bile rise. What was she doing here in the middle of the night? she asked herself, wiping her fingers on her skirt. She should never have answered her beeper when Landis called. She should be home, reading in bed with the kind of man who casually ran his hand over her knee every chapter or two. She examined her fingers again, squinting. The glare of the streetlamp caught the knotty scar that ran on the underside of her forearm. She turned her wrist, momentarily mesmerized by the rim of gnarled flesh. She thought about Finn. She had walked away from her best shot at love to be here, on this dirty, dangerous corner in Crown Heights with blood on her hands. It was a warm summer night but she felt an ache, a kind of forlorn longing, settle into her bones like a fever.

"What did you say, Steve?" Manuel was standing behind the camera, making clicking noises with his tongue. She heard Landis panting in nervous fear over the IFB. She felt outraged, imagining how he would insult her in front of her colleagues at the morning meeting. To her right, a pair of transvestite hookers with matching Diana Ross wigs looked as if they were about to start slugging it out.

Landis's voice came back, too loud in her ear. "You got to get the voodoo angle. If we drop a single Nielsen point, I'm dead!"

She heard Andrew Fink's voice. "This isn't newspapers, Kate, it's television. There's nothing on paper to read and reread. If it isn't larger-than-life, the average viewer will open another beer and forget everything you say. This is what you can do. Make the wildest claim you can, then temper it with your next few sentences. That way, the overall impression you give is correct."

"Can I do that?" she asked Fink skeptically.

"You have to," he said firmly.

She squared her shoulders like Katharine Hepburn and took a breath. "I'll go with the voodoo, Steve. It'll run like this." She faced the camera and gave a fake smile.

"A Brooklyn man was found dead in his bathtub tonight surrounded by decapitated animals in what police said may be a ritual killing. But police sources say they haven't yet ruled out the possibility that the wounds were self-inflicted."

"Don't say *decapitated,* say *headless,*" Steve corrected her without hesitation, giving no sign that he was aware of Fink's words. "And be more graphic about the wounds."

Her shoulders sagged. "Steve . . . I'm about to become the victim of a sex crime. Let's just get this done."

"Right," said Landis. "Countdown, two minutes. Cuing up."

Twenty-five feet to her right, a station wagon stopped and the passenger-side door swung open. One of the Diana Ross hookers clambered in. Kate watched as the BABY ON BOARD plaque in the back window began to sway.

"Three, two, one," Fink counted down. Manuel gave the sign. "Okay, go."

# 8

Finn sat in his dark apartment in front of the television with an open beer. The sound was turned down and the radio blasted a heavy-metal song that was indistinguishable from the one before it. He was going to sit here and drink beer, not moving or feeling, until he fell asleep or had to report to work, whichever came first. He decided he didn't care if Bigelow and the rest of the guys hated him. He didn't want to think about what might have happened to Versos. What was done was done. He didn't want to think either about Bigelow taking money from Chinese gangsters. What the asshole members of his group did on their own time was their own business. He didn't want to know about it. He didn't want to think about anything at all.

He wondered how his life had gotten so desolate. Other cops he knew from the bar had wives and children and summer vacations at Disney World. They sweated through teacher's conferences and Little League. He thought, at some point, his life would begin to expand again. But for the last two years, it seemed to Finn that he was just stumbling from one empty room into another.

He had been sitting there for so long that when the doorbell rang, he thought he was hearing something on the radio.

"Jesus, I got to clean this place up," he said, kicking a beer can on the way to the door. It was probably someone collecting for something. Sisters of the Sick

and Poor. PAL, Girl Scouts. They all came to him.
Finn wondered if an angel working for the United
Way had marked his doorframe with blood, indicat-
ing CHARITY SUCKER LIVES HERE.

"What?" said Finn, surprised to see Bigelow at his
door. "What are you doing here?"

"We couldn't find you at O'Brien's. Aren't you
coming out with us?" Bigelow smiled as if they were
the best of friends, but his fingers were rubbing
together nervously.

Finn put a hand to his forehead and felt wrinkles.
Five hours ago, Bigelow had acted as if they were
blood enemies.

"C'mon, Money and McCoy are waiting in the car.
Johnson's old lady wouldn't let him come. Put on a
jacket, for God sake. You look like shit. And we got
reservations at Peter Luger's for end-cut steaks."
Bigelow pulled out a thick wad of bills and waved
them in front of Finn. "My treat."

Finn gave him a slightly dazed smile and Bigelow
seemed to relax.

"You sure I don't need my wallet?"

Bigelow winked. "Leave it at home with your shield
and your gun."

After a long, sodden dinner, McCoy decided he
needed target practice. An hour later, Finn watched as
Bigelow, Money, and McCoy stood in the moonlight,
shooting rats with their service revolvers on an abandoned stretch of beach at Arverne.

"I can't believe Rockaway is part of New York
City," said McCoy, squinting down the barrel. "This
reminds me of the town in Texas where my grandmother lived."

"Except these city rats would carry off a car if they
smelled cheese in the glove compartment," said Bigelow, sticking a small spoon under McCoy's nose.
McCoy inhaled deeply and then squeezed off a shot.

"You missed," said Finn. Bigelow extended the
cocaine spoon to Finn, nodding. Unsure what to do,
Finn mimicked McCoy and inhaled. It felt as if he

were packing hot gravel into his sinuses. Then his lips released into a smile.

McCoy squeezed off another shot. Finn heard the far-off chunk of the bullet entering the sand. He could hear things from fifty feet away. Rats scurrying, papers crackling in the breeze, the distant sound of a car horn.

"Missed again," said Finn, forgetting his good jacket and stretching out on the sand. He felt his jaw clenching and a little swarm of butterflies flapping their wings in his gut. He grinned at the thin slice of moon and raised one arm. "Detective John Finn. The un-de-feated rat-shooting cham-peen of Brooklyn."

"I'll get one," McCoy said defensively, accepting another noseful of cocaine from Bigelow.

Finn looked around at the steady, regular faces of the men in Group C. He couldn't believe he had been so paranoid about them. It happened sometimes to cops. Finn knew a detective in Bushwick, Tony Basely, who was so paranoid that he secretly tapped his home telephone. Every morning, Basely drove to work listening to a tape of his wife complaining about him to her mother. No, these were his only true friends. Some strange stuff had happened, but he had to believe there was a good explanation. Women could leave you and break your heart, but these men were the only thing he had to hold on to. There was no telling how far Finn would have sunk if Bigelow hadn't stepped in and reminded him how to be a man. They watched out for each other and they did their jobs. If they didn't run in and break up a drug deal, no one would. Some people saw them as the garbagemen of society. But Finn knew they were the best friends he could have hoped for.

"Remind me never to ask you to cover my back," said Finn happily. Then he remembered that Money was sitting nearby. He looked up and saw his friend slumped against an abandoned piece of hurricane fence.

"What the fuck's wrong with Money?" Finn asked. When no one responded, he heaved himself to his feet and staggered over to where Money sat. In the moonlight, he could see that Money's color was bad. The young cop's jacket was off and one of his shirtsleeves was rolled up. In his arm was a syringe full of blood.

"Jesus Christ, Money," screamed Finn. Bigelow came up behind them and expertly plucked the syringe out of the young man's arm.

Bigelow turned to McCoy and said, "Let's take him to the house."

Less than five minutes later, they were dragging Money up a set of elegantly patterned stairs to a house in Neponsit that Finn guessed must belong to a movie producer or an investment banker.

You could tell from the outside that the owner was loaded. Instead of a regular light over the door like all the other houses in Queens, the walkway was lit with small lanterns shaped like Japanese pagodas. The rest of the house was accented with spotlights that picked up the extravagant waterfront sunroom and the wide picture windows. It was as if the owner wanted to show you, night and day, what a rich bastard he was.

Finn was taken aback when Bigelow pulled a set of keys out of his pocket and opened the front door.

"Who lives in this house?"

"What do you mean?" Bigelow said, smiling. "You've been here before. It belongs to those guys you met."

Finn nodded vaguely. He felt as if he had stepped off a curb and fallen into a manhole. Finn rubbed his forehead to hide his panic. He didn't ask Bigelow, "What guys?"

Aside from some expensive-looking curtains, there wasn't a stick of furniture in the house aside from a grimy refrigerator and two telephones. From the closet, McCoy produced a blanket and a stained pillow and eased Money down on them.

From the living room, Finn gazed out the picture window. Still feeling the effects of the cocaine, he watched the Coast Guard boats twinkling on the water.

Over his shoulder, he saw McCoy and Bigelow

arguing in the other room, but something stopped him from joining them.

"I'm going to find the can," he called. Bigelow waved as he picked up the phone.

Finn walked down the long, empty hallway. Behind the first door on the left, he found a green marble bathroom with a water-stained sink. He flipped on the light switch, turned on the water, closed the door, and continued to explore.

The first door on the right led to a bedroom with full views of the ocean. The second bedroom looked the same, with lesser views. Across the hall, Finn found a small, unused sauna. The fifth door was more difficult to open. Slightly unbalanced, Finn pushed against it and the door gave.

The walls of the room had been stripped down to the struts, and a reinforced steel hatch had been laid into the floor. He found a light and turned it on. It was a storage compartment. But storage for what?

The closer he got to the hatch, the more he noticed a powerful odor in the room, something familiar that got in his nose and made his eyes water. Remnants of cocaine were racing through his heart, stoking his brain to think more clearly. His heart began pumping furiously. He felt cool sweat on his hairline. The identity of the smell drove into him like an arrow. He knew it from drug raids. The room reeked of heroin.

He turned off the light and walked quickly back to the bathroom to turn off the water, then joined the others. They were talking quietly now about the Mets' chances for the pennant, and Bigelow was dividing a stack of bills into five small piles. When he saw Finn, he grinned easily and casually swept the bulk of the money into his jacket pocket.

"You need some walking-around money?" Bigelow asked him, extending a few twenty-dollar bills. Finn hesitated and then realized he was afraid to refuse.

"Sure," said Finn, stuffing them into his back pocket. "I'll get it back to you on payday."

Bigelow smiled and shrugged.

Finn was relieved when Bigelow loaded a groggy

Money back into the car. Finn could hardly hold up his end of the conversation as they drove back to Brooklyn. But McCoy and Bigelow didn't notice. They were blasting "Lido Shuffle" on the tape deck, casually talking about old times.

"The neighbors saw us bring in the photo equipment. They knew it was five guys going in and out. So when the old lady knocked on the door of the surveillance apartment to complain about the noise, we didn't know what to do." McCoy explained for the third time as Bigelow smiled indulgently. "If she came in and saw the cameras pointed out the window, she might tip off our targets. But if we didn't let her in, she'd be suspicious, too. But Versos, he came up with a great idea. He called out, 'Just a minute. We're getting dressed.' Remember? It was great. The neighbors put two and two together and decided we were making gay porno films. They sure left us alone after that."

Some instinct for self-preservation squeezed a stiff laugh out of Finn's lungs. As Bigelow pulled the car up to Finn's apartment building, McCoy was adding details to the story and laughing. Bigelow was absently singing "Lido, whoa, whoa, whoa, who-o-a" along with the radio.

Finn stood in front of his condominium, smiling, until Bigelow's taillights disappeared around the corner. Then he fell to the curb and was violently sick.

# 9

By the time Kate got to J.J.'s Upper West Side apartment, it was midnight and she was soaked to the skin. She had spent the evening at Breezy Point broadcasting from the middle of a wild summer thunderstorm. Manero wanted to save his hair for the top story at eleven, so every hour, when the sitcoms were preempted for a weather update, Kate crawled out of the van and stood in the rain reiterating the weather bureau's storm warnings and pointing out wave heights. The more the wind blew and the larger the waves crested, the more crowded the beach became. Urban surfers, looking for the perfect curl, donned their wet suits to protect them from the polluted water and headed for the waves when the weather got bad. They were ruining Manuel's shot, and Kate was glad when a few large bolts of lightning sent them scurrying back to their cars. Covering a summer storm was a difficult assignment. The wind made Kate look terrible on television. She held her microphone in one hand and tried to keep the IFB in place with the other. That left her hair, which was wild on a mild day, blowing across her face, almost obscuring it. A quick glance in the monitor confirmed to Kate that she looked like a tumbleweed to millions of viewers across the tristate area. But she struggled on, getting a sky-to-horizon lightning bolt as a backdrop on the nine-o'clock "Special Weather Broadcast."

"That's great!" shouted Landis from the control table when he saw the lightning.

"Now he'll want you to do it again for the eleven," intoned Fink through the IFB.

But while the weather was the top story on the six-o'clock broadcast, by eleven the storm had dissipated to a light rain.

J.J. opened the door to her apartment. "There is nothing television does better than a good weather story," she said. "I'll get you some dry clothes before we start."

"Forget the mobbed-up judges, political scandals, and gun control," said Kate, walking into the apartment. "When the wind blows, I'm on the case." After Landis found out how much overtime Manuel had accumulated staking out the judge in the social club, he'd refused to authorize any more. "When I want you to investigate a judge, I'll let you know," he had said, sneering and dismissing her with a flick of his hand. At that moment, Kate felt like calling up Solomon Randall and begging for her old job back.

J.J. returned with a baggy summer sundress. "Here, try this." She held it out for Kate. "Tough day, huh?"

"Lousy day. I'm an experienced reporter. What am I doing covering wave heights?"

J.J. looked at her. "It's the kind of story that television owns. It can definitively answer the kind of existential questions that make casual viewers into faithful viewers. Like, will the storm turn into a hurricane? Are the planes late at LaGuardia? Will my boat wash away in a freak high tide? Never mind news from Sarajevo. That's newspaper stuff. People want to know about larger forces than themselves. They want to know how bad the rain is going to get."

"Yeah. Don't forget serial killers and ritual slaughter," said Kate, thinking of the voodoo suicide. Her face burned. "Maybe that isn't the kind of news business I want to be in," she mumbled almost to herself.

J.J. ignored her, handing her a towel. "You've been

doing good work—a lot more on camera than anyone ever anticipated. I hear Bartlett is very pleased."

"Thanks. I've been studying my tapes. I can tell I'm getting better. I just don't look like the other television reporters."

"Nothing that a good cosmetic surgeon can't fix," said J.J., laughing when she saw Kate's expression. "You're doing fine. I caught you a few times tonight. Barbara Walters you're not. But you looked appropriately rain-soaked and bedraggled. A little makeup and some practical advice and you'll be ready for prime time.

"First things first. Burn all your natural-fiber clothing. No cotton. No linen. They wrinkle in the van and look like hell. Get a boxy blue polyester jacket and pearls. It will look great on television, and you can wear it over a bathing suit and still look professional."

Kate looked dazed as J.J. continued, "Now, makeup. You need to see a professional stylist. But until you get the station to hire one for you, remember, put foundation on every surface of your face."

"I'm not an actor," wailed Kate.

"And your cameraman's not a magician. They've been lighting you in a flattering way, but some days there won't be time."

"Yeah," said Kate glumly.

J.J. stopped her rapid-fire lesson and looked her in the face. "You're not happy?"

"I don't know. Yeah." Kate paused, not wanting to seem ungrateful. "I'm happy to have a job. And this one is better than I could have hoped for. Even my dry cleaner gives me respect now. But I miss newspapers. Maybe I've had a charmed life, but at thirty-two, I've finally learned the meaning of the word *regret.*"

"You regret jumping to television?"

"What choice did I have? I needed a job and I could have done a lot worse."

"What then? What do you regret?"

"There was a time in my life when I walked away from relationships, from friends, people who cared about me. I never gave them a second thought."

"Are you talking about John Finn?"

"I'm surprised to hear myself saying it, but, yes, after all this time, I still miss him."

"I'm not surprised. It was always my opinion that you made a big mistake when you let him get away."

"Are you kidding? You never said that before."

J.J. shrugged. "Did you ask me? No."

Kate was confused. "But I thought that, you know, he was a cop. Not like, you know . . ."

"You didn't think your friends would approve of someone who got their BA in night school? It took me a long time to figure out that I couldn't live for what people thought of me."

Two years ago, J.J. had moved in with a graphic artist named Judy. J.J. shyly introduced Judy as her housemate, which seemed like some throwback to sorority days considering Kate knew J.J. and Judy shared a one-bedroom apartment. "Kate, wake up. You can't measure your boyfriends by your mother's yardstick anymore. It's enough to find someone you like. It's enough just to be happy."

J.J. produced a yellow tackle box full of elegant-looking bottles and tubes and resumed the lesson. "Don't use eyeliner on the bottom of your eyes. You'll look like something caught in the headlights. Define your lips with a lip pencil, then brush in the color. Throw out all your hats so you don't come to work with hat hair. Keep styling gel in your pocketbook, and always stand with the wind on your face or you'll get sideways hair like you did on the beach tonight."

Kate stared down at her damp hands. J.J. stopped.

"You can't just think about it. You have to try. Try to be happy."

"It's not so easy. I saw him, you know, on a story my first day at Channel Seven. He made it pretty clear he hated me," she said, reflecting. "Still, I was thinking about calling him, you know, trying to make amends."

"Make a kissing mouth," J.J. ordered, and began to paint Kate's lips. "No, don't call him. It's too easy.

After what happened, you've got to show him that he can put his trust in you."

"Think I should send him flowers?"

"Make the face again," J.J. instructed. "No. Too corny." She handed a small hand mirror to Kate. "But you'll think of something."

"What if I don't?"

"Kate, you've been in love with a guy you haven't seen for two years. You'll think of something."

# 10

Finn was relieved to be late for the surveillance-training seminar. Versos's getting shot behind a locked door had jolted him. But now, the image of Bigelow's stash house was like a black cloud trapped beneath his brow. He was agitated and confused, afraid if he started chatting with his buddies, he might blurt out something about heroin and Chinese gangs.

In the dismal classroom, members of Group C and Group D were seated, fingering their newly issued Nagra tape recorders. No one looked up when Finn squeezed himself behind an empty desk.

He sat directly behind Johnson and to the rear left of Bigelow. Once he was settled, he picked up his tape recorder, opened his surveillance manual, and was horrified to find that his hands were shaking. He dropped the book and clutched his hands together.

He loved Bigelow. Loved him like a brother. And he couldn't believe he'd gone from being a hard-ass cop to being a criminal. A crooked cop, he murmured to himself. Rotten. Not a grass eater, either. A meat eater. The phrase stuck in his trachea, and he squeezed his eyes shut.

Face it, he chided himself. We're not talking about a free lunch and a case of Scotch at Christmas. If Finn could believe his eyes, his best friend was taking money from the Chinese mob. Not only that, he had the keys to a Rockaway stash house. That could only mean that he was involved in the drug trade up to his ears. Meat eater. He said the words slowly, silently.

Finn rubbed his forehead, feeling Bigelow's taint sink into him. Maybe I'm wrong. But what if I'm not? What have I become? A meat eater? No. An assistant meat eater? No. More like a meat eater's asshole buddy.

A grand jury wouldn't make such a fine distinction.

What did that make Johnson? he thought. What did Money know? Johnson looked over his shoulder and Finn realized that he'd made a noise.

Their instructor, Nick Albina, hooked him with his glinty eyes and nodded.

Finn wanted to bury his face in his hands, but instead he stared at the book in front of him without seeing a single word.

What would Albina do in this situation? Finn asked himself. Albina's instincts for self-preservation were sharp. Before he was put in charge of training narcotics cops, Albina had been a legendary undercover for about twenty years. The constant anxiety of setting up stings on high-level Colombian drug dealers had had a peculiar effect on him. He continually wore a distracted half-smile, part wary and slightly amused, as if he were listening to his own laugh track. Finn once had a beer with Albina's old partner, who told him that the only way to get Albina's full attention was to pull a gun on him.

This evening, Finn noticed, Albina was more focused and enthusiastic than usual since he was teaching the part of the course he loved. How to work undercover.

"You have only your hidden tape recorder and your wits. And tape recorders can go dead," Albina said as he smiled at some internal memory.

"You drink, you talk, you socialize with these people. Sometimes you get to be a friend, but you never forget what they are. Dangerous criminals."

Finn felt more alone than he ever had in his life. It was as if his skin had been burnt away in a flash fire and the protective layer that separated him from the rest of the world was gone. He tried to think of someone he could talk to, but no one came to mind.

Sure, there was Fat Tony, his old partner, but he had retired upstate and was running his own security business guarding 7-Elevens. He liked a couple of guys from the Eighty-third, but he hadn't really kept in touch since he got reassigned to Narcotics. There was Blinky, from the old neighborhood, but Finn didn't think he had a current phone number for him. He felt a cold finger on his heart. Since Kate had walked away, there was no one. No one he could go to. Finn felt a sharp point of pain, the progeny of the dull ache he felt every time he put his lips to a glass of beer or a brandy or a shot of Scotch. No one. As the truth pressed down on him, Finn found himself staring at the back of Bigelow's head. For the first time he noticed Bigelow had a small tonsure of thinning hair shining under the fluorescent light. The smartest, most fearless, most daring, and maybe the most corrupt cop Finn knew was quietly going bald. He couldn't take his eyes off the spot. It was like a sign from God that Bigelow was vulnerable in ways he didn't even know about.

"You got to have two sides of your brain operating at once. On one side, you're a cop, someone entrusted to enforce the law. On the other side, you're a criminal."

Finn looked at Albina and the back of Bigelow's head. "You talk like a criminal. You act like a criminal. You think like a criminal," Albina was saying.

Finn picked up his surveillance tape recorder and smiled. He had a crazy idea, almost a joke really. Taping his friends. Chances were, it would come to nothing. One of these days, Bigelow would explain what was going on and Finn would tell him about the tape and they would have a good laugh.

Finn squinted at the bald spot on Bigelow's head.

If there was something going on, then the tapes would be like having insurance against a flood. Finn knew that if the high water came, he would get wet. But a tape recording might be the little pile of sandbags that would keep the river from washing him away.

Albina was pounding his fist into his open hand and his eyes were flashing.

"At the same time, never let one side of your brain eclipse the other. Never forget which side you are on."

# 11

Kate sat in front of a large bank of CDs blowing a little tune through her lips. She was in the library, which was visible from the main floor through a set of double glass doors. The eleven-o'clock broadcast had finished, and only the skeletal crew who put together the midnight headline show remained in an otherwise dark and silent newsroom.

The library at the *Daily Herald* was known as the morgue, a damp catacomb of yellowing file folders stuffed with news articles and haphazard piles of reference books. There was nothing dead about Channel 7's library. For starters, it was jammed with the brightest and fastest computers in the information business. And the databases were frightening. There was an alphabetical list of every name printed in every telephone book in every state in the country. There was a CD filled with real estate records indexed by state and last name of the property owners. There was a car-registration database and a database that provided credit information on your subject right down to his monthly finance charges.

Kate knew she'd come to love tracking down mobsters in this room. The carpeted library was more spacious than her cramped Tercel. Nobody wore guns or directed their bodyguard to shove you off the sidewalk. And it was so efficient.

Tonight, her target wasn't a hidden partner in a construction firm, it was John Finn. She bit her thumbnail and paused. She was taking J.J.'s advice.

She was going to try to be happy. She just had to figure out where to begin.

"Follow the big money," she said to herself, and selected the real estate CD. She pressed the POWER button and fed the disc into the computer. In the time it took her to input Finn's name, she learned that he still owned his old condominium in Bay Ridge. And he still had a ways to go on his mortgage.

She fed the address into the phone book logs. After they broke up, he changed his number. For the last two years when she had called information on a whim, the operator had told her the number was unlisted. Tricky. She rubbed her forehead. Then she selected another CD. It was a compilation of major mailing lists. If John Finn had sent away for Ginsu knives, ordered shirts through the mail, or answered a sweepstakes, the information he supplied to the company would have been sold to the makers of this disc. Ya! she almost shouted. He had supplied his telephone number to one telemarketer or another. Now she had it.

She looked at her reflection in the blank green screen and felt like a stalker. This was creepier than burglarizing someone's house, she thought. It was like sneaking into their apartment and photographing their most private papers.

She quickly scrolled through DMV and jotted down Finn's social security number. Now it was time to see what was really going on in his life. She tapped into the credit-information line and fed the computer what she already knew about him.

She wondered about the ethics of spying on an old lover. She heard her very proper Katharine Hepburn voice begin to scold. She jabbed the EXECUTE button. Forget it. She wasn't backing down. Too bad about privacy. Scientists used to believe disease was caused by bodily humors. They thought the world was flat. Times change. Certain concepts fall out of vogue. In truth, she reminded herself, Finn's privacy was gone long before she started feeding CDs into this machine.

She split the screen to get a full accounting of his monthly credit cards. On the right, she saw that American Express had frozen his account and shipped his debt to a collection agency. On the left, she saw that his Visa card was overextended. He'd started getting in debt over his head a few months after they broke up. He'd had a squeaky-clean credit rating until then. She wondered if it was just a coincidence. She began flipping one screen after another. He wasn't spending his money on a brand-new wardrobe. Most of the charges were from bars and restaurants. One bar, O'Brien's in Brooklyn, seemed to be responsible for the bulk of his debt. She wrote down the address of O'Brien's, then cross-referenced it in the phone log.

She quickly dialed the number that appeared on the screen.

In the background, she heard the unmistakable clatter and clinking of a busy bar.

"Is John Finn there?" she asked, testing.

"Who's this?"

"Rhonda."

"Well, he's not here yet, and when he arrives for his nightcap, I won't be happy to see him," snarled the bartender.

Kate hung up the telephone slowly and smiled.

# 12

Ordinarily, Kate wouldn't have set foot in a bar like O'Brien's. Ordinarily, Kate wouldn't have chosen Marilee Woodward as a drinking buddy either.

Marilee, a twenty-eight-year-old education writer, had left her renovated Victorian house, her staff job at the *Atlanta Constitution,* and her investment-banker husband for a job at the *Herald.* Now Randall was turning the once-respectable newspaper into the *National Enquirer,* and Marilee was looking to forget her troubles in the arms of anonymous men. Tonight she had her blond hair pulled back in a headband and she was wearing a cheerleader's pleated miniskirt and a halter top. Kate was hoping Marilee's cheap, queen-of-the-hop looks would act as a kind of shield to keep Kate from being recognized. It was getting to be a fact of life. Total strangers looked at her and nodded as if they were glad to see a familiar face. About twice a day now, someone broke through her cocoon of anonymity and asked her point-blank, "Aren't you the lady on the news?" Kate was learning to smile, friendly enough not to rebuff a potential Nielsen family viewer but distant enough to avoid breaking her stride.

"What are we doing way out in Brooklyn at this dive? When I moved from Atlanta, I thought by now I'd be drinking Dom Pérignon on Broadway." Marilee made her dumb-blonde looks work for her. She had a sharp tongue and an almost photographic memory, but she prefaced even the most biting question with a toothy, innocent smile.

"Your paycheck from Randall won't stretch that far. Besides, I'm looking for someone," said Kate, nervously chewing the inside of her cheek. She caught sight of Marilee's well-muscled back in the mirror behind the bar. It would almost have been better to risk being recognized than to be in the company of Miss Aerobics.

Kate motioned to the bartender. "A beer," she shouted above "A Horse With No Name," which was blaring from the jukebox. Not a flicker of recognition in his eyes, she noticed. Obviously, O'Brien's wasn't a pocket of dedicated Channel 7 news fans. So far, so good.

She checked her lipstick in the mirror. Lipstick, what a stupid invention, she thought. Kate was always forgetting to scrape it off her teeth until Landis's final countdown. Last week, when she was reviewing one of her tapes, she was appalled to see that she had managed to smudge her lipstick in such a way that she looked as if she had a harelip.

She stared at Marilee's rosebud lips. Marilee would be perfect for television.

"I'd like a Sex on the Beach," said Marilee.

The bartender didn't move. "Not me," he said, "too sandy."

Marilee looked confused.

"She'll have a Scotch," said Kate hurriedly, and the bartender moved off.

The bar was filling up. Men in their thirties and forties came to escape the clammy summer humidity, lean on the dark oak bar, and drink a beer. They talked about the Yankees' prospects and pretended, if only for an evening, that their waistlines weren't expanding, that the mortgage wasn't due. They came to forget a discomfiting truth—that of all the things they planned in their lives, only a few would actually happen and those, largely by luck.

"So tell me," said Marilee, downing her Scotch and

leaning forward conspiratorily, "is this guy you're looking for, like, your boyfriend?"

"Was. Was my boyfriend." But I was too caught up trying to get a front-page story to know when I had a good thing, she almost said. Instead, she smiled, grinding her teeth. "Maybe he will be again."

Her eyes followed the bartender, who seemed to be scolding a patron at the other end of the bar.

"If you're going to threaten me," he said, "you'll have to drink somewhere else." Kate felt her cheeks turn red. He was talking to Finn.

Finn looked bewildered, as if the family dog had bitten him instead of fetching the morning paper.

"What's gotten into you?" Finn replied, oblivious to Kate. "Can't a man have a drink in peace? What is it, male menopause? The change of life?"

"I'm warning you now, that's all," the bartender said, grudgingly sliding Finn a Scotch and a beer chaser.

It looked as if Finn had arrived at O'Brien's with his entire unit. Kate recognized a few of the faces from Versos's shooting. She noted a massive mustached man who seemed to be their superior. She tried to remember what the crime-scene sergeant had called him. Biggs? Doug Biggs? She identified Mark Money, the one who was put on modified duty after the Versos shooting, from the picture that had run in the *Herald*.

They didn't seem to be mourning their fallen comrade, thought Kate. In fact, they seemed positively jovial.

She elbowed Marilee. Both women moved two barstools toward the men. They were talking about the Yankees. Something about the left-handed starters. Kate hated the way men dissected sports into meaningless phrases. "The Night Chicago Died" came on the jukebox and Kate watched Finn slap two broad backs and stagger back toward the busy men's room. She gave Marilee a sign and followed him to the back of O'Brien's. She waited impatiently beside one of two darkened telephone booths until Finn walked unsteadily out. He didn't see her. She watched in amazement as Finn stepped into one of the booths, deftly opened his shirt, pulled out a microtape, and turned it over.

After quickly buttoning his shirt, Finn left the telephone booth. By the time he joined two skinny redheads talking in the back of the bar, he'd already affected a drunken sway.

The noise inside the bar had become deafening. It was almost eleven o'clock, and the men clustered around the bar were drinking with the grim determination of marathon runners.

"Theodore and I are going back to Manhattan," Marilee announced when Kate returned, gesturing to a bearish man wearing a feminine-looking gold cross at his neck. Kate felt as if the evening were spinning out of control. She wanted Marilee here with her.

"You're going home with a stranger?" said Kate dumbly.

"It's better than going home to Atlanta," said Marilee, hoisting her perfect body off the barstool.

Kate leaned into Marilee's blond hair. She wanted to say, "Don't leave me here alone," but she was too proud. "Don't forget to use a rubber," she said instead.

"Don't tell me your friend is leaving you on your own," said a voice. It was Finn's boss. She remembered his name. Dougie Bigelow. Kate took in his walrus mustache and his large, menacing jaw. There was something overwhelmingly masculine about this man. He practically exuded high-octane testosterone. Something about him scared her and attracted her simultaneously.

She forced herself to smile.

"It's happened before," she said engagingly.

Bigelow clapped his hand on her shoulder.

"Well, we can't have you drinking alone, come and join us. What's your name, honey? You look mighty familiar."

Kate didn't wince. "I'm Kate."

"My name's Dougie Bigelow. I'm a narc, so don't offer me a joint." The rest of the men laughed and Bigelow pulled her close. "You really do look familiar. Did you go to Fordham?"

"No," Kate said too quickly. She swallowed. "No, I didn't."

"Strange. I know I've seen you before. What're you drinking, Kate? School's out and we're ready to party."

Finn turned and found her standing with his best friend. She could feel his eyes bore into her. She ignored him, trying to size up the situation. If he was wearing a wire on his friends, he must be in a world of trouble. Having her pop up in his life again would be the least of his problems.

She sipped the beer Bigelow had ordered for her.

"Your friend was pretty," Bigelow said, giving her a sincere smile. "But not as pretty as you."

"I can't compete with Marilee. She's the authentic belle of the ball." Kate was so distracted by Finn she was having trouble keeping up her end of the conversation.

Finn pushed between them. "Let me buy your new girlfriend a drink." He was talking too loud.

As he reached into his pocket for money, a shoving match lit up behind them. A man built like a refrigerator surged against Finn. Kate saw his hand reach involuntarily for his shirt, then heard his tape recorder clatter under Bigelow's barstool.

She and Finn both looked down and she heard Finn gasp. Out of the corner of her eye, she saw Bigelow leaning down to retrieve whatever had fallen under his chair.

She took a deep breath, sloshed her beer on Bigelow, and in the confusion, allowed her handbag to empty onto the floor.

Silence spread through the bar like cheap cigar smoke. All eyes were trained on the five-by-four-inch tape recorder under Bigelow's seat, which was quietly recording the awkward coughs and sniffs of the crowd.

"Ah, sorry about the beer," she said to Bigelow, who wasn't smiling anymore.

Bigelow reached down and picked up the recorder between two fingers as if he were holding a rat. "What do we have here? Is this IAB among us?"

Kate could feel the icy stares from around the bar. She smiled nervously, stuffing her papers and folders back in her bag.

"Sorry, that's mine. I'm a reporter, Channel Seven news," she announced in a steady tone. "I always carry a tape recorder."

"Is it always on?" asked a voice a few feet away.

"Oh, is it on?" she asked, forcing a smile. "That's odd. I hope I didn't wear out the battery."

She turned to Bigelow and took the tape recorder out of his hand. His face was dark, almost swarthy, and his eyes warned of violence.

"Well, thanks for the beer and the compliment," she said, pleased her voice didn't shake.

Then she turned a straight back to the silent men and walked out of the bar.

# 13

She sat behind the wheel of her Tercel at the dark edge of the parking lot for forty-five minutes before Finn finally staggered out. He elaborately scratched at his pants and waddled toward her car. When she was sure no one had followed, she threw open the passenger-side door.

"Get in."

He collapsed into the seat like a man who had been rescued from drowning.

# 14

She had moved to a larger apartment, Finn noticed. This one had a dining room, French doors, and stripped-oak shutters. But the interior was unmistakably Kate's. He recognized the oatmeal couch and the blue overstuffed chair. He had lain in his own fusty sheets imagining this room so often that now he almost felt as if he'd been here before. He smiled when he saw the familiar piles of newspapers stacked up under the furniture. Above the couch hung a framed headline: REPORTER STALKED/STABBED BY SERIAL FIEND. He was lost in a wave of memory.

She looked around. "You'd think my decorator was William Randolph Hearst," she said, trying to make funny small talk, but he barely heard her.

Two years ago, she was his girlfriend. He'd come to her old apartment and made crazy love to her. He didn't know she was being stalked by a psycho named Dominick. He'd watched from her bedroom as Dominick burst through her front door and stabbed her. Then Finn had shot Dominick to death.

"You moved," he said simply.

Kate looked at him. "Yeah. My landlord was such an asshole. She kept my entire security deposit to repair the bullet hole in the kitchen sink."

Finn smiled thinly. In the fantasy he had played and replayed in the last two years, Kate's apartment was the same but she had changed. In the fantasy, she could see the kind of man he was. She could understand that his heart beat only for her and she loved him for it. In the fantasy, she wouldn't want to leave him, ever.

"You want a drink?" she asked.

"I'll have what you're having."

She looked at him, thinking of his bar bill at O'Brien's. "I'm having seltzer."

She placed two crystal glasses on the table and put Finn's silent tape recorder between them.

"So?" she said.

He stared at her, willing himself to be immune to her electric sexuality that rolled toward him like thunderclouds.

"What can I tell you?" He shrugged slowly.

She smiled, but not a happy smile.

"Well, I'd like to know what you've been doing for the past two years. I'd like to know why you changed your telephone number and never returned the messages I left at the precinct." Finn felt her currents running fast through his limbs. He knew he'd better leave, but he was frozen in his chair. She had a power over him. And two years ago, she had used that power to destroy him. Kate saw him freeze up. "And, if you don't want to answer any of those questions, I'd like to know why you are wearing a wire on your friends." She finished quietly. "What's going on?"

He wanted to tell her everything: Bigelow taking money from the Chinese, his suspicions about the way Versos died, his sick feeling watching the men in his unit pretending Money had done the shooting, the stash house in Rockaway. But if he said it out loud, then he would have to believe that his best friends in the world were worse than three-quarters of the criminals he had locked up in sixteen years on the force. And he'd learned a few things about Kate. She was a reporter before all else. With her, everything you said was fair game for a story. Once he told her, she'd have about twenty-five questions, each harder to answer than the one before.

He felt stones of anger in his gut. He'd learned an even harder lesson about her. She was a bright girl, very bright, but there were some things she never recognized. Like the fact that not so long ago, he would have done anything for her. She never saw that. He had come this far. Sitting in her apartment was like licking an iron post in midwinter. He was stuck. In order to get free now, he'd have to rip off a tender piece of himself and leave it behind. He rubbed his forehead with an open hand. Be smart, he instructed himself.

"Listen, I'm trying to help you." Kate was sounding desperate. She wanted him to say something. "I saved your skin at O'Brien's. I don't even want to think what your so-called friends would have done to you if they knew that the tape recorder was yours."

The current between them ceased abruptly.

"Okay, now we're even," said Finn.

She looked mildly stunned.

"So, that's it?" she said after a long moment. "You want to call it a draw?"

He realized, with a start, that he had power over her, too. She wanted him. He looked at her boldly.

"You're looking for a story, right?"

"I went to O'Brien's looking for you." In spite of himself, Finn began to smile. "But I wouldn't turn away if one landed in my lap."

He closed his eyes, feeling something like eggshells cracking in his chest. It was the little soft feelings for her he thought he'd put away forever. He wanted so badly to have someone on his side he felt a physical pain. He took a deep breath. It's Kate, he told himself. The girl who walked away, the reporter.

"I had a fire in my apartment," he said. "I fell asleep while I was cooking a hamburger and almost burned down the building." He wasn't going to play her game. He was holding hard to a wedge of anger and sarcasm, trying to keep some distance between them.

"The fire department came and everything. It was terrible."

She looked at him helplessly but said nothing.

"My building manager has been on me to pay for the water damage to the apartment below." He was rambling.

She pushed back her chair, walked a few steps, and stood behind the chair where he sat. He was prepared for her to tap him on the back and show him the door. Instead, she rested her fingertips tentatively on his shoulders, just barely touching his shirt. Her touch traveled straight to his belly and then lower. He felt himself respond as quickly as a hormone-dipped teenager. He wanted to drag her hands over his face. Take her in his arms. Smell her skin, taste her, hide forever. He was afraid to turn around and look her in the eye.

Her voice was above his head. "John, you have a right to be angry. And I don't know if you can believe this, but there are things about me that are different."

He spoke to the air. "Yeah, new job. I saw you on the television. I always told you that you'd be a big success."

Above his head, she smiled in the air. It was true. He had always acted as if he expected great things from her.

"That's not what I'm talking about. Right now, I'm not working a story, I'm trying to make sense of what is in my heart. But before I go any further, there are a few things I need to know." She walked around to the side of his chair so she could see his face.

"Like what?"

"When I saw you the other night when your friend was shot, I thought you might be in trouble. Now, seeing you with the tape recorder, I'm sure of it. You're in trouble, right?"

Finn made his mouth tight.

"This isn't for a story?"

She held up two fingers. "Cub Scout's honor."

"Then, yeah, I guess you could say that."

"Serious trouble?"

Finn nodded. He felt his confusion lightening. It was the Roman Catholic principle. Conscience was the burden of carrying your troubles alone.

"You can't tell me about it?"

"I will when I can."

"Okay, but I'm not naive. You're wearing a wire to record some kind of criminal activity." Tension was between them like glass. "Did you commit any crimes?"

Finn heard screaming in his ears. Now, all his lapses came back to him. The blackouts, the nights that faded to white when he woke up in his bed or on Bigelow's couch. The stories he heard Money and Johnson tell about their adventures when he could not remember a single detail.

He stalled. "These things are not black-and-white," he said slowly. "You can find yourself in a strange place and things are happening"—he shrugged—"that are beyond your control."

She studied him. "Did you commit any crimes?"

He wanted to bury his face in his hands and weep. What he meant to say was, "I don't know." But if he acknowledged it out loud, it would only make it worse.

He looked down at the polished wood table. "Of course not."

She exhaled heavily. Then her hands were on his shoulders, turning him, bringing him close, soothing him. Her face was inches from his nose. His synapses were firing like bottle rockets on the Fourth of July. He felt pressure building in his groin and didn't think he could walk to the door if she told him to. He felt a surge of longing for her so strong that he gripped the armrests of his chair.

"Now I have something to tell you." Kate paused. "I made a mistake two years ago. I didn't know it, but I was chasing something I already had. I realize now that you were offering me something precious, but I didn't even recognize what it was. It took me almost a year to figure it out, and another ten months to get up enough nerve to do something about it. But here I am. Before I make a fool of myself, let me ask you two more questions. The first one is, Did you really love me way back when?"

Finn tilted his head back at her. He didn't trust his voice. Kate waited. He was surprised to see that she had tears in her eyes.

"I did."

Then she pulled up her shoulders stiffly, bracing herself again. "You don't have to answer, but what I really want to know is, Do you think you could love me like that again?"

Her hands were around his neck and running up the stiff brush of his hair. He leaned into her, letting her hands move smoothly along his cheek. He guessed that she was looking for traces of the old John Finn. The one who had once loved her. He didn't know if he would be able to find that man again and he was afraid. He kissed her, hoping that she couldn't tell how much fear was roiling inside him. If she picked up on it, she didn't seem to mind. Each of her kisses went more deeply than the last.

# 15

"Try red, it always looks good on television." J.J. and Kate were arguing in a spacious dressing room at Saks. J.J. was shoving suits at Kate through the swinging doors.

"Forget a little red suit," said Kate, who was wearing a bra, panties, a pair of white athletic socks, and an expression of pure exasperation. "I'll look like Nancy Reagan."

Kate knew she shouldn't be complaining. She'd begged J.J. to go shopping with her. As a teenager, Kate had been an overweight bookworm and summarily rejected her mother's attempts to get her to wear "weight control" girdles and smocks. Instead, she settled into a wardrobe of sloppy jeans and oversize sweaters that saw her through college. She threw in a few nice jackets, skirts, and omnipresent garters once she got a job at the newspaper, but basically she had worn the same style clothes since she was eighteen. That wardrobe wasn't going to work for television. When Kate reviewed her first stand-up for Manero, it was obvious that, sartorially, Kate was out of her league.

"Nancy Reagan happens to be very telegenic," retorted J.J., hanging the suit on one of the hooks.

"No. No. No," bellowed Kate from the dressing room. J.J. rolled her eyes in unison with the aging saleslady, who looked as if she had styled her hair with a whisk. "I'm not wearing a suit with puffy sleeves. I'll look like Sandy Duncan." The saleslady shoved a few more multi-hued suits into Kate's dressing room.

J.J. continued, ignoring the fact that Kate was edging into a teenage temper tantrum. "Two years ago, I covered a former-first-lady press conference. In person Nancy looks like a vicious little prune, but on television she looks like a movie star. Even her facelift is tailored for television."

A younger saleslady had joined the other, gawking.

Kate stuck her head out of the dressing room. She was wearing a mustard-colored jacket. J.J. gave her the thumbs-down. "Can plastic surgeons really do that? Cut your face for television?" Kate asked seriously.

"I'm inquiring," said J.J., who now made it a yearly ritual to have her features trimmed so that to television viewers, she never aged a day.

There was silence from the dressing room, the sound of a zipper, and then a wail. "Forget this red suit. No way. It has gold, double-breasted buttons. I'll look like *The Nutcracker.*"

"Remember, clean-cut and boxy shoulders. Makes you look honest," answered J.J. encouragingly.

When Kate emerged from the dressing room, the salesladies nodded in approval.

"I am honest," said Kate. "No matter what I wear."

"I said look honest," said J.J. "How does it feel?"

"Like I have a senile husband and a middle-aged daughter exposing herself in *Playboy.*"

Kate turned to the three-way mirror and frowned. She had to admit, she looked fabulous. Her jet-black hair contrasted dramatically with the rich red of the jacket. The skirt fell a few inches above the knee, setting off well-toned calves and strong ankles. The cut of the suit was more tailored than anything Kate had ever owned, and it made her look like a gleaming advertisement for corporate America. Kate could barely recognize herself.

She imagined Finn's look of surprise if she greeted him in an outfit like this. He'd probably think he'd knocked on the wrong door. Kate frowned and looked around the dressing room for a telephone. She wanted to check her messages to see if he'd called. Taking him to bed last night was a mistake, she thought. By the time they got between her sheets it was clear he didn't trust her. He was holding back too much. A few hours later, they were both sad and sorry. She wanted to lick his ear and promise him that things would get better, but it was almost dawn and she was sure they weren't going to get any better right then. She had waited until he dressed quietly, kissed her, and slammed the door behind him. Then, as she listened to the birds calling out to each other at dawn, she cried.

Pulling back to the present, she reached for the tag at the sleeve. She almost dropped to her knees with sticker shock.

"This suit costs fifteen hundred dollars," she whispered to J.J.

"You can afford it on your salary," mouthed J.J. back, then she turned to the saleslady.

"She'll take it," said J.J. "Now let's get shoes and accessories so you can wear this little getup to work."

When Kate got to the station at three, she could have been wearing a Saks shopping bag for all anyone noticed. The evening's top news story was already on fire in Queens. "Flames are shooting one hundred feet in the air," Landis told her, quoting from the promos that had just run. He hustled her out of the newsroom before she could even check her telephone messages. An oil tanker had run off the road and crashed into a paint factory in Maspeth, stopping traffic on both sides of the LIE. The driver was already dead, and several night-shift workers at the factory were still unaccounted for. Mancro had been at the scene for a little over an hour but was threatening to walk back to Manhattan if the station didn't send a limousine to pick him up first.

"Hook up with your crew in Maspeth," said Landis. "We're doing promos every fifteen minutes until the six o'clock show."

About two miles from the paint factory, traffic

stopped for good. Kate abandoned her Tercel on the side of the clogged road and walked the rest of the way in her new pumps. By the time she located Manuel, the little toe on her left foot had an enormous blister, and sweat was dripping into her bra.

"Where's Manero?" asked Kate, taking the IFB Bernie handed to her.

"Gone," Bernie said, then turned back to his dials, looking exhausted.

In the still summer evening, the smoke and fumes from the oil tanker and the burning factory hung over the block in a thick, carcinogenic blanket. Every now and then, a tongue of fire would jump into the air, propelled by yet another combustible chemical released into the deadly brew. Grimy firefighters from as far away as the Hamptons sat exhausted on the curbside, chugging on tanks of oxygen. A cluster of print reporters hung listlessly behind blue police barricades, coughing in the fetid air. The only people who didn't seem affected by the disaster were a crowd of teenaged boys in baggy pants and polo shirts who lurched and stumbled around the rescue trucks as if this were their own private disaster movie.

Kate checked her watch and began setting up for the five forty-five promo. Manuel, his face stained with soot and his fluffy hair flattened with sweat, tried to set up a background shot that would capture the fire and avoid the teenagers.

Three minutes before the countdown, Kate brushed her hair, touched up her makeup, and then limped over to the group of print reporters.

"Jesus, is it Halloween already? What are you supposed to be? Nancy Reagan?" It was Rob Grant, Kate's nemesis from her days at the *Daily Herald.* Kate hoped that the shock of seeing her legs in sheer stockings and pumps would be too much for his sclerotic old heart. She willed him to have a coronary on the spot, but to her disappointment he kept breathing. She turned to face an old-time *Post* reporter, Patrice Mackenzie, who gave her a hostile stare.

"Hey, Patrice. Are you okay? You look exhausted," Kate said. "What's happening here? Do the fire officials think they can contain it?"

"You on your way to a garden party or something?" Patrice said pointedly. Kate flushed. She was embarrassed to be wearing a $1,500 suit to a fire. Working for television suddenly seemed like a stupid, vacuous job. She didn't want to do a promo, she wanted to write this story for a newspaper.

Kate felt tears in her eyes. Patrice softened and threw her head to the left, gesturing for Kate to walk and talk. "It goes like this," she said rapidly. "The fire had spread through the paint-mixing facilities and into the research area. We don't know what is being released into the air, but everyone in a four-block radius is feeling sick. Haz-mat is making the proper notifications, and I think they are about to start evacuating the blocks around here." Kate had whipped a notebook out of her pocketbook and was jotting it all down. Patrice paused and Kate looked up. "Kate, I know your heart's in newspapers. Did you have to start looking like *them* right away?"

Kate started to respond but then saw Manuel gesturing to her frantically.

She shrugged at Patrice and limped back to do the promo.

"Four, three, two," Landis was counting down.

Kate took her place in front of the camera and began to read from her notes.

"The fire has been raging out of control since two-thirty this afternoon when an oil tanker . . ." Just then, one of the teenagers who had been horsing around on the sidewalk in front of the factory jumped into the frame directly in front of Kate. Manuel's eyebrows shot up. He waved the boy off, but the kid just stood there with a wide, stupid grin on his face. Kate stepped forward, placing her arm around the boy to guide him away, trying to keep reading her flimsy script. "I'm on TeeeVeee," the boy squawked. In the IFB, Kate could hear Landis groaning. Another teen jumped into the frame at her right and joined the chorus. "I'm on *TeeeeVeeee*!" he said. Kate cut her promo short.

"Back to you," she said tersely.

When the red camera light went dark, she yanked her arm away from the boy.

"You little jerk," she spat out. "What do you think you're doing?"

The teen gave her a goofy smile and gestured toward Rob Grant. "That man said he'd give ten dollars to every one of us who got on TV."

Kate looked at Grant, who smiled and gave her the Nazi salute.

"C'mon, Manuel, let's try to get a shot from the other side of the factory." She gestured to a faraway stretch of sidewalk.

It took longer than they thought to bring in the signal again, and Kate could hear the intro song to the six-o'clock broadcast before Fink was able to lock them in. At the start of the countdown, Manuel gave her the sign that he'd established a clean microwave transmission.

Landis was counting again, "Five . . . four . . .," when Kate saw those two boys along with a small pack of others rounding the corner. "Don't look now," she said into the microphone. "But we might be getting a few more human projectiles into the frame."

Landis reacted first. "God damn it! I don't want those little shits messing up my top story. Get Bernie to break their legs," he sputtered. "Okay. You're up. Go."

Kate smiled into the camera and nervously began reading.

"The factory began burning out of control around two-thirty this afternoon after a tanker burst into flames and . . ." Kate could hear footsteps: the teenager was running toward her. She didn't let her eyes leave the camera. The boy opened his mouth in a warrior yell: "I want to be on *TeeeeVeeee*." As soon as his fast-moving body became visible in Kate's peripheral vision, she stuck out her arm. It was a protective gesture, one she made without thinking. The boy's chest impacted on her hand and she gave him a quick, reflexive shove. Instead of being pushed out of the frame, he lay on the ground at her feet, stunned.

Kate continued to read. "So far, the driver of the tanker, whose name is being withheld until his family can be notified, is confirmed dead and several others are missing." As Manuel cut to the tape, Kate could hear laughing and groaning in her IFB. Andrew Fink was laughing.

"You laid him out, Kate, you laid him out on live television," he said, chortling. She pulled the IFB out of her ear and, defeated, climbed back into the van. Manuel was laughing so hard he couldn't straighten up. Bernie was wiping tears from his eyes. Kate stared at her hands and willed herself to be transported to a place far away. But when she looked up, she was still in the Channel 7 van. Manuel placed a sympathetic hand on her shoulder but she shrugged it off, reaching to pick up Landis on the microphone.

Landis was groaning. "We're getting phone calls from viewers all over the tristate area. They don't care about the fire. They care about the boy. They think you've killed him."

# 16

The wait at the DMV was less of an orderly line than a lynch mob.

"I've been here two hours," yelled one lady shrunken to the height of a mailbox, leaning on a walker and waving a computer printout.

The bored clerk wore dreadlocks and a flashy tie. He regarded her with contempt.

"She's probably too old for a license anyway," he said loud enough for the lady to hear.

Finn hated when young people treated old people badly. It was just a thing he had. He'd always tried to respect old people. It wasn't always their fault that they ended up the way they did.

He pulled out his black leather folder and showed the clerk his shield.

"I need to check an old ticket, part of a homicide investigation. Eighty-third Precinct."

The clerk's eyes widened, and Finn wondered if he'd killed anyone lately.

"Got to talk to my supervisor and she's out to lunch."

"It's only ten."

"She likes to eat early."

"Listen, I can't wait all day. I could get a subpoena and force you to hand over this information."

It was a blunder. He couldn't really get a subpoena. And he knew this ridiculous civil servant would jump at anything that sounded as if it would generate more paperwork.

"Of course, while I'm getting that," Finn continued smoothly, "I could also check warrants, run your sheet and your prints. See if there were any hits."

"No need for that," the clerk said, smiling nervously. "Let me show you to our records room."

That's more like it, Finn thought as he followed the clerk down the long hallway, away from the angry motorists.

"This here is the morgue," said the clerk. He flipped his hand toward three dozen dusty file cabinets, each filled with copies of tickets written by the fleet of traffic agents who patrolled the streets of New York.

"Of course, we don't get every ticket. Half the time, the agents write 'em, then lose their copy so there's no official record. Sometimes the computer just chews 'em up and never spits them out. Sometimes you get five tickets for the same infraction. Sometimes a ticket gets misfiled. It's like it never existed." He looked at the room with Finn. "Good luck."

After twenty minutes of looking, Finn's stomach started to growl. There was sweat on his upper lip. He had showered this morning when he returned from Kate's house, but it didn't seem to do any good. Water seemed to bring out the hidden effects of too much binge drinking. Instead of feeling relaxed, he felt anxious about taking Kate to bed. Being with her was like watching a death match between the pit bulls of his soul. He would have slept with her even if it meant it was his last night on earth. But the closer he got to her—the real-life flesh-and-blood woman—the more he felt the hurt that had been cutting into him for the last two years. He was a grown man, married, divorced—no children, but that was his ex-wife's choice, not his. He was a detective in the NYPD. He was as tough as they come. But he could never have walked away from her last night, not the way she wanted him. It made him almost physically sick to admit it, but he knew if she left him again, something inside him would break that could never be repaired.

He pulled out of his reverie to smell a sweet, sick funk coming off him. He still couldn't find the ticket.

Four hours later, he was still looking. It was a job for a machine, fumed Finn. What was the point of computers if he still had to dig through dusty, mismatched files like some kind of paper-sniffing dog.

It took him a good hour to figure out that the files were listed by car registration, and another hour to find someone who could cross-reference Bigelow's name with his registration number. After that, it was forty minutes to find the file cabinet containing the right month and year.

When he found the ticket, the only emotion he felt was relief that he could stop and go home. It wasn't exactly key evidence. But at least it was something more than a hazy, alcohol-soaked hallucination, a boozy dream. He inspected the traffic agent's scrawl. At nine P.M. two weeks ago on Wednesday, DOT officer M. A. Franklin had tagged Bigelow's car for parking in front of a hydrant. The address was 5020 Eighth Avenue in Sunset Park. Right in the heart of Brooklyn's Chinatown.

# 17

Kate was sitting in her office simultaneously watching two competing broadcasts of the evening news and waiting for Landis to come into her tiny office and fire her. The flames from yesterday's fire eventually consumed the paint factory. The black smoke ruined her $1,500 suit. The young hecklers, agents of that bastard Rob Grant, destroyed her career. One of the tabloids had even carried a still of Kate straight-arming the boy. Even J.J. couldn't save her. She checked her home answering machine. Day number two. No calls. She'd struck out with her boyfriend and was watching as her second job in four months faded away.

She stuck her head out of her office and scanned the newsroom. From her door, she could see more than a dozen television screens turned to various evening comedies and dramas. Every person left in the newsroom had red-rimmed eyes from watching too many images dance across too many screens. She sat back down at her desk.

No job, no paycheck. I'll be homeless and alone, she thought. She imagined herself dressed in rags, begging in front of the *Daily Herald* building. And my big play for romance crashes and burns before my eyes.

Why hadn't Finn called?

"You almost ready for our talk?" It was Landis, vibrating like a tuning fork. He had snuck up on her somehow.

"Sure," she said, feeling sick. She tried to make it sound as if she weren't facing the guillotine. "God, what a day I had yesterday. I could use a good bottle of wine and a plate of spaghetti." She looked at her boss and smiled. For two hours, she had been imagining the ugly words that would pass between them. It was almost a relief to think he'd finally fire her. She kept jabbering, a pathetic attempt to make a friend of the grim reaper. "And I could also use someone to pick up my new jacket from the tailor, put fresh milk in my refrigerator, and make my bed. You know, Steve, what I really need is a wife."

He smiled at her. "Can't help you organize the PTA, but let me take you out to dinner. I know a great place on Forty-ninth Street."

Kate was shocked. She had expected something to come out of his mouth like, "Clean out your desk and never set foot in the newsroom again." She pulled at her wild forelock. Landis stared at her, shaking. She noticed his dark, curly hair, his well-cut aquiline nose. She looked at his shoulders, hoping he didn't work out. Jogging was fine. Squash, too, as long as he didn't take it too seriously. But forget Nautilus and free weights. She had had it with those ropey gym rats in the eighties, desk jockeys who discovered their hidden athletic ability by sharing sweat with a bunch of yellowing steroid addicts. Her hand flew to her mouth. Just because he wasn't firing her didn't mean he was Adonis, she scolded herself in her Kate Hepburn voice. This was Landis, the man who mocked, screamed, cursed, and fired frightened assistants for bringing him cold coffee. If he was handsome, so was Jack the Ripper.

She forced herself to recover. "Sure," she said, not sure at all. "I'd love to."

Forty minutes later, she was sitting in Patsy's, an old-style Italian restaurant in Midtown decorated with seventies-style mirrors and pictures of Frank Sinatra hugging Alonzo, the maître d'.

"Welcome, Mr. Steve, so nice to see you." Alonzo's squashed features hid a mind adept at remembering faces, corporate affiliation, and political ranking, and at never mixing up drink preferences or interchanging the names of wives and mistresses.

"Nice to see you, too, Alonzo," replied Landis absently. But Alonzo was not to be put off. Doing an Italian version of a Stepin' Fetchit, Alonzo unfurled his white handkerchief and was waving it at Landis as if he were dusting a centerpiece. Landis looked pleased and followed another waiter to a large empty table.

"Tony," Alonzo cried out urgently. "Bring Mr. Steve his drink." He said it as if Landis had his own wine cellar at Patsy's. Landis accepted a martini and ordered antipasto for both of them and a bottle of wine for Kate. It occurred to her that he might be a regular. It shook her up a little that Landis had a life outside the station. The waiter flourished a bottle of Chianti like an obstetrician producing an infant son, then poured a glass. Landis drained his martini, and before he lowered it to the table, a waiter had appeared with another.

"We're thinking about assigning Manero a new producer," Landis said. Kate saw the dinner plates get bigger and then smaller in the candlelight.

"What? Why?" Was this some kind of ritual humiliation? He had taken her out to dinner to fire her?

"Bartlett thinks your work is very good and so do I. As long as you don't go off on any more investigative tangents"—he was talking about staking out the judge in Ozone Park—"or kill any young hecklers, we want to send you out on your own."

Kate raised her glass. "Cheers," said Landis. Kate sipped, smiled, and watched the candle flicker.

"I want to keep Bernie and Manuel," she said quickly.

Landis sighed. "They'll be here when you and I are both gone."

He sampled the antipasto and took long gulps of his second martini.

"Word has filtered back from network. They've got their eye on you." Kate's eyes widened in surprise.

"Wow. Great." Then she exhaled. "Sometimes I feel like I can hardly keep pace with televised news."

"No one can," Landis said, suddenly philosophical. "It's technology out of control. As anyone who works for CNN can tell you, we produce too much information for the human mind to absorb." He finished his martini and began drinking wine. "It can drive you crazy."

"Is that what happened to Vic Manero?"

"No, his problem is that he absorbs nothing. He's a total idiot." Kate could see that alcohol was making him steadier and his eyes were humid. "But look at me, television has sucked me dry. I'm just a shell of the man I thought I would be. I drink too much. My wife divorced me, I have two children who don't even send me a birthday card. I behave like a ruthless maniac, when in fact, deep down, I'm a nice guy."

Kate tried not to stare. He was trying to sell her, but on what? On Steve Landis? She ignored the pitch, batting the conversation to safer ground. "I wouldn't say you have nothing. You have a fast-paced, high-paying job in the best city in the world." What a crock, Kate thought. People only said New York was the best city in the world when they lived in Jersey or were about to move to Seattle where you didn't have to think what might happen to your car stereo on any given night. "Plus, you have the respect of your peers." They both knew that was a lie. Nobody respected Landis, but most everyone in the local news division feared him. But after all, Kate thought, less than an hour ago she was rehearsing ways to beg him for her job. A little routine flattery seemed like the least she could do.

Kate nibbled at the antipasto, hoping Landis was too hungry to keep talking about his inner child. But to her exasperation, he would not be stopped. "I feel like I'm two people," he said, a stuffed mushroom tucked in his cheek. "The video madman everyone sees in the newsroom, and a regular guy who likes a good bottle of wine, a well-written novel, and a warm fire."

Kate wanted to laugh at his Hallmark depiction of masculine contentment, but she realized in a flash that Landis was speaking with more than a hint of desperation. "I'm forty-three years old," he said. "When do I get to be happy?"

She nodded, chewing slowly so she didn't have to answer. Landis ordered dinner for both of them and continued to muse. "The only person who seems to thrive on television is Andrew Fink," Landis added. "Somehow he's able to do it and maintain his equilibrium. He's a lesson to us all."

Kate was about to ask about Fink when Alonzo began fussing with such intensity that most of the diners in Patsy's stopped eating and looked up. The United States attorney for Brooklyn, Brian Mahoney, and five pale aides in dark suits and close-cropped hair had just walked in the door. As a group, they looked like a faculty meeting of a Jesuit high school.

Landis stood up and stretched out his arms. Mahoney strode forward and embraced him as if their children had just announced their intention to be married. Alonzo and the other waiters pushed another table up and pulled chairs around it so the feds could join them at their table. Kate found herself sitting shoulder to shoulder with a dark-haired young man with dead brown eyes and thin lips permanently curled in a sneer. It was Mark DeMaris, Mahoney's heir apparent.

"Yes, of course, I've seen you," DeMaris said to Kate. "Very nice to finally meet you." He politely left out the fact that she had written two large, unflattering articles for the *Herald* about his failed prosecution of Genovese family capos. She let the comment go. She had found that assistant U.S. attorneys spoke in parsed phrases, devoid of detail, as if their breakfast order at a greasy spoon could be grounds for appeal. But, tonight, words were flowing out of DeMaris like any cheap politician. He spoke about *his* office and *his* prosecutors, all but announcing his appointment as interim U.S. attorney.

"I'm sure we'll be seeing much more of each other,"

he said. Kate smiled and nodded, her attention drawn to Mahoney, who was talking business with Landis.

"Maybe a judgeship," Mahoney was saying, "but I'm definitely going out on a high note."

Kate looked at DeMaris quizzically. "A big one," he whispered confidentially. His boss was locked into conversation with Landis. "They'll be plenty of media interest."

"Mob?" she said, immediately wishing she had a notebook.

DeMaris shook his head. "Bigger."

"Big white-collar stuff?"

"Sexier."

"Tell me."

DeMaris waited until Alonzo had walked away.

"Police corruption."

"Protection rackets?"

"And more."

"Drugs?"

DeMaris winked and gave her a wide smile. "Call me. Let's have lunch."

# 18

Kate stared at her Day-Timer. It was Saturday, July 14, four days since she had slept with John Finn. She dug a finger absently into the sweaty waistband of her gym shorts. Four days. Not even a telephone call. She looked at her machine again. The message light wasn't blinking. She stubbed her toe against her heel and kicked off her Adidas. Then she peeled off her damp socks. Even a step class with the Lycra maidens of Park Slope didn't take her mind off Finn.

The telephone rang. Kate lunged. It was Nina, her best friend from college and mother of Kate's eighteen-month-old namesake.

"No, not yet," Kate said. Nina had been keeping the vigil with Kate. "I know, four days. Maybe he's been busy." She mentally wondered if he had plunged into some kind of downward spiral, a lost weekend that started Wednesday morning. Half-laughing, Nina suggested Kate check the hospitals. She considered it, then, remembering his credit-card records, wondered if she should call O'Brien's.

"Maybe he's fallen prey to the dreaded PCR," grumbled Kate.

"PCR?"

"Postcoital reconsideration. You married types don't know anything about it, but it's a syndrome among men who can't commit," Kate informed her lightly. "But at the very least, he could call."

Nina made the ritualistic comforting sounds innate to close girlfriends. Kate felt her cheeks get hot.

"Maybe getting back together with him was just a silly fantasy." She felt her eyes fill with tears. Then, she heard a click and realized it was her call-waiting signal.

"Damn, Nina, let me get this." She heard the sound again. "It's either the station or a telephone solicitation. Those are the only calls I get these days." She heard the sound again.

"Kate, it's John Finn."

She opened her mouth but felt her throat close like a hatch.

"Kate? Are you there?"

She took a breath. "Ah, hi, John." She exhaled, thrilled that she had formed words in English.

"I'm sorry I didn't call sooner but I've been really busy."

"Oh, I've been out of town for a few days," she lied airily. She hadn't gone live since the day of the fire so who would know? "I had so many messages I didn't get a chance to sort through them."

Even as she lied, she mocked herself for being petty. Kate Murray. Living the life of the internationally renowned television journalist. So fast-paced. So glamorous. No one had to know she ate moo shu chicken and watched reruns of her segments on her VCR. Then she remembered Nina on the other line. "Could you hold on a minute, John? I have another call." She said it as if she were talking to the White House on the other line. Let him think state secrets were discussed on a connecting piece of fiber optics. Eat your heart out, Detective. She hit the receiver button and thought she heard Nina's patient breathing.

"Oh my god, I can't believe it," Kate blurted out excitedly to Nina. "He finally called. After all that waiting, all that fretting, he called me. He called me." She had her fist above her head and drove her elbow downward. "All right."

"Kate." She stopped dead. It was Finn. Somehow she hadn't broken the connection. "Oh, God, hold on."

"Hello, Nina. Jesus, I can't believe . . ." But somehow she had managed to disconnect Nina. She was about to hit the receiver again when she stopped. In ten seconds she'd hung up on a friend and made an idiot of herself to the man that she had recently decided mattered most. She was completely deflated. She paused before she hit the receiver to pick up on Finn. How could she possibly recover? What could she say? She wanted words to read on a page. A script in front of her so she could get through the segment. But she had nothing. It flashed through her mind that she could just hang up and let the machine answer when he called back. She thought of J.J. telling her that she had to try to be happy. She wondered what Katharine Hepburn would do. Florid with embarrassment, she tapped the receiver and picked up Finn's call.

She dropped her chin and decided to go for Emily Post politeness and abrupt and total amnesia. "How kind of you to call," she said as if he had arrived in a top hat and tails on the arm of Edith Wharton.

She could hear him grinning into the telephone. Think Emily Post, she commanded herself. Think Kate Hepburn. He lingered over the pause, relished her discomfort a little too long, she thought, momentarily peeved. But when he spoke, his voice was filled with weight. "Kate, I felt terrible about how we left it the other night."

"Oh?" she said noncommittally, unsure whether he was about to break it off with her or invite himself over for a rematch.

"You know I'm in a difficult situation at work right now," he said obliquely. "And seeing you has put me at war with myself."

She felt her heart fracture and she discarded Emily Post like a rag.

"Don't break it off with me, John," she said, anguish tearing through her voice. "I've waited so long to see you again."

He sounded surprised, then happy. "I don't want to break it off."

"You don't?"

"No, I just need to go . . . em . . . slower."

She exhaled. "What do you mean, slower?"

He paused. "I don't know. The other night, it was like we were trying to pick things up where they were two years ago. I can't do that. We have to start again. That's why I was calling. I wanted to ask you to go out with me."

"Go out with you?" she echoed numbly.

"Yeah, you know, on a date."

# 19

As he sat in the cramped van, Finn took a drink from a small metal flask and tried to remember how long it had been since he had gone on a drug raid perfectly sober. It must have been a long time, because he'd forgotten how horrible it felt.

He had vowed to do this without a drink, but the waiting washed away his resolve. None of Group C's undercovers were buying drugs. Their job was, at the given signal, to help the members of Group D make arrests. Everything about the operation was beyond their control. It wasn't even going to go off on time. They'd been sitting in the surveillance van for hours until Group D's undercovers finally got their connection to show up with the drugs. Every minute that passed made Finn feel sicker. He'd been a cop long enough to believe that tragedy is random; if your number is up, no one can protect you from the pain coming your way. Drug raids only heightened the potential for the kind of pointless violence he wanted to avoid. He stared at the men around him. Every man who ran from the van into the target apartment would have the same lousy odds.

He looked around at the steady, regular faces of the men in Group C and wondered how much they knew. No one asked for a drink or acknowledged that Finn was getting drunk. It was as if they had all agreed that it was something that would never be discussed. Finn wished he could remember exactly what things he was supposed to remain silent about. He had agreed to play a game without learning the rules. After yesterday's trip to DMV, anxiety was layered into the very air that he was breathing. He wasn't sure what he'd wanted to find when he went there, but anything that bolstered his shadowy memory of Bigelow and the Chinese gangsters made him feel nauseated. When he left DMV, he had been so deeply frightened that he called Kate. That was a mistake. He wanted her more than he could express, but his instinct was warning him to stay away and wait for his life to fall back into the same dull, destructive, comforting rut he had been in for two years. Yet another voice was sounding a warning that he had been down too low too long. He felt a mechanical ticking in the tape recorder and felt sicker. He must be an idiot to be making secret tapes. These were his buddies, for Christ's sake.

McCoy was reading aloud from the *Daily Herald*.

"The new United States Attorney Mark DeMaris took a hard line on corruption today, saying it would not be tolerated at any level, from a public servant to a police officer to an elected official."

"What the fuck does that mean. D'ya think he's talking about cops?" whined McCoy.

"Never believe anything you read in the media," said Johnson. "Didn't this guy just get appointed to be a federal judge?"

"That was his boss, Mahoney. This is the new guy, DeMaris. And mark my word, DeMaris is going to run for mayor," said Stephen Lee, who wore a red bandanna around his neck, which called attention to three fiery hickeys he was trying to hide. "Politicians, reporters, they're hand in hand. They'd sell out their grandmother if there was something in it for them."

Finn felt the sound of the ocean in his head.

He shuddered and then realized that Bigelow had directed a question his way.

"Sorry, what?"

"Still on the hard stuff I see," said Bigelow, smiling. Finn smiled back, disarmed. "I said, what do you think of the story?"

Finn held his breath, feeling the tape recorder

pressing on his kidneys like a fist. He shrugged, turning his palms outward.

"Probably bullshit. U.S. attorneys' jobs are more political than the Queens DA. Those dirtbags at IAB will listen to anyone who wants to bad-mouth a hardworking cop. And the feds are not much better."

Finn looked up and was relieved to see that the members of his group were nodding in agreement.

But there was no time to relax. A squawk came over the radio. Lee flung open the van door, and Group C bolted for the target apartment on the fourth floor. They moved across the enclosed cobblestone yard in precise formation, graceful and controlled.

By the time Finn got through the door, other cops had secured the first floor. Finn saw Bigelow duck up a back stairway and followed. McCoy lagged a few steps back.

On the second floor, McCoy grabbed a muscular, bald man running across the landing and began to beat him. Finn stopped, caught his breath, and reasonably sure there was no longer any danger, followed Bigelow.

By the time they arrived on the fourth floor, the main target of the sting had already been whisked away for interrogation by a member of Group D. A young undercover stood holding a gun on one of the dealer's underlings and their cache of cocaine. Bigelow, bristling with authority, dismissed the young cop and stood in front of a table full of money and Ziploc bags containing cocaine. Finn shook his head. He must have been wrong about Bigelow. Even the way he moved, you could tell that he had the confidence of the meanest animal in the barnyard. He was a real cop's cop.

"Go on, son, they need you on the second floor. We can handle this," said Bigelow, and the young cop clomped down the stairway.

Bigelow nodded to Finn, then turned to the suspect, who was scratching his head nervously, as if he had fleas.

"See that fire escape over there?" Bigelow asked the

suspect. The young man nodded uncertainly. Bigelow raised his hand and brought the full force of his swing down on the man's neck.

"I want you to climb down it, and if you look back, I'll shoot you and say you were trying to escape."

The suspect scratched again, gave Bigelow a single uneasy look, and ran for the window.

Bigelow began searching through cabinets until he found a ragged-looking pillowcase in a utility closet near the sink. Bigelow began to fill it with the cocaine.

Finn almost staggered with shock.

"Bigelow, is this some kind of setup? What are you doing?" Finn hissed.

"What am I doing?" said Bigelow slowly. "What does it look like I'm doing?"

"Well, Albina would say you're breaking the chain of custody on the evidence. This stuff has to be inventoried."

Bigelow placed another bag in the pillowcase.

"I'm not taking all of it. I made sure nobody had time to count it. I'll throw it on the roof and pick it up later. They'll never notice it's gone," said Bigelow, all business. Then he recovered his bravado. "And let me tell you a thing about Albina. He doesn't know all the things I know."

Finn looked down the hallway, seeing shadows moving at the far end. He was terrified that someone would come and arrest them both.

"Albina doesn't know all the things you know either." Bigelow's eyes were shining and his face was mottled with excitement. "We spend all day tracking down these dealers, and you know what? They're laughing at us. Jail time doesn't mean a thing to them. What's a five-year sentence if you're making millions?" He gave a hard laugh. "The only way you can hurt them is to take their product." He hefted a bag. "Or their money. It's the only thing they understand."

Finn flinched. Bigelow didn't look like a hero to him anymore. His big mustache and wide jaw made him look like a wolf. His mouth was smiling but his eyes were pinched and greedy, like the faces of the old men who hung around OTB. Bigelow was more than a grass eater. He was more than a meat eater. He was omnivorous.

Finn felt revulsion soak him like a cold rain. Then he was outraged and the emotion connected him to a rapid chain of memories that he had cauterized and forgotten. At seventeen, outside of an after-hours bar he had taken on two bikers armed with a broken-off Michelob bottle. He'd needed twenty-five stitches but he'd survived. Then there was that murderous scum Marvin Plank from the Eighty-third Precinct who'd put a gun to his temple and pulled the trigger. Finn wasn't even injured that time. And two years ago, he'd fatally shot the man who'd stabbed Kate. That was the hardest, but he'd lived through that, too. He had survived too many close calls to let another man pull him under. He was in a slump but he wasn't dead yet.

Finn's entire consciousness became focused on the five-inch square of flesh and adhesive tape supporting a sound-activated tape recorder in the small of his back.

"Bigelow, what the fuck, man. You're going to get caught. You're going to get caught *stealing the drugs.*" He said the words so loud and clear that he wouldn't have been surprised if Bigelow realized that he was being taped, pulled out a gun, and shot him right there.

"You think I'm afraid of some IAB losers or a blowhard U.S. attorney?" Bigelow had stopped tossing bags into the pillowcase. "I'm not afraid of them. You don't have to be either. You know why we don't have to be afraid?" Bigelow's voice was soft and sure. "You know why?"

"Why?" Finn wanted Bigelow to keep talking. He was setting his trap, getting everything on tape. "Why aren't you afraid of getting caught?"

Bigelow held up a bag of the white powder and squeezed it like a woman's breast.

" 'Cause we're fucking good cops, that's why."

Finn looked at Bigelow. Then he looked down the hall.

But Bigelow pressed him. "Did you hear what I said? I said we're fucking good cops." Bigelow gestured to Finn with his chin. "You're a good cop. I'm a good cop. Now you say it."

Bigelow's face looked like an overfilled balloon. He looked dazed and Finn wondered if he'd been sniffing cocaine. Bigelow took two steps closer to him and angled his face toward Finn. "I said, say it." He was less a man than an overpowering menace.

Finn didn't want him any closer. If the tape recorder clicked or Bigelow's hand touched Finn's back, Bigelow would discover the wire.

Finn stepped sideways.

"Bigelow, this is stupid."

"Say it." Bigelow was on him now, his lips were inches away, screaming. Finn could feel Bigelow's spit fall lightly on his cheek.

"C'mon, Bigelow, don't be crazy—" Finn drew a breath involuntarily as Bigelow threw his arm around his shoulders, more restraining than embracing him.

"God damn it, I said say it. Say it or you'll find out how fucking crazy I am." Bigelow's hand was less than twelve inches away from the tape recorder.

"We're good cops," said Finn breathlessly.

"Louder," screamed Bigelow, gripping Finn.

Finn sucked in air.

"We're good cops."

Bigelow released him. He moved quickly over to the window and threw the pillowcase onto the roof below.

Bigelow turned and gave Finn a thumbs-up. "We're the greatest."

# 20

He had arranged to meet Kate at five o'clock in the Japanese tea garden in the Brooklyn Botanic Garden. At five-twenty, Finn began to sweat. After yesterday's drug raid, he thought he would be dulled to the usual urban annoyances, but as he sat stuck in traffic, anxiety was tearing into him like a chain saw. Any New Yorker would wait fifteen extra minutes for a friend. Even the most punctual person has had his or her travel-time estimate vaporized by a sick passenger on a subway train, a jackknifed tractor trailer, or a cabdriver who knows his way around Khartoum better than Brooklyn. You can explain a fifteen-minute delay by shrugging and saying, "Traffic." But anything later than fifteen minutes becomes a personal insult. Finn leaned on the horn and heard a snarl of horns in response. Even if he double-parked, he was still ten minutes away. And he wasn't even sure where the tea garden was once he walked through the front gate. No way she would wait for a half an hour. She wasn't that kind of girl. He felt defeated. Suddenly, the traffic became a symbol for all that was wrong in his life. He knew he should be driving on a sunnier street again, but he was stuck here in a fumey hell and there was nothing he could do about it.

He'd wanted this evening to be perfect. When he thought about it later he realized he meant what he'd said when he'd told her that they had to begin again. He didn't call her after she took him to bed because he wanted to turn his life around before she got any closer. But every day that passed, he felt himself being sucked deeper and deeper into a black swamp. He grimaced, thinking of the night they had spent together. She scared the shit out of him the way she could peer into his soul. The first question she asked him was whether or not he was dirty. The truth was, as hard as he tried, he simply couldn't remember. And he could never let on to her how seriously his memory had been corroded by drinking. He felt so deeply ashamed. He didn't want her to know he had sunk so low.

He could taste the funk in the back of his throat. He needed a warm Scotch and a cold beer, but he didn't dare take a drink. He saw the flashing lights of an ambulance stuck solidly in traffic ahead. He swore quietly, then loudly, then gave full throat to his anger. He hammered the steering wheel with his fist. A bedraggled bum in a wheelchair begging from car to car pulled his wheels backward in an elaborate show of giving Finn wide berth. Finn leaned on his horn again. He edged his car too close to a cabdriver, then heard the sound of grating metal as his fender scratched a two-inch snake onto the yellow paint.

"Shit, sorry," yelled Finn, backing up and lightly bumping the car behind him. He didn't even look back.

By the time he got to the front gate, he was sprinting. He needed to see her like he needed no one else before. It was a few minutes before six. He was sure she would be gone and he felt like weeping.

He jogged by two granite plinths, a row of benches, and through a grove of gracious, old cherry trees. As he skipped down a well-tended path, the only thing he heard was the rhythmic rasp of a hedge clipper. He ran along a little pagoda-topped fence until he saw the brown bamboo of the teahouse almost obscured by leafy green cones of wisteria. He slowed down, a momentary hostage to its unusual beauty.

Although he'd grown up in Brooklyn, he had only discovered the Botanic Garden two years ago when his second cousin, Bobby Monahan, a priest from

County Kerry, had visited him. Bobby was an amateur rosarian, a rose buff, and he raved about the Brooklyn Botanic Garden's rose garden as if it were the Super Bowl. Although Finn found Bobby's affection for the flowers absurdly feminine, he was taken by the peacefulness of the place. At the time, he thought it was the sort of romantic spot he wanted to bring Kate to and cursed her for leaving him. With the sun pitched behind the leafy trees, he was choking on a wave of bitter irony and self-loathing.

"Ah, Kate, I've lost you again," he said, feeling a sob in his chest squeeze him like a boa.

"Are you talking to yourself, John?"

He stopped still and saw Kate sitting inside the teahouse, the red shrine reflecting on the still, green water behind her. She looked so beautiful he wanted to fall on his knees and bury his face in her lap.

"You would have walked right by me." She was smiling, as if she were expecting him exactly two minutes before six.

"I am so sorry," he said lamely. "Jesus, I can't believe the traffic getting here."

Kate smiled and looked around. "I'm glad to see you," she said simply. She stood up and linked her arm in his as if they were cousins instead of sworn enemies who just started sleeping together. He tried not to feel the gnarled flesh of her forearm, but it was rough against him, forcing his mind back in time. He imagined running his tongue along that scarred section of skin and telling her how very very sorry he was that he couldn't stop Dominick. He dug his nails into the palm of his hand to bring him into the present. He had asked her here to start again, not exorcise old ghosts.

"I thought you would have gone," he stammered as they walked toward a giant fountain encrusted with different species of water lilies.

"I would have waited all night." There it was again. Just like that moment in her apartment when she said, "I went there looking for you." A simple, direct declarative statement. I want you. Once he would

have killed to hear her say it. Now, the words made
him feel the weight of the trouble he was in. He
couldn't believe he'd ever wanted to go slow. He
wanted her now, now, here on the verdant paths of
the Botanic Garden. He leaned down and kissed her,
hungry, crazy, wanting to escape from himself. "I
have other plans for you tonight," he said, his mouth
grazing her ear. "They don't include much waiting."

Four hours later, he was sitting on her couch,
sipping some kind of sweet herbal tea and admiring
the way candlelight brought out the blue-black highlights in her hair. They hadn't jumped on each other
in the Garden. Instead, they had eaten dinner in an
empty Italian restaurant, their forks in spaghetti and
their ankles intertwined under the table. It was the
kind of meal where every time the waiter cleared
Finn's plate, he found himself thinking that he was
twenty minutes closer to getting into bed. When she
finally locked the door to her apartment, he was ready
for her from the moment the back of his hand
brushed her nipple. Afterward, he watched her glis-
tening bare back as she walked across the bedroom
and turned on the air conditioner. He was ready for
her again before her dark hair splashed against the
pillow.
    Now Kate's knees were thrown over Finn's thighs
as she put her head back and laughed, pointing out a
particularly unflattering picture of her as a gawky teen
in her high school yearbook. He was in a different
world, far away from drug raids and the guys in
Group C. From Bigelow. It was the way he should
have spent every night of the last two years. With her
hair close enough to brush his face, he felt that
nothing could harm him. He wanted to hold on to her
the way she was this moment, before she could walk
away. He felt a desire for her distilled to almost
painful urgency. Her arm fell from his shoulder to the
small of his back and her finger found a bead of
adhesive stuck to his skin.
    She suddenly shivered.

"Are you still making tapes?" she asked quietly.

Finn couldn't answer. She was too smart not to spot a lie. He was sure she would walk away if she knew the truth about his life.

"Kate, don't ask me questions like that." He was aware of how serious he sounded.

The smile left her face.

"Why?" she said softly.

"It's important to me."

She waited without speaking, but Finn could feel her drawing away. He tried again.

"I know better than to tell you what to do," he started. "But I want to ask you, as a favor, to me. For us." She smiled at the word *us*. "I know you want to help me, and by your nature, you always want to know what's going on. But don't try to get involved in this thing, this thing that's happening to me."

She stood up and paused as if she were thinking of a way to respond.

"I want to be with you," she said. "Your girlfriend. If something bad is going on, I want to know all about it."

"What if I promise to tell you as soon as I can. Would that be enough?"

She paused. "When would that be?"

He shrugged, unable to speak.

Kate looked him in the face without comprehending. "John, I'll tell you honestly that I think you need help. And I think you're a good and moral man. Whatever is wrong, I'm sure you can make it right," she said solemnly. "You'll end up going to IAB or the Department of Investigation. You'll end up getting the help you need."

Finn was startled. He had been running around with his head in a cloud, and like a grand master at chess she was figuring out the next steps he needed to take. "What makes you say something like that?"

"Your tape recorder told me."

He didn't want to let her in any farther. He looked around him, absorbing every detail of the warm apartment. It occurred to him that it was the first place he had been in many months where he was sure nothing could hurt him.

"I'll do what needs to be done. But I'll do it. On my own. I need you to stay out of it."

"What am I supposed to do meanwhile?"

"Be there for me. Be my harbor."

She was smiling at him again, pulling him close. Her smooth cheek was against his chest. His safe harbor.

# 21

Finn was so nervous he couldn't take his eyes off Lt. Kevin Sorenson, the IAB inspector investigating Brooklyn Narcotics, and, as a consequence, sat on a video camera someone had left on a frail green couch next to the wide desk.

"I guess I broke it," Finn said lamely, handing him a lens and a lens cap that had separated from the body of the camera. Sorenson, that smug little prick, never even smiled.

Sorenson closed the door; the soundproofed room reminded Finn of a crypt. Finn was more completely and thoroughly frightened than he had ever been in his life. In the past, being scared was tied to drug raids. It started with a feeling of apprehension that built up over an hour or two and climaxed in about three minutes of bloodcurdling fear. But this was different. He had gone to sleep in Kate's arms and woken up terrified. But there was no going back. Finn knew he had to stop Bigelow. The shower and shave did nothing to calm him. He'd driven to IAB headquarters on Livingston Street in Brooklyn grinding his teeth, his breath like a bramble in his throat. He was turning on another cop. A cop who'd saved his life. A cop whom he had called his best friend.

He had known for some time that IAB was looking at Brooklyn Narcotics. It wasn't exactly a secret. Sorenson, whose red face and overinflated chest made him look like a fire hydrant, had interviewed Bollini before Versos was shot. Of course, it was supposed to be hush-hush, but since they met in a glass-doored office in the middle of the day, they might as well have announced during roll call that Brooklyn Narcotics was being watched.

Swept along by jets of adrenaline, Finn settled on the green couch and had to suppress a hysterical laugh. Facing Sorenson in IAB headquarters was like flipping through *National Geographic* to see pictures of big game. Sure, he believed that rhinos lived in Kenya. They just had no connection to his life. It was the same way with IAB. Good cops didn't rat out other cops. Cops who helped IAB were the lowest of the low.

But now Finn figured he had no choice. Kate was right. It was too big for him to handle alone.

"Why are you here?" Sorenson asked finally.

Finn didn't answer.

Sorenson looked at his watch.

Finn started. "I heard you were investigating Brooklyn Narcotics. I thought maybe you needed help."

"You mean *you* needed help," said Sorenson promptly.

Finn, fighting for composure, said nothing.

"The question is, what's in it for us? Why should we talk to you?"

This wasn't the way Finn imagined it. Going to IAB was an end move. The last thing you did. Sure, your career would continue, but your life in the department was over. Now, Sorenson was making it sound as if there were some kind of qualifying exam before you could slit your own throat.

Finn's shoulders were hunched and he tried to relax them. He took a breath. This was going to be harder than he thought.

"Alfonse Versos is dead."

Sorenson shrugged broadly. "An accidental death. We're looking into allegations of corruption."

Finn waited for Sorenson to explain. Then it dawned on him that Sorenson hadn't tied in the shooting with any of the corruption.

"You think it's a coincidence that cops in Group C

are stealing drugs and one of them just happens to get shot?"

He knew he was making a mistake. IAB brass would go to any length to promote the myth that there was only one bad cop on the police force at a time. Pockets of corrupt cops were bad for the department's standing in the community and with the City Council. Occasionally, they made cases on individuals— mostly cops with drinking or drug problems. They only went after precincts or divisions when a blue ribbon panel like the Knapp Commission or the Mollen Commission shoved them into it.

"The file on Versos's shooting is inactive."

"This must be a joke."

"Not at all."

Finn paused a moment, trying to collect himself.

"So what if I can tell you differently? What if I can prove to you that Versos was shot by a cop—not by accident, but to keep him from talking to IAB."

Sorenson looked him over slowly. "I don't think we'd be interested in talking to you."

Finn felt the top of his head blow off. It was too late to save himself. Without saying it, Sorenson had made it clear that Finn was the human sacrifice. IAB had already made a case against him.

Sorenson's eyes seemed to get smaller. In answer to Finn's silent question, he opened his drawer and pulled out a manila folder with several smaller folders inside it. "We didn't need much. It says here you were investigated twice two years ago. Once for a gun discharge, and another for a self-defense shooting. Says here you once had a close relationship with a newspaper reporter. Was that before or after you started showing up to work drunk?"

Finn had come to the wrong people for help. These were cops who sniffed the sheets and called it a police investigation. These were the guys who followed you home or to your local bar. They had gotten a lot of complaints about police corruption in Brooklyn Narcotics. But instead of rooting it out and admitting that the department sheltered, even promoted, bad cops, they were going to make a case against Finn. It would be something minor. A small, contained show of blood. Nothing to attract additional press inquiries. Nothing to ruffle the chiefs. It was as if they were planning to open a chute and expected him to fall so fast that no one would hear him scream.

Finn felt his fist clench and he stood, pushing the balls of his feet against the floor. It was an old street fighter's move, establishing balance in the seconds before the first swing.

"There's a hell of a lot more going on in Group C than a drunk detective. I'm not going to be the fall guy for the whole unit." Finn's voice was ragged.

"What you want has very little to do with it at this point. We'll do what's good for the police department."

"I have tapes."

Sorenson opened his top drawer and hit the OFF switch on a concealed tape recorder as if he were killing a bug.

"Give them to me. That's a direct order."

Finn let the molecules of silence bounce between them. Sorenson, for all his chesty attitude, was dissolving.

"You have to give them to me."

Finn shrugged. "But you've already made your cases in Brooklyn Narcotics. You know what's going on. Nothing I have on tape could surprise you or make it seem to the feds that you weren't doing your job. Could it?"

"Don't try to play games," said Sorenson, but Finn cut him off.

"Just remember, if I get indicted, the tapes will tell their own story."

"I would advise you that there are certain things that are best kept inside the department. It is in the best interest of the police and your best interest as well."

That's what Bigelow had said. Keep it in the family. It was Finn's cue to go. They can open the chute, he thought as he turned to leave, but they can't make me step in.

# 22

Kate was doing a stand-up in front of the moldering Bronx Courthouse for a pretaped segment to commemorate the first anniversary of a bribery scandal that had sent two Bronx judges to jail. She finished her scripted comments and looked seriously at the camera as Manuel, who was wearing a WILL WORK FOR SEX T-shirt, pulled back so he could get a full shot of the once-majestic building behind her. As he tilted the camera, a four-foot piece of the marble cornice broke off the courthouse and fell square on the roof of a corrections department van on its way back to Riker's.

"Oh, shit," Kate said, then cringed when she realized that Manuel had probably left the audio on and she had just ruined their tape. "You get that?"

Manuel said nothing but by way of an answer held the camera on the crushed car. Kate scrambled to the bottom of the steps. Two corrections officers had pulled the driver out of the van, unhurt. But his passenger, a prisoner named Darryl Amram, was killed instantly. It should have been the happiest day of Amram's life. A jury had just acquitted him of stabbing a young bartender to death. Amram was being driven back to Riker's to be processed for release. Just as it was becoming clear that Amram had been crushed to death, the mother of the bartender, an enormous-breasted Irish woman with a mop of gray hair styled like barbed wire, walked out of the courthouse, surveyed the carnage of her son's killer, and began to applaud.

Kate let Manuel get a closer shot of the corpse through the shattered back window of the van and then ran up the steps to interview the mother.

"The jury was out for two days, we thought we had 'im," she said as if she were describing a baseball game. "Then, Jesus, Mary, and Joseph, the idiots decided to let him free."

"Your son being killed must have been a terrible tragedy for you," Kate said.

"Ah, yes," the woman said absently.

"And was the acquittal a painful experience?"

"Terrible, terrible."

"How do you feel now that the man who was accused of stabbing your son was squashed before your eyes?"

"It's like I always said, God has a way of taking care of these little things."

Kate struggled to maintain a serious expression when she wanted to click her heels together and do a victory dance. This story would be the equivalent of sending her résumé to Dan Rather.

She saw that back in the van, Bernie was already looping the tape to go live at twelve. Even Andrew Fink allowed himself a long, low chuckle when he got the feed.

"Great work, great," he said. Although Kate had never laid eyes on him, she considered Andrew Fink to be her best friend at the station. He was the one she trusted the most. Almost every day, she invited him for a cappuccino or a drink, and he always made a vague acceptance. But whenever she was in the newsroom, the door to the microwave room was locked. When it wasn't locked, Fink was nowhere to be found. She imagined he had a full life. He probably had a wife and child stashed away in the suburbs. Still, she felt as if she could tell him her problems even if he thought a personal disaster meant the Volvo wouldn't start.

"I do it all for you," she said, flirting. "When are we going to have that drink?"

"Someday soon," said Fink without conviction.

By the time she sat down to a late lunch with Mark DeMaris, Kate had fielded three calls from producers of syndicated shows like *911* and *Top Cops* making bids for the exclusive rebroadcast rights to the "chunked murderer."

"You're having a good day," Mark DeMaris said as she slipped behind the banquette at Smith & Wollensky. It was the kind of seating arrangement Kate hated. Instead of looking at your dining companion you stared out at other people eating their food as if they were the floor show. It was the kind of steak house where politicians came to make their public deals. And where elected officials brought reporters for on-the-record interviews. Kate guessed she wouldn't get a single usable tip out of DeMaris.

Now that he was the boss, DeMaris had replaced his coal gray, nondescript suit with a dapper Italian cut. Kate wondered if he was having gray streaked into his hair at his temples to make him look more distinguished.

Kate smiled. "A bad day for the acquitted murderer. A good day for Kate Murray."

"Well, sometimes justice is handed out in strange ways."

She looked at him. It was an odd thing for a prosecutor to say.

She waited for him to say something more, to give an indication of why he wanted to meet with her. She bit back the urge to pepper him with questions about the corruption investigation. He said nothing. She said nothing. The moment lengthened. Then he broke into his getting-to-know-you patter. How long had she worked at the *Herald?* What did she think of television? Like he really cared.

The waiter, a hulking man wearing a blood-smeared apron like a butcher, came by to take their order. Kate fumbled with the menu, ordering the first thing in the diminutive salad column. With a flourish, DeMaris order a prime rib. She looked at him as he spoke. Political animal, she thought. He radiated ambition like a flamethrower. And something else, something self-satisfying and unlikable. Assurance that he would get his way. She wondered if he tyrannized his wife. Probably. Some guys could never really disguise their belief that they were entitled to slightly more than their share. She found him repulsive.

She pulled out of her reverie when the mayor's top deputy mayor, Norman Taylor, strode over to the table. "Nice to see you," he said, sticking out his hand. And to Kate's utter surprise, she saw his hand was extended toward her. DeMaris, however, was not as quick and had already formulated an answer. "Great to see *you*," he answered for Kate. Taylor didn't give a sign that he had noticed. "Great story today. The fellow who was chunked in the Bronx. Great television."

Kate tried to be gracious, but Taylor had already turned to DeMaris. "Nice to see you, too," he said with the voice you might use with someone who had just kicked your dog.

She watched them. Two germs, bred for chemical warfare, ready to start attacking each other. By the time they settled again, DeMaris seemed genuinely animated around her. As if he were factoring in Taylor's opinion of her over his own. Aside from the crazy ME's assistant and her fear of being recognized at O'Brien's, Kate had never dwelled much on the idea of fame. Now here it was, befuddling her lunchmate. She liked it.

The waiter brought their food. Kate had just wrapped her lips around a slippery piece of chicken when Rob Scott, the anchorman, slapped her on the back.

"Great story, Kate," he said, oblivious to DeMaris. "We're going to kill 'em in the ratings tonight."

When Kate introduced DeMaris, he fell over himself to be charming. Scott hardly nodded. Away from a teleprompter, Scott was actually a very limited guy with few interests beyond his salary and Q ratings. One lawyer was the same as the next for him.

When Scott walked away, Kate could tell something had definitely changed with DeMaris. He was meeting her eye more directly, as if he were eager that they be seen as equals. She smiled.

"What I really want is to serve the public," DeMaris was saying. "At a level that affects the very fabric of the city."

"Like what?" she said uneasily.

"Well, it has been my dream to be mayor and I'm confident I can make that happen."

"Why are you announcing your candidacy to me? I would have thought you'd want this in the *New York Times* instead of on Channel Seven."

"I do want it in the *Times*. But I also need the opportunity to let the good citizens of New York learn about my record."

This was it. The pitch. She tuned her ears.

"That means plenty of attention in the media."

Of course, idiot. He wants to be on television. She didn't like DeMaris enough to do this dance with him.

"There is an expression I've heard around court. I believe it's 'quid pro quo.'" She waited. DeMaris didn't flinch nor did he rush to respond. Yes, he was certainly a player. She continued, "First thing I need is an advance on your biggest story. The police-corruption story."

"After the indictment, it's public information."

She shook her head. "I know that, but if you give me the basic outline of the case now, I can start working on a ten-minute segment instead of a ten-second mention. It couldn't help but improve your image as fighting young prosecutor."

His eyes seemed to settle on Kate's. She smiled her best dazzling, top-of-the-eleven-o'clock-news smile.

"What would you need to know?"

"Precinct?"

"Brooklyn Narcotics."

She forced herself not to react. She thought of Finn saying "don't get involved."

"Specifically?"

"Cops working for the Ghost Brigade."

She whistled low. "IAB involved?"

"They don't know a thing about our probe."

"How many people involved?"

He shrugged. "Maybe two, maybe six, maybe a dozen. We'll know within a few days. We'll talk again before we finish off the investigation."

# 23

Finn thought it was strange that Dan Yumor had gone from being a computer programmer to an FBI agent. It was stranger still that Yumor, the first white-collar worker from a family of dirt farmers and refrigeration repairmen, was assigned to the unit that covered Asian organized crime. Yumor never seemed interested in anything beyond his son's Little League team and the crabgrass in his front yard in Toms River, New Jersey. He brought bottled water with him when he was forced to work overnight details in New York City, and no amount of teasing would persuade him to spend money in a restaurant that didn't serve Salisbury steak. His car had a bumper sticker that said EAT YOUR IMPORTED CAR.

But every cop Finn asked said Yumor knew more than anyone else about Brooklyn's Chinese community. He'd studied the gangs as if they were a new computer language. His office was filled with flow charts, graphs, and mug shots.

Ordinarily, Finn would have gone to the public library before asking the FBI for help, but Yumor was a cousin of his ex-wife, Sandy. After the settlement her divorce lawyer pried out of him, Finn figured his ex-relatives owed him a big favor.

"Nice to see you, Dan," he said, sliding into the booth at the diner where Yumor had insisted they meet. "How's Sandy?"

"Well, the doctors think it's twins."

"What? She's pregnant? Jesus, she just got married!" said Finn, unable to imagine Sandy's hard little hips and taut stomach swollen with a child.

"Three years," said Yumor defensively. "They've been married three years. And she's not getting any younger."

Finn could see that Yumor thought Finn was insulting his cousin, so he changed tack.

"Of course. That's great. I'm happy for her, really happy. Just shocked. You know, my wife."

"Ex-wife," Yumor said, not backing off.

"Of course. Listen, when's she due? Don't forget to call me when she delivers. I'll send flowers," said Finn, trying to soften him. "I always wanted kids. Sandy was the one who wanted to wait."

He thought of Kate holding hands with a chubby-legged toddler and felt wistful. Yumor motioned to a waitress. Finn ordered coffee black. Yumor asked for brewed decaf, not Sanka, with milk, not cream. The waitress wrinkled her nose and sloshed two cups in front of them.

"So what do you need to know about Sunset Park?"

"Well, I'm looking into an incident in a building there. It looked like gang activity."

"What location."

"Five-oh-two-oh Eighth Avenue. Above a café."

Yumor whistled. "It's the Ghost Brigade headquarters. Whatever it is, back off. Don't waste your time on it."

"What do you mean?"

"I can't say. It isn't my case. I only supply the intelligence information, you know, background, mug shots, who's who."

"C'mon."

Yumor leaned closer. "Keep it under your hat, but it's an open investigation. The triads are shipping tons of heroin into New York and distributing it through Dominican middlemen. We don't know how it's getting past our borders, but the triads must have brought the Ghost Brigade in on it—a kind of insurance policy to make sure the drugs get to the Dominicans. So we're sitting on them. Figure it'll be a good time to make a RICO stick."

Finn thought of Bigelow, the wad of money, and the table full of Chinese men. The Ghost Brigades were buying some insurance of their own. Bigelow was working for them.

He felt his balls retract and his stomach seize up.

Oblivious, Yumor sipped his coffee and grimaced. He gestured for the waitress, who pointedly ignored him.

"Let me ask you one more thing," said Finn, feeling sweat dripping down his pant leg.

Yumor stuck out his chin. "Sorry, I already said too much."

"One thing. I got to know. Is there surveillance on five-oh-two-oh Eighth Avenue?" If the FBI saw Bigelow there, they also saw Finn stagger up the stairs.

"Sorry, buddy, can't tell you. I don't work for your outfit." He put up his hand and snapped his fingers for the check. The waitress looked down her long nose at him and stormed into the kitchen.

"For God's sake, Yumor. A life could be riding on this." Finn didn't say the life was his. "Is there surveillance?"

Yumor turned his eyes from the swinging kitchen doors.

"They're watching it, Finn. Watching it hard. Round the clock. No one gets in or out without agents knowing about it."

# 24

Kate and her old friend Nina walked through the gates of the Central Park Zoo. Behind them, marching with the fierce concentration of a West Point cadet, came Katieanne, Nina's eighteen-month-old daughter. Kate was scheduled to cover a Democratic fundraiser tonight and was dreading an evening given over to rubber chicken and long, predictable speeches. It was a beautiful, hot day, and to quell the uneasy sense that summer was passing her by, she had arranged to meet Nina and Katieanne for lunch at the zoo.

Kate was surprised to see that Nina, who prided herself on her impeccable clothing, looked wrinkled. She had circles under her eyes and an unidentifiable food stain on her tank top. She was at her wit's end with Katieanne.

"There I was in the middle of the laundry-soap aisle of the A & P with Katieanne writhing on the floor," said Nina, shuddering at the memory.

"What was the problem?" said Kate absently.

"She wanted to take off all her clothes in the supermarket. I wouldn't let her." Nina shrugged ironically. "Okay. Call me an abusive mother. I didn't want her naked at the A & P." She paused. "I remember before I was married I would hear kids screaming on airplanes or in restaurants or in a supermarket. I'd think to myself, 'What's wrong with the parents of that child?'" Nina was crying. "Kate, do you think there is something wrong with me?"

Kate patted her friend on the shoulder. "Listen,

Katieanne is going to be a strong woman. You wouldn't want it any other way. You did fine. You're a good mother."

Nina turned to stare at her daughter with a mixture of wonder and fright. Katieanne wasn't what anyone would call an easy child. She had an elfin face and the will of a freight train. She had burned out two baby-sitters in her first year and brought her parents to the brink of divorce by consistently sleeping four and a half hours a night.

Just then, Katieanne caught sight of the sea lions splashing in their tank, and she darted forward into the crowd, her little Reeboks dancing over the pavement in a way that defied gravity. Instinct took over and Nina dashed after her daughter. Kate smiled. She could see a lot of Nina in the little girl. When Kate first met Nina, she was dropping out of Syracuse University to become a dairy farmer on an Israeli kibbutz. Later, after they both graduated, Nina did an abrupt about-face and landed a job at a prestigious Wall Street financial firm. In short order, she married a buttoned-down lawyer named Samuel Fecks. Nine months after she was wed, Katieanne was born, and Nina, with great energy and enthusiasm, became a full-time mother. Until Katieanne, Nina had taken each turn in her life with complete equanimity, as if dairy farming in Israel were a natural steppingstone to being the wife of a straitlaced lawyer.

Katieanne broke away from her mother again, running toward a fenced-in piece of tundra, rapturously screaming, "Po' beys!" as two mammoth white bears lumbered out of their fake snow cave. When Nina caught up, her daughter began pulling on her pant leg relentlessly, demanding to sit on her mother's shoulders for a better look at the bears. Wearily, Nina complied. Kate stared at Katieanne's small head resting on Nina's like a feminine totem pole, thinking they looked like the emblem of family life in the 1990s. It was a life Kate had, in the past, outwardly scorned and lately inwardly feared she might never enjoy.

Nina tried to pick up the strain of an adult conversation. "I was talking to an old friend of mine from work. He's a broker. He said you have him bewitched. He watches Channel Seven every night in hopes of seeing you."

Kate felt prickly heat on the back of her neck. Nina continued, "Do you want me to introduce you? I mean, in case this thing doesn't work out with Finn."

Kate dodged Nina's unspoken questions. Nina was usually her confidant, but right now, Kate didn't know what to say about Finn. She reached down to peel some gum from the heel of her pump. "Why haven't you mentioned this fan of mine before?" Kate said suspiciously. "Is he married or something?"

"Something."

"What?"

"Just separated."

Kate groaned. "This is your idea of a date?"

Nina shrugged. "I took a chance. I don't know that many thirty-five-year-old virgins."

"Jesus, Nina," said Kate, then she realized that Katieanne was staring at her full in the face. The toddler leaned down and shouted into her mother's ear, "Jesusnina." Nina looked shocked and Kate tried to stop herself from smiling. Katieanne sensed she had stumbled onto a punch line. *"Jesusnina,"* she mimicked Kate perfectly, her high voice carrying through the crowd. "Jesus, Nina. Jesus, Nina." Two old ladies turned and began to whisper. Nina blushed and Kate mouthed, "Sorry."

Nina hustled Katieanne toward the concession stand. Balancing bottles of seltzer and orange juice, they sat on steel benches and began gnawing on lukewarm hot dogs. Kate felt hemmed in by the frenetic energy of so many small, hungry children. Nina didn't notice. She was trying to stop Katieanne, who had quickly gobbled a hamburger, from eating spare french fries she had found squashed on the tiled floor.

"I used to want her to eat natural, unprocessed food

with no preservatives," said Nina. "Now I'm happy if
it's food that someone hasn't stepped on."

"We all change our minds about what's important,"
said Kate, thinking of Finn again.

"Yeah? What about you? D'you ever think about
having a family?"

Kate shrugged. "I think about it, but it doesn't
seem to be happening." There was more heartbreak in
her voice than either woman had expected.

"Not that I'm an advertisement for maternal bliss,"
said Nina, trying to lighten the moment. "If I'd
known"—she pointed to Katieanne—"I never would
have left my day job. Being a full-time mom is too
hard."

Kate nodded sympathetically. "I wouldn't have the
nerve to be a single mother. I guess I'd need a stable
relationship. Even then, I'm not sure about the logis-
tics of working and raising a child. I'd need a lot of
help, or have to teach them how to drive a microwave
truck very very young."

Katieanne had given up on squashed french fries
and climbed into Kate's lap. She wiped her runny
nose on Kate's jacket and snuggled her head under
Kate's chin. Her little hand crept up behind Kate's
ear, and she began to rhythmically stroke Kate's hair
as if she were petting a sheep. In less than a minute,
Katieanne was asleep, a heavy, warm lump on Kate's
shoulder. A change came over Nina when she saw her
daughter's eyelids. She straightened up, tucked in her
shirt, and attacked the food stain with a little leftover
seltzer. Kate felt the child's warm breath.

"Maybe you won't be a mom. You'll be Katieanne's
glamorous Auntie Kate reporting from far-flung ports
of call," whispered Nina.

Through her thin jacket, Kate felt the child's rapid
heartbeat. She thought of her empty apartment and
her silent answering machine. "Yeah," she said.
"Glamorous Auntie Kate."

# 25

It was another drug raid, and the talk he had had with Dan Yumor two nights ago, combined with a cruel hangover, fell on Finn like so many little blows raining on the back of his neck. The other cops in Group C were acting like pallbearers at a funeral. There were no practical jokes, no good-natured teasing, no animal noises over the radio. It seemed to Finn that every man in the unit just wanted to get through the raid quickly and without incident.

They were working again with Group D, taking out a drug dealer, Earl Figley III, and his lieutenants Aubrey Rose and Michel Collins and their operation. They'd set up a series of command posts in the Cypress Hills housing project. The problem was that Figley had grown up in Cypress Hills and knew every path, tunnel, and bullet mark in the interconnected brick towers. And half of the men in Group D were new to Brooklyn.

"I got a bad feeling about this," Stephen Lee murmured, only half-listening to the "chalk talk" as the undercover stood in front of a blackboard pointing to doorways in Figley's primary command post, apartment 9V in the East Tower. Bigelow, his eyes half-closed, hummed the lyrics to "Oh, It's So Nice to Be with You."

After mug shots of Figley and his top henchmen were passed around, Bigelow assigned Finn to watch the back entrance of the tower. Bigelow assigned Lee to surveillance detail. Lucky bastard, Finn cursed him quietly. He got to sit inside a van parked half a block away.

"How come I didn't get surveillance detail?" Finn grumbled.

"All that fellatio has finally paid off." Lee grinned as he slipped on his Task Force jacket.

"I love all the things you say and do," hummed Bigelow, ignoring the men.

Two hours later, Finn was standing in a quiet courtyard, wondering who had come up with the idea of housing poor people in towers. It didn't make any sense. It wasn't as if the real estate values in the area around the Cypress Hills projects were inflated. In fact, half the buildings on the surrounding blocks were abandoned. Drug dealers controlled the block. Most decent people walked quickly from the subway to their homes, counted their children, and closed the door firmly against the gunfire that burst through the ambient hum of urban living. Those people left on the street hated cops. Muggers, petty thieves, and junkies, they had been the recipients of thousands of casual beatings. Relations between the street people and the cops had gotten so bad that the street people looked past your uniform or your task force jacket and saw you as a chance to even up the score. The cops responded by traveling in pairs even to get coffee.

Finn started counting the windows of the project. Most of the people they stuck in the high-rise housing were single mothers pushing strollers or old folks depending on a walker. When the elevators were broken, which was most of the time, stairs restrained them as effectively as a locked prison door.

He checked his watch and listened. The raid should be going down just about now, but he couldn't hear a thing. No shooting, no muffled shouts. Maybe he'd get lucky after all and Group D would make all the collars and leave him out of it. Then it would be just another quiet summer night in Brooklyn. He squinted at the sky and thought he saw a star peeping through the yellow-tinged cloud.

Finn was totally unprepared when he looked back to earth and found himself staring at Figley's number two lieutenant, Aubrey Rose.

Rose looked startled, too, but he was traveling at a velocity inspired by fear. He butted into Finn without slowing down. Finn sprawled onto his ass.

He heaved himself to a squat and radioed for backup.

"Male, five feet ten inches. Approximately one hundred seventy-five pounds." Finn eyed the fleeing figure. "Carrying what looks like a nine-millimeter."

He listened as the 10-13 code, officer in need of assistance, went out over the division radio. Then he set off trotting after Rose, pausing only for a second when he saw Rose duck into the North Tower.

"In pursuit of armed suspect," Finn shouted into his radio. "Entering west side of North Tower, first floor, requesting backup." What Rose didn't know is that tonight, the Cypress Hills housing project was crawling with cops. Finn's radio call would summon a battalion in a matter of minutes.

Finn let his radio drop against his side when he heard the bang of a steel door. He stuck his head down the hallway and saw that Rose had disappeared behind a door marked BASEMENT. He was struck by the silence from his radio and realized that no one had answered his call. Usually when a cop radios a 10-13, the airwaves are bombarded with acknowledgments. Nothing gets a cop moving faster than a fellow cop in trouble. Finn swiveled his head and, in the dim light, tried to imagine the thickness of the walls. Maybe no one got his signal.

He dashed down four steps. He was overtaken by the scent of spilled bleach as he passed through a utility room and rounded a brace of scarred-looking washing machines. He thought he heard Rose's footsteps. He ducked back toward the dryers. Finn heard another door slam, then nothing. Finn heard the scrape of careful footsteps nearby and felt his scalp crawl in horror as the room where he was hiding went dark. There was either someone far ahead toying with the circuit breakers or someone in the same room standing next to the light switch.

"Requesting backup. C'mon, c'mon," he pleaded into his radio, trying to keep his voice low. Where the hell was his backup? He couldn't stay where he was, so he stuck his hands past a sheet of cobwebs and found a dirty door handle. With his weight on his hip, he forced it open and stumbled into one of the project's interconnecting tunnels.

Since crime took control of the projects, no one used these tunnels anymore. They were dimly lit and scattered with long, dusty cobwebs and silt-covered beer cans. Finn ran unevenly along the tunnel, listening to his ragged breathing. He rounded a corner, then pushed on.

He stopped suddenly, aware of some movement ahead of him. Was it Rose or just a rat? He felt the nauseating tickle of the sticky, dirty webs on his cheek. He looked at the crumbling ceiling, imagining being buried under the rubble of a twenty-four-story apartment building. They could dig for twenty years, Finn thought, and never pull him out.

His eyes jumped into the dimness ahead, trying to follow another faint sound. Then he heard the clang of the steel door behind him. He sucked in the fetid air. It was a squeeze play. He was stuck in the middle as the bad guys slowly advanced on him from either direction.

"Request assistance, foot unit in utility tunnel between West and North Tower," he pleaded. "Oh, please, somebody hear me, I'm in a hell of a mess." Then he knew. The men in his unit could hear me. But they'd decided not to respond. It was an old cop trick, guaranteed to break even the wildest maverick or the most regulation-bound whistle blower. They simply left him alone in a moment of fear. The message was plain. Do it our way or you fight the streets alone. Bigelow was a criminal but he was still a cop. Somehow, he'd sensed that Finn was turning away from him. Finn felt fear percolate into his bones, then rage. He imagined the members of his group listening to him plead for help. He thought of the way they would be sitting in the van, looking shyly at Bigelow, waiting for him to smile. They would be shocked, of course, if Rose shot Finn to death in this tunnel. They would drink and be maudlin at his funeral and tell each other what a good cop Finn had been. They simply couldn't get to him in time to stop the shooting, they'd say.

Who would come to his funeral? His parents were both dead. His neighbors were probably signing petitions to evict him even now. Fat Tony would make the trip down. Sandy wouldn't come. She'd be out buying a double stroller, and besides, he wasn't sure she thought much about him anymore. The very men from Group C who were responsible for his death would turn out in force. He thought of a western he had once seen where one of the cowboys died of typhoid alone on the wild open prairie. The cowboy turned his horse loose, finished the water in his canteen, and murmured the only prayer he knew until his eyes rolled back in his head and the only sound was the whistling wind. At that moment, Finn knew exactly how the cowboy felt. Then, somewhere, his adrenaline-flooded brain threw out the sound of Kate's laugh. Finn felt his heart, which had been frozen in Lucite like a ghoulish paperweight, begin to beat again. There were two things that Bigelow and the men from Group C didn't know. Kate Murray was in love with him. And he had enough incriminating tapes in his apartment to keep a team of federal prosecutors busy for a year. Finn felt the strength rise in his arms. More than anything in the world, he wanted to get out of this tunnel to see the stars again, to turn his life around, to hold Kate one more time. But all he saw was blackness.

He heard the sound ahead of him get louder. Aubrey had doubled back for the confrontation.

Finn slid his hands over the damp mortar until he found a small recess in the wall for some kind of equipment that had been pulled out and sold for scrap years ago. He crouched down and pushed his body into the space. He wasn't hidden, but at least he wasn't standing there like a target dummy waiting for Aubrey to pump a slug in his heart.

He held his breath as the footsteps got closer. He saw Aubrey's shadow looming and his heart began to push through his chest.

But when Aubrey Rose rounded the corner, he had his hands over his head.

"D-d-don't shoot me, I'll give up my gun," Rose stuttered.

Finn stood up rapidly and advanced on Figley's lieutenant. He frisked the boy, secured his weapon, and then struck him in the jaw with the butt of his gun.

"Don't make a sound, you little mongrel," he whispered to him. "Didn't your mother ever tell you not to run from cops?"

The boy looked at Finn and whimpered.

Finn cuffed Rose, put his gun to his shoulders, and made the boy walk back down the tunnel in case Rose's partner shot first and tried to separate out the police officers later. As they heard the footsteps approaching, Finn realized it wasn't a good idea. Rose was too thin to provide Finn with any type of protection. He crouched down, pulling Rose down after him like a human shield.

Finn whispered to Rose, "Tell him there are cops all over the tunnel and he should run away."

"Fade, man," shouted Rose, obeying the pressure of Finn's gun in his back, "the place is crawling with five-ohs."

Finn could see the outline of a small man in the shadows walking toward them. He slowed. Finn's head was spinning.

"Police!" he called out. "Don't take another step."

"Don't shoot," said a familiar voice. "I'm the cavalry sent in to rescue you."

And Stephen Lee stepped out of the shadows.

# 26

The sky was a flat, clean blue and the birds were knocking themselves out calling from tree to tree. It was the hottest day of the summer so far, and Kate felt her shoulders relax as if she were slipping off a sweater. She always felt better when she drove through the Victorian gates of Green-wood Cemetery. She waved to the guard. When she was making a quick visit, she drove to the Ninth Avenue gate, which was nearer the neat, symmetrical lines of headstones that marked the newer graves. But today was Sunday, her first full day off in nine days. She parked her car near the elaborately carved waiting room at the Fort Hamilton entrance, stuffed her beeper in the glove compartment, grabbed a handful of this week's papers, and set off to find Edith's headstone.

In life, her grandmother Edith Murray, a tiny woman with a fast mind and a big heart, had been her counselor, her personal barometer, and her biggest fan. One night last fall she had called Kate to discuss a series Kate was writing for the *Herald* on foreign-made automatic weapons. Then she went to bed and died, peacefully, in her sleep.

It was the end Kate had wanted for her, but she missed her terribly. After two months or so, Kate started going to Green-wood Cemetery for the same weekly visit she'd made to Edith's apartment, and later her nursing home. At first she felt silly, sitting by the blank, snowy grave. But after the plain headstone arrived, Kate gradually began to enjoy the trip.

She passed the gravestone of the Mafia princess, a twenty-foot tableau of a woman collapsed on pink granite steps clutching a bouquet. One of the bowed old maintenance men had told her that the deceased, as he called her, had scorned her lover, a powerful member of the Black Hand, and decided to marry an exporter. The enraged mobster had her rubbed out on the way to her wedding, and she died, the maintenance man told Kate, on the steps of the church.

Kate pulled a carnation off a newer grave and stuck it in the Mafia princess's hand. She passed by Al Jolson's grave and the plot where vaudeville performer Billy Warwick interred every member of his troupe, from the Midget to the Fat Lady. She skipped past Charles Scribner's beautiful neo-Gothic gazebo, and the sculpted mausoleum that housed the inventor of Nathan's hot dogs. She spotted the six-foot flaming crucifix in gray marble, a more ostentatious emblem than Edith would have tolerated but a useful landmark for finding Edith's plain grave.

She settled herself on a little stack of newspapers. It seemed appropriate to bring them here. Although Edith would've encouraged her to take the television job, her heart was always in the printed word. Even if CBS had handed Kate Dan Rather's job, Edith would have preferred her to write a front-page story for the *Herald*. Television was for Jackie Gleason and "This Is Your Life." To Edith, the written word meant power. Even when her eyesight was failing, Edith read every article that carried Kate's name.

Edith would understand how uneasy Kate felt about her new job. When she worked at the *Herald*, she felt as if newspapers were her destiny. Now, since she started at Channel 7, all she had to do was watch ten minutes of Oprah and her freak of the week and Kate was awash in self-doubt. Television was a medium for people who hungered to be recognized by millions. These days, Kate just wanted a decent paycheck, a steady guy, and hopes for the future.

Far away, Kate heard the jays calling and she watched the breeze carry a few late rose petals to the ground. It was a picture-perfect day. But instead of feeling relaxed, Kate felt her mood slide around like a jazz horn. She wondered if she was premenstrual and realized with a start that she had lost count of her cycle. She thought nervously of making love with Finn. She always worried more about AIDS than birth control, assuming, because she'd never been pregnant, that she couldn't conceive a child.

"Hello, Edith. It's a beautiful summer day." Edith would have called it "grand." "In spite of my ambivalence, television has been going very well. With J.J.'s help, I've been doing more on-air work than I ever imagined. Kids on my block call me the 'news lady' when they see me on the street." She decided not to mention that problem at the paint factory.

She sighed. "But the real news is Finn. Again. He's back in my life." Edith had always liked Finn.

"I hardly recognized him when I saw him. He looks much thinner and more, I don't know, haunted." She was surprised at her choice of words. "Things are different between us now. For one thing, he's not doing all the pursuing. I figured out what you meant when you said I had to trust in love"—she lowered her voice confidentially—"and I went after him." She paused, smiling a little. "But he seems different to me." She considered. "Part of it's that he doesn't trust me because, you know, the way things ended the last time." She took a deep breath. "And the other part of it I can't quite put my finger on. He says he has trouble at work, but it's more than that." She realized when she spoke how much Finn had changed. "Two years ago, he was the most solid guy I ever met. Bedrock. Now"—she fluttered her hand—"I get the sense he's all twisted up. He doesn't know who he is or what he's doing." The more she talked, the more agitated and unsure she felt. But she pushed herself gently, as Edith would have done. "Yeah, it's a difficult time for him. His unit is under investigation, but as far as I know, he's not helping the investigators. When I asked him about it, he said not everything was black-and-white. What does that mean? I mean, I thought the people he worked with were corrupt. Now I'm starting to wonder if he's, you know, tainted."

She heard the reedy scream of a siren grow closer and then begin to fade. She heard a car backfire and the unmuffled roar of a New York City bus chugging its way up a hill. All around her were solemn, ancient headstones. Slabs of granite unmindful of the weather, the current mayor, levels of airborne PCBs, and the teenagers who snuck over the fence to smoke pot. Below these markers were bodies, and below the bodies were other bodies. The rolling hills of Greenwood Cemetery were made of the rich loam of composting New Yorkers. She was sitting in the city of the dead. She looked at the flaming crucifix and squinted at the name carved at the base. His choice of gravestones was gaudy, but who was to say what kind of man Eduardo Carlucci was? What difference did it make if he was good, moral, and kind or a lying, conniving bastard. She squinted to read the lettering above his name: "Beloved father and husband." It was not like there is any truth to epitaphs. She had walked the paths of Green-wood Cemetery for almost a year and had never seen one that said, "Asshole to the End." No matter how you carried yourself through life, it all ended the same way. Inhale, exhale, then nothing.

Kate heard Edith's voice and imagined her spidery fingers running through Kate's unruly hair.

"Look in your heart. You know the answer." That's what Edith would say. She was convinced that her granddaughter was born with all the wisdom and talent she would ever need.

"Edith, my heart tells me he's a good man." She stared out over the gravestones. Integrity was an organic part of the Finn she once knew. It'd been like an essential organ. It was etched in the retina of his eye, laced in the feathery cells of his liver, and linked in the white spools of his spine. She wondered just how much he had changed.

Then she thought of Mark DeMaris, shining with ambition, and Landis, edgy and fickle. She heard the breeze whisper through the new leaves. DeMaris said cops in Brooklyn Narcotics were working with the Ghost Brigade, but no matter how many times he said it, she stubbornly would not let herself imagine Finn working for the Chinese gangs.

She wiped her face with the palm of her hand. Denial. It was a strange sensation. Like night blindness. She remembered an interview she had done with the bedraggled wife of a convicted serial rapist. The wife stumbled down the steps of the courthouse like a sleepwalker. Her husband was a loving man and a good mate, she told Kate. She had no inkling he had been committing two brutal rapes a day. Kate didn't believe her. You sleep next to a man, you share his dreams and you share his nightmares. Even if you can't admit it to yourself, you have a sense of what he is capable of doing. "I had no idea he was committing these terrible crimes," the woman started to say. Kate looked up from her notebook, intending to nod her head in encouragement. Instead, she found herself staring in the woman's eyes, and Kate took an involuntary step backward. The rapist's wife hadn't just suspected. She had known and allowed it to happen. The woman understood what Kate saw and put her hand on Kate's arm, sobbing and begging. In spite of herself, Kate had pulled away. The woman's hot tears fell on Kate's hand. "I should have made him stop."

Kate inhaled the smell of cut grass. Some people commit crimes. Other people allow crimes to be committed. She wondered where that woman was today and felt sorry that she hadn't offered her a few kind words. Perhaps, Kate thought, it was all a matter of degree.

# 27

It was four A.M. by the time Finn returned from processing Aubrey Rose. His scorched apartment had been burglarized. The few orderly corners and drawers he had managed to establish since the fire were returned to rubble. It was a professional job. Not one of your typical ax-down-the-door-and-take-anything-electronic crackhead specials. No, this was painstaking. The lock on the door had been removed with the clean deliberation of a locksmith. Finn pulled his gun and walked through each room in the apartment. He was aware that the burglars were long gone but that his apartment might still be watched. With the shades open, IAB could see exactly what he checked first. He put his gun away. He cursed Sorenson. It was a typical IAB response to a report of police corruption. They leaked the fact that he had tried to cooperate, then broke into his apartment to steal the tapes. Finn felt a bead of sweat on his forehead. If they'd gotten the tapes, all was lost. There'd be nothing to stop IAB from bringing him up on charges—drunk on duty, misuse of a firearm, some piddly counts to ruin his life and get him bounced from the department. Kate, whose laugh had kept him alive tonight, would quickly learn how far he'd fallen. There was nothing to keep her from walking away. He knew he couldn't live through it again. He shut the door and pushed a chair against it. He walked over to the living room window and pulled down the shade. Then he poured himself four fingers of Scotch. He drank it but his

anxiety only increased. Then he poured himself two
fingers and managed to hack two ice cubes out of the
ice tray. He threw those into the tumbler as well and
swirled it, making a circular motion with his hand. He
walked through his small apartment, pulling shades
and closing curtains. When he was sure that he could
not be seen from outside, he walked quickly to the
black lacquer cabinet he had bought with his first
detective's paycheck. He surveyed the three-foot line
of tightly packed rock-and-roll albums he had col-
lected since he was fourteen. His fingers skidded over
the corrugated spines. His heart was pumping like a
gusher, but perversely, he wouldn't let his fingers go
directly to the Rolling Stones albums. If the burglars
had found the Rolling Stones, there was no hope left.
The only option was for Finn to eat his gun.

He pulled out one or two records to check them for
soot and water damage. Seeing soot on a Derek and
the Dominos album was like seeing flames lick your
family album. There were a lot of memories here. It
seemed as if every innocent chapter of his life had a
song that accompanied it like a musical score. Songs
like Bad Company's "Feeling Like Making Love." He
opened the jacket cover to the *Straight Shooter* album.
Every time he heard that song he was seventeen again,
sitting in the mandatory Monday-morning Mass at St.
Sebastian High School, quietly humming the most
blatantly sexual lyrics he had ever heard. Without
looking at the Rolling Stones records, he slid the Bad
Company album back into its spot. These old LPs
were dinosaurs, eclipsed by cassettes and compact
discs and whatever other technology was just around
the corner. But there was something romantic about
the glossy black plates. Throwing them away would be
like willingly forgetting his childhood. And what
about Rod Stewart's *Every Picture Tells a Story*. He
pulled out the record. He used to love this guy. He
loved everything about him, the way his voice dipped,
coarsened, and went sweet again. He loved the fact,
too, that Rod always got the girls. He saw a lot of
action for such a funny-looking man. Finn felt the

weight of his gun in his underarm holster. He wondered if he could actually make his finger squeeze the trigger to end his own life. He wondered if dying from a self-inflicted gunshot wound would hurt. He pulled out another album. That was the problem with the cops in Group C. They listened to that sappy seventies trash Bigelow liked instead of real music. They didn't have any heroes like Rod Stewart. They thought good old music was the Village People.

By the time his finger stopped at the Rolling Stones, Finn could taste vomit. He didn't want to die. When he pulled, the entire Rolling Stones collection from *England's Newest Hitmakers* to *Voodoo Lounge* came out in a chunk. Everything looked exactly the same as it had been three nights ago when he returned from talking to Yumor. He had chopped out the middle of the jackets and epoxied the cardboard sheets together to form a secret compartment. He opened the double album *Exile on Main Street,* whose cover acted like a lid for his makeshift hiding place. The tapes were safe. Finn sank back on the couch, stared at the wall, and sipped Scotch.

He fell into a twitchy sleep but awoke a little before nine A.M. when the horrors struck. Anxiety jolted him like a baseball bat striking his skull. Seconds ago, he'd dreamed that he was standing in the heroin storage room in Rockaway. Then he was on a drug raid, running into the target apartment. He watched Versos, his friend, lying on the floor. He saw Bigelow standing over him, his gun still in his hand. Then Sorenson was taking him away in handcuffs and he was in a prison. Bigelow, now one of the guards, was standing over him, drowning him in a lidless, steel toilet bowl. Then the scene switched and Finn had his service revolver on the patch of skin between his brows. He was sobbing. He pulled the trigger and watched as the bullet eased down the barrel in slow motion, tearing into his flesh layer by layer.

Finn's heart was pounding. He felt his eyelids roll back in his head. Fear, scampering on little rat feet, crawled up his torso. He wouldn't be able to sleep again. He could hear his hoarse breathing, too fast and a little uneven. Maybe he was having a heart attack.

He groaned and reached into his jacket to locate his shield and gun. His fingers searched for the familiar weight. He had played his records and drunk Scotch for a few hours, then he remembered nothing. Maybe he had passed out. Maybe he had taken potshots at pedestrians from his window. He was dimly aware that most people took waking up for granted; some even greeted the day with a kind of optimism. Finn didn't know where they got the nerve. He found his gun and his shield about the same time he felt shooting pains in his left shoulder.

"What the fuck is going on?" he said aloud. His stomach was on fire and the taste of whiskey hung like a deadly taint on the back of his throat. He got out of his bed, leaving an indentation on the tinged sheets. He tried to take a deep breath, but the smell of stale smoke made him gag.

He staggered to the kitchen and blindly grabbed the neck of a bottle. As his fingers fastened around the cap, the pain in his chest became so intense that his knees buckled. He slid down and slumped against the cabinet.

The pain was tearing at him now, making his hands shake as he tried to twist the bottle cap. His fingers felt thick, as if he were wearing a baseball mitt.

Desperate, he put the bottle in his mouth and twisted off the cap with his teeth.

From across the room, he caught sight of himself in the mirror and was shocked to see the feral desperation in his face. He was grotesque and absurd.

"I'm trying to get drunk before I die of this fucking heart attack," he said aloud. "Just so I don't have to face it alone."

He began to laugh but the pain in his shoulder made him scream and wrenched tears between his gasps.

"Jesus."

When the pain abated, he lay on the floor, perfectly still, waiting for it to come back. He stared at the ceiling, wondering if he would die. Then he wondered if he'd have the strength to kill himself if he couldn't turn his life around.

He stood up. His clothes were clammy with sweat. He stepped out of them.

Naked, he folded himself back into bed. He lay supine, his head on the pillow. He pressed his knees and ankles together. Then he pushed his elbows against his ribs, taking inventory of his body parts. Even the sensation of the sheet against his skin was something, a little indication that he could feel anything at all.

# 28

Finn listened to the sound of his knocking echo through Money's split-level home and reverberate down the silent suburban block.

He pounded on the door again, hearing slow shuffling from inside. He leaned over the stairway railing, but the view from the picture window was blocked with heavy curtains.

The door swung open, catching him off balance.

He held up a six-pack of Heineken.

"I was in the neighborhood, Mark. I thought we could grab a beer."

Money, who wore drooping gray sweatpants and a dingy T-shirt, squinted at Finn and looked at his watch. It was four P.M. "Sure," said Money, gesturing him inside.

Even with the curtains drawn, Finn could see that Money was wasting away. His cheeks were gaunt and the laugh lines around his eyes had deepened into furrows. Money grabbed a dirty-looking flannel shirt and pulled it over his T-shirt, despite the oppressive heat of the mid-August day. Finn looked around. He guessed immediately that Money's wife had left and taken most of the furniture. Cops' wives were like the canaries coal miners used to carry into the pits, he thought, the first ones to react when their husbands entered the danger zone. The house was empty except for a worn wall-to-wall rug and two BarcaLoungers facing a six-foot television screen. Money heaved himself into one of the chairs and pointed the remote at the screen.

Finn pulled an opener from his pocket and popped the lids off two of the green bottles. Money took his eagerly. For a moment, Finn was transfixed by Money's Adam's apple bobbing as he swallowed the beer. He felt the powerful urge for a drink. He breathed in the familiar yeasty aroma. This morning's anxiety attack had convinced him that he had to cut down on his drinking, maybe stop altogether. But watching Money, restraint and need battled each other as if his left hand had decided to arm-wrestle his right hand. Now Finn's mouth was eighteen inches away from the rim of a beer bottle. Saliva sprang along his molars. He stared down at the single unblinking eye of the green bottle and watched a bead of condensation slide down the bottle neck. He knew if he had a swallow, he would be lost. He felt an ache in his hand and realized he was clenching the beer in a death grip. He let the bottle slide silently to the floor.

"How've you been?"

Money yawned. "Not bad. The PBA got me a lawyer and he thinks everything is going to work out fine."

"Good. That's good news." Finn looked around. "Where's Nancy?"

Money stared as a familiar-looking actress promoted her latest movie on the Oprah Winfrey show.

"She left me about six months ago, moved back to Virginia with her folks."

Just the opposite of Kate, Finn thought, who seemed to pop up when he was in trouble. He let Money's answer pass without comment.

"What are you doing out in suburbia? I thought you lived in Brooklyn."

Finn smelled his own boozy smell from last night's Scotch. The adhesive tape holding the tape recorder to the small of his back was tugging at his sparse body hair.

He had come this far, he couldn't lose his nerve. It was a Hail Mary play if ever there was one. Money was the weak link, he was young and an addict. If Finn couldn't get Money, the rookie of Group C, to tell him what was going on, none of the others would give it up. Finn was about to use his best interrogation technique. Any cop who had set foot in a detective's squad room would figure out what he was doing in about fifteen seconds. He was counting on Money's being too young and too stoned to catch on.

"I was doing an errand for Bigelow this morning," Finn lied. He let the implication hang in the air. A slightly larger than life-size version of Suzanne Somers giggled her way through a promotional interview. "When I got finished, I stopped for a drink, got to talking—you know how one drink leads to another—met a girl . . ." Finn waved his hand, hoping he sounded like his old self. He had always been too drunk to remember sober what he sounded like when he was drinking.

Money didn't hesitate. "Yeah. Errands for Bigelow can be a lot of fun."

Finn was in. He feigned surprise. In his mind, he fell to his knees and silently praised God. "You've helped him out with this . . . thing of his?"

"Sure, all the time," Money boasted. "Whenever he needs anything done, he can always rely on me. He's my boss. He taught me to be a cop's cop."

Finn slipped into the patter of questioning he'd used in the homicide squad, measured, friendly, smooth enough so the subject didn't realize that he was doing the giving and you were doing the taking.

"Well, it's a new one to me." Finn smiled broadly. "And the money is good. How long've you been working with him?" Money, living in an empty house with only Oprah for company, seemed anxious to talk.

"Since I got to Group C. I'd just finished my shift and Bigelow and I were coming out of the precinct and we found this kid breaking into my car." Money leaned forward in his chair to tell the story. "My brand-new Datsun 280Z. You know how annoying that is? Well, I went ballistic. We cuffed him and patted him down, and lo and behold, we find about a couple of grams of cocaine on him. I said, 'Shit. He'll be ROR'd in three hours.' But Bigelow says, 'Hold on,' and he runs to his car and comes back with baking soda and a Baggie." Money smiled at the memory. "Throws a pinch of coke in with a handful of baking soda and vouchers the whole evidence. Bigelow explained to me how the lab tests for the presence of cocaine, not the purity. That bastard got busted for carrying a quarter pound of cocaine. Made him look like a major distributor. He got seven to fifteen years." Money leaned back, smiling proudly. "Which is about right for breaking into my car."

"How old was the mutt?"

"Seventeen."

Finn nodded, feeling sick. He had been to Attica a few times to pick up prisoners, and it always made him think of a human kennel. He thought about a boy spending fifteen years there for a few grams of cocaine. He felt sure he needed a drink.

He forced himself to smile. "Bigelow knows how to hit 'em to make 'em fall down and stay down."

But Money continued, "To celebrate, Bigelow and I went out and snorted up the rest of the coke. We had ourselves some party. We cut two lines and snorted them off the dashboard of a patrol car."

"Some party."

"Yeah, that was earlier. Now, since the spring, he pays me straight time, per job. Just like police work. Except I'm moonlighting and Bigelow is my boss."

Money grinned at Finn, then his gaze shifted to the television.

"Why didn't you ever let me in on it back then?" asked Finn, trying to keep the conversation from drying up.

"You were at the stash house with us. Bigelow hands you money all the time. I figured you knew all about it."

Finn struggled not to give in to his panic. "I didn't remember seeing that house until the night you passed out," Finn said quietly.

Money looked at Finn. "You're a drunk," he said matter-of-factly. "No one expects you to get things straight. Bigelow said he couldn't trust you, but not because of the booze." Money smiled. "I think the reason is that, underneath it all, Bigelow thinks you're a choirboy."

Finn needed to get back in control. He smiled and shook his head in feigned amazement.

"I can't believe that's what he thought of me. After what I've been through with you guys? I mean, Christ, I owe Bigelow my life."

Money started to shake. It took Finn a few seconds to realize he was laughing.

"Yeah, the stickup kids in the bodega. Bigelow saved your life all right." Money was wiping his eyes with the back of his hand.

"What's the joke?"

Money started to shake again. "Two weeks before, during a raid, Bigelow pulled a couple of shotguns out of the target apartment and put them in the trunk of his patrol car. He needed to get rid of them. About an hour before you walked into that bodega, Bigelow sold those kids one of those shotguns. Then he collared them."

Finn felt his stomach turn over. No wonder the kid didn't run.

Finn forced a smile and a yelp that he hoped sounded like a laugh. "You guys should have told me, let me in on the joke. I thought we were buddies." Some joke.

"I tried to tell Bigelow you were that way," the cop said lamely. Then he stood up and dragged his feet toward the bathroom. Finn could hear him crashing around inside the medicine cabinet. In a moment, he returned with a plasticine bag, a heat-sealed syringe, and a black leather belt. He pulled up his flannel sleeve and Finn saw that the underside of his forearm was a map of bruises.

"I'm surprised Bigelow brought you in on this now," said Money, sitting down on the Barca-Lounger. "He's been so nervous about this big delivery. He says solid gold is going to wash up on the Neponsit beach on Labor Day weekend and make him a rich man."

"I don't know why he chose Labor Day. Aren't the beaches a little crowded?"

"Not at night," Money crowed. "This plan is pure genius. At night over Labor Day weekend, the coast is like the BQE, packed with pleasure boaters on their last big overnight trip of the summer. Guys fishing and drinking beer and listening to the waves rot their Fiberglas hulls. The Coast Guard is so busy answering distress calls from the weekend whalers you could get a tugboat to pull the Statue of Liberty to Staten Island and the Coast Guard wouldn't even notice."

Finn smiled, encouraging. "But it's Chinese heroin," Finn ad-libbed, thinking of Yumor. "Won't the Ghost Brigade have him whacked when they find out he's ripping them off?"

"They'll be afraid to kill a cop. It'll bring too much heat down on them. Anyway, I doubt Bigelow is planning to stay around after he gets the shipment."

Finn was concentrating on the tape recorder now. His nerve endings were so jangled, he could almost feel the wheels of the little machine turning.

Money held a lighter under a spoon filled with heroin. The commercial break was over, and Oprah, looking slightly overweight, was holding up a small hairy mutt that had survived a Midwestern flood by living in a trash can.

"How'd he get so tight with the Ghost Brigade?"

Money smiled but he didn't risk laughing. He needed to keep his hand steady. "It's a good story. They tried to have him killed after he ripped off a Dominican dealer named Francesco. You know Bigelow, he can charm a charging elephant. He got the hit man to introduce him to the *dai lo,* and the next thing you know, they're business partners."

"What a guy."

Money was suddenly suspicious. "Why are you asking me all this stuff? I thought you said Bigelow brought you in on this."

Finn knew he was close to the edge. "Ah, he mentioned something about Rockaway, but I didn't want to push it. He seemed sort of paranoid." Finn put on an injured expression. "That hurt me. I mean, if you can't trust your friends in the department, who can you trust? Right?"

It was a false note, but Money was too caught up in his sordid ritual to notice. Junkies, Finn thought. They only worry about getting high. It was disgusting what a man could do to himself, how far someone was willing to go to deaden his pain. Money was willing to give up his wife, his job, his principles, and allow his best friend to be killed in front of his eyes. Finn felt his anger building. An addict's world is big enough for only one man. Just him and his pain and the thing that can take that pain away. He hated Money, hated him for being weak. Hated him for being an addict. He looked at his colleague, sitting in his dim living room in his empty house shooting heroin at four P.M., and knew they were exactly the same.

"Yeah, a cop's cop will never let you down," said Money. Finn watched him slip the needle into a scab and pull back the plunger until the syringe filled with blood. Finn stood and yanked back the curtains on the picture window.

"Why did Bigelow shoot Versos?" Finn said quietly. His loathing for Money was packed like mortar between his words.

Money didn't even look up until he had emptied the syringe into his arm. When he turned toward Finn, the weak afternoon light made him look like a cadaver. Finn repeated his question.

"Why d'ya want to talk about that?" Money didn't deny it. He didn't even act surprised. The camaraderie between them drained away. If Money were a suspect, he would demand to see his lawyer. But he wasn't a suspect, Finn thought. He was a scumbag. Finn leaned over and hit Money hard in the head with his fist. Money just stared at him, and Finn guessed he was waiting for an explanation. Then Finn realized that Money was simply waiting for the drug to take hold. Waiting for his familiar oblivion. Waiting to be pulled like a blind puppy to a warm milky nipple. Finn felt like breaking the kid's arms.

They had killed Versos. Every one of them had done it. "Why didn't you try to stop him? He shot your friend, for God's sake. What's the matter with you?"

Money looked at him, slack-eyed. "No one wanted it to happen," he whined. "But you know Versos. He was so pig-headed. He'd contacted someone in IAB. All Bigelow wanted was Versos's word that he wouldn't turn rat. When he wouldn't give it to them, I guess he couldn't risk keeping him alive."

Finn hit Money again in the head. "It wasn't like we all agreed on it, or anything," Money tried to explain, covering his head with his hands. "I guess Bigelow decided it needed to be done."

Finn's fingers stung with every slap he laid on Money. But instead of fighting back, the kid kept getting limper and limper, sliding off the chair to the floor, not quite covering his face well enough to keep Finn's fists from his nose. Finn was enraged. His back ached, and he held Money's T-shirt, suspending him a few feet off the floor.

"And if Bigelow decides tomorrow that you're the next to go," Finn screamed at Money, "should I cover up for him? Should I let everyone think he shot you by accident? You're such a good cop. Tell me, what should I do?"

Finn felt as if he needed more oxygen, as if the stale air in Money's rooms had been used up by all the pointless rationalizing that had gone on between these walls.

"What? Is Bigelow mad at me or something?" Money seemed anxious, but then the narcotic hit his brain and he smiled, his last words trailing off.

Finn kicked an empty Heineken bottle across the room and walked out of Money's house.

# 29

That afternoon, Finn crouched next to his Rolling
Stones collection and pulled the small pile of tapes
out of his secret compartment. The fire damage to his
apartment had never seemed worse. With the humid
mid-August air pressing in on the screened-in window, he could see the black plumes and smell the
charred kitchen walls from every room in the one-
bedroom apartment. It had been a long time since he
had stood in the living room in the evening, perfectly
sober. The problem with not drinking is that if you
weren't drunk or so hungover your skull could barely
contain your brain, you noticed the wreck the rest of
your life had become. The skin on Finn's knuckles
was broken and his shoulders ached from the beating
he had given Money. What he really needed was a
drink. He stared at the liquor cabinet and then
averted his eyes, as if he had seen something shame-
ful. He sat down on the soot-stained couch and
rewound the latest tape in the recorder.

"No one wanted it to happen," Money's guttural,
drugged-out voice filled the room. "But you know
Versos. He was so pigheaded. He'd contacted someone in IAB."

Finn popped the tape out and labeled it carefully
with a pen: MARK MONEY: AT HOME IN HICKSVILLE,
AUGUST 23RD. He moved to put it with the others,
then stopped. The tape was evidence that Bigelow had
killed a cop to protect his drug business. He thought
of Versos. He thought of the dead prostitute with the

key to Bigelow's house. He knew exactly how his supervisor was wired now. He was a psychopath. He had no conscience. Finn felt fear like a large, heavy hand on his shoulder. The tapes weren't safe here. And neither was he.

He couldn't stand it anymore. He walked to the refrigerator, opened a beer, and tried to think of somewhere to hide them. He had a locker at his old gym, but sometime in the last two years he had let his membership lapse and they hacked off the lock and threw away his sneakers. He could call his old partner Fat Tony, but Tony was smart enough to steer clear of this kind of trouble. He had to hide the tapes, find someplace another cop, a desperate, crazy one, would never think to look. There was only one place he could go.

# 30

Kate was weary and a little nauseated by the time she arrived home from the station. As she got out of her black Tercel, she noticed that her stockings had a run that extended from her shin to her knee. Stupid to have to wear stockings in the summer. It was one of those unbearable August evenings when the heat of the day lay on the sidewalk like a belligerent rhino, refusing to move or be moved. She had spent the day interviewing victims of a stock fraud and wondering how involved Finn was with the corruption in Brooklyn Narcotics. She was prepared to spend the twilight hours huddled around her air conditioner, surfing through sitcoms, flipping through *The New Yorker,* worrying whether Finn would be all right. She didn't even notice him sitting at the top of her stoop looking upset and vulnerable until she had her foot on the first step.

"Whoa! What are you doing here?" It wasn't the way she had imagined greeting him. She held up the memory of their last conversation like a flash card. Had they made plans for tonight? She would've remembered. His face broke into a grin of pure joy. Kate smiled. Then she saw a pint of Johnnie Walker wrapped in a paper bag next to his thigh. She squinted at him. The bottle was open. He was drunk.

"I came by to see you," he said, slurring slightly. Despite the heat, he was wearing a light wool sports jacket and his hairline was dark with sweat. "Are ya gonna invite me in?" She motioned for him to follow her. He smelled like menthol shaving cream, leather, and smoke, a smell she was learning to associate with pleasurable sex. She shivered a little. Then she smelled the booze. When she'd locked the front door behind them, she absently tilted her head for a greeting kiss. Then she flung her briefcase on the couch and kicked off her shoes, but Finn didn't take off his jacket.

Her mind was spinning. "Excuse me," she said, reaching under her skirt to release her garters and stripping off her stockings with great relief. For a moment he watched her hungrily, then he averted his eyes, pretending to study the cover of her *American Gardener* magazine, a gift from her mother, who still wouldn't acknowledge that she lived in a co-op in Brooklyn.

"I'd offer you a drink but it looks like you already have one." She wanted to say something nicer but she was unnerved. All day long, she had been thinking about Finn. She just wasn't prepared to find him on her stoop with an open bottle of Scotch like some kind of degenerate wino.

"I'm going to change," she said, and headed into her bedroom.

Finn waited until her bedroom door shut, then walked unsteadily into her kitchen. He opened her cabinets and scanned the contents, disappointed to find that she appeared to do at least a nominal amount of cooking. It would have been better if she stored winter sweaters among her pots and pans like Sandy used to do. He opened a few more cabinets. On a top shelf he saw four old-style canisters marked FLOUR, SUGAR, TEA, and SALT. She probably didn't do much baking. Up-and-coming television reporters didn't have time to sit around waiting for the dough to rise, he thought. He emptied the flour onto the counter. His hands were shaking and he was dismayed to see that the flour formed little mushroom clouds and left white dust on everything in a two-foot radius.

Damn. He looked around for a sponge but couldn't find one. He took the tapes out of his pocket. He didn't want to do this, to involve her, but he couldn't help it now. With luck, she'd never know what he was hiding in her house. He grabbed a handful of Ziploc bags from a drawer and shoved the tapes into them. Then he put them on the bottom of the canister and, using his hands as a scoop, put a three-inch layer of flour over them. He slid the canister back to its out-of-reach spot. He wet a paper towel and began to scrub the counter, but it only made the flour turn to gray paste. He bent down and blew the remaining flour dust into the sink, smelling the Scotch on his breath. He heard a sound from somewhere in the apartment. Trying to move quickly, he turned on the water. The flour from his hands had settled on the front of his jacket. He was sweating in earnest now, running his hands under water and patting the jacket. He could hear her bedroom door close. He gave the counter another quick swipe and then shoved the sticky paper towel into his pocket. He turned to face Kate. There was no time to check for traces of flour.

"So, how was your day?" he asked her. She was wearing bike-messenger pants and an oversize T-shirt. Finn thought that if she had returned wearing a black, see-through bra and a G-string, she couldn't have looked sexier. He was trying to sound casual, but he was sure his face was giving him away. He wished he hadn't had so much to drink.

"Great, I did a react on a stock-market scam and the whole segment got bumped by a promotion for *Inside Edition* on UFOs. I hate trash television."

He let a minute pass. "How about I take you to a nice dinner?"

She put her hand to her mouth. "No, I've been feeling sick. Must have been some bad seafood."

He walked over and gave her a long kiss, feeling a rush of love and a wave of self-doubt. He didn't trust himself to keep talking. She pressed into his lips, then pulled back suddenly. His mouth tasted like a Scotch-

and-fear cocktail. Kate was confused. She wanted to
make him feel welcome, but it seemed that this man
in her apartment, this man who two days ago melted
every solid surface of her body, was somehow a
stranger. She looked into his eyes and thought of a
story she once covered for the *Herald*. A woman
passing on the sidewalk near a construction site had
her legs crushed when a crane toppled from its
support and pinned her. Kate was the first reporter at
the scene. The weight of the twisted steel pressed on
the woman's arteries, keeping her from bleeding to
death. The woman was alert but mute with shock.
Only her fingers, blindly reaching out for the hand of
an EMS worker, communicated "I'm alive!"

She put her arm around him and her hand slid to
the small of his back where he had kept his tape
recorder strapped. Instead of the machine, she felt the
pint of Johnnie Walker he had stuck in his pocket.

"Don't worry, I'm not recording you," he said
lamely.

"You gave up making tapes?" She said it slowly, as
if she were trying to understand a foreign language.
"What's going to happen now?"

Finn closed his eyes. He wanted his life with her to
be far away from Bigelow and drug raids and dirty
cops. But here he was, bringing that filth into her
house. Now he knew he couldn't stop the circles of his
life from intersecting. He felt shame burn into him as
if he had squeezed a hot wick. "I haven't stopped. I
just have what I need for now. But do me a favor and
stay out of it." He couldn't tell her the truth. He was a
hypocritic phony.

She stared at him, and her questions held him at
bay like a hungry cannibal.

He shrugged. He pulled the pint of Johnnie Walker
out of his pocket and loosened the lid. A terrible
recognition was dawning on Kate. Sure, Finn had
changed. He was thinner, more intense, better in bed
every day. But he was also full of excuses and ways to
protect what she could see had become his most
obsessive and pleasurable pastime—drinking. She'd

been around drunks before; her Uncle Natey, a few reporters at the *Herald,* Officer Slezwouski—the cop who'd called her on the telephone and asked her to spell his name right and then jumped off the George Washington Bridge. Finn had changed all right. He was a stone drunk.

She looked at the way he pulled hungrily at the bottle. She loved him more than ever and wondered if she was going to be sick.

"I bet you don't even know what you're going to do now, am I right?" she asked.

Finn was silent, wondering for a moment how she knew. From outside, they could hear street noises. Dog walkers lingered, enjoying the summer air. Kate could hear the jovial noises of teenagers hanging around the all-night deli on her corner.

Finn took another drink.

"I went to the Academy with a guy named Marty Suggs," he said instead. "He became a diver for the Emergency Services division. Once a week, he'd put on his wet suit and dive into the water around New York City and try to recover a body part or a handgun from two feet of mud and sludge at the bottom of the river. Parts of the East River and lower Hudson are so polluted, Marty had to wear a miner's light on his head, and even then, he had zero visibility. He couldn't see more than six inches in front of his face. But Marty loved that job. Nothing made him happier than to wake up and find that it was Monday morning and he had to go diving."

Kate watched him.

"One day, he is looking for a handgun off the Thirty-fourth Street Heliport in the East River. The water is almost black as night, even though it was noon. Swimming almost blind, Marty runs into a metal fence." Finn put up his hand as if he were resting it on a wall. "It wasn't the first unexpected thing he had run into down there. He doesn't think much of it. He turns and swims in the other direction." Finn put his hand up again. "He runs into the same metal fence. He changes direction, another fence. Now he's starting to panic. He puts his hands over his head and realizes the same metal grating is over his head, and in that second, he knows he's trapped. The job he loved turns into a cold, black hell."

Finn took a sip. The bottle had defeated him again. He knew now, he would never stop drinking.

"What happened to him?"

"He eventually figured out that he swam into a big cage, like the kind they used to keep the lions in at the circus. Using his hands, he traced every inch of that cage. He had about two minutes of oxygen left when he found the hatch to swim out again."

"So the story had a happy ending?"

"Maybe."

"Marty's all right?"

"He never went diving again. He walks a foot patrol now in Washington Heights."

Kate felt the outline of his arm against her through her thin shirt. She was filled with a wild sexual longing that soaked through her doubt and frustrations.

"Why did you tell me that story?"

"I'm trying to explain something to you."

"What?"

"Sometime in the last two years, I swam into a lion cage."

"But what do you want me to do? I want to help you and you won't let me," she said, her eyes filling with tears.

"You are helping me, and you don't even know it."

She was choking on her words. "I would do anything for you." He took another drink, hardly aware of what she was saying. He felt a slackness across his chest as it suddenly felt easier to breathe. When he looked up, she was staring at him hard. "But you've got to do something for me."

He held her gaze.

"I want you to stop drinking. Go to AA if you need to. But put down that bottle."

His mind was shifting and he felt under attack. He

shook his head no. She didn't know what she was asking.

She started to cry for real. "Won't you at least try? You know by now I only want the best for you. Why don't you trust me?"

Finn felt the whiskey burn in his stomach. He felt a cold draft in his heart. His mouth began talking before his brain could stop it.

"Why should I trust you? You walked out on me, remember?"

She looked as if he'd hit her. "That was two years ago."

Finn shrugged.

She drew herself up. "So that's the answer? That's it?" She leaned in close to him. "Well, let me tell you, John Finn. That isn't good enough. I love you and I don't want to end it this way."

Her eyes were still wet but her fists were on her hips now. She looked tough, Finn thought. She would have made a good police sergeant. But she kept talking. "So the question I have is, 'What are you going to do?' You, acting like a drunk, working with a bunch of criminals, behaving like you don't have an iota of respect for yourself or for me. Ask yourself, where are you going to be in five years? Are you going to be with me? You don't even know, do you? You've been living from day to day and drink to drink." He felt a pain in his chest. Bull's-eye. How did she know these things? "I get the feeling that the only reason you're here right now is that I won't let you go . . ."

"Into the gutter. Is that what you were going to say?" said Finn, suddenly furious.

Kate looked shocked. "No. That wasn't what I was going to say at all."

The depth of Finn's despair began to dawn on her for the first time. She continued a little more softly, "I was going to say that I won't stand by and let you commit suicide."

He pulled out the empty bottle of Johnnie Walker again and stared at it. He wished he had something to chase it with. A beer, a brandy. His head pulsed.

But Kate had already stood up and was herding him toward the door.

"John Finn, I want you to go now. When you come back, I want you to tell me if we'll be together in five years."

"Kate, I'm in the lion cage, Kate."

"The only thing keeping you in the cage is you," she said, sidestepping him so that he was standing on the threshold of her apartment.

"Kate . . ."

But she had already closed the door.

She stood in front of the open refrigerator watching the cold fog rise off the wilted lettuce and Tupperware until she began to cry. Why had he come here? Why? She closed her eyes and reached for a Michelob. Then stopped and poured herself some orange juice instead. Crying was a relief after almost a week of feeling pent up. She walked into her bedroom and shut the door behind her. "What am I supposed to say?" she said aloud. "I'll love you even if you're a fall-down drunk working for the Chinese mob." She sloshed a little of the juice onto her T-shirt and, disgusted, decided to change it. She crossed her arms and grabbed the bottom of her shirt to lift it over her head. The movement immediately sent a wave of tenderness through her breasts. She noticed this afternoon that her skirt band left a little red imprint around her waist. Maybe it was time to buy a Stair-Master. Maybe it was a return of PMS. She never gained back the weight she'd lost in her late twenties. After she turned thirty and stopped anticipating her monthly period with chardonnay and green M&M's, her weight never even fluctuated from week to week. She wiped the tears off her cheek with the back of her hand and looked at her body in the full-length mirror, naked except for the black stretch shorts. She thought of the nausea that had been dredging the bottom of her stomach. She counted the number of times she had had unprotected sex with Finn. She slapped the juice glass down so hard on her bureau that she spilled it again. "Oh my god, maybe I'm pregnant," she said out loud. Then she looked in the mirror again and knew. "I'm pregnant."

# 31

Finn sat in his car in front of Kate's apartment, pulling on his bottle. He wanted to knock down her door, go straight to the kitchen, and grab the tapes out of the flour container. But it was too late. Too late. He took another drink. She had read his tea leaves, all right. He fiddled with the radio, listening to snatches of Roy Orbison from some oldies station just out of range. He took another drink, feeling his lips loosen on the mouth of the bottle. She'd asked him to stop drinking. Just like that. She didn't know that he had been trying not to drink since the day he saw Bigelow's stash house. He simply could not. It was hard even to admit to himself, and once Kate found out, she would leave him again and never look back. Almost automatically, his hand dipped inside his coat pocket to get the leather folder that covered his shield. He locked it in the glove compartment with his wallet and his gun. When he slammed the compartment, he felt something inside him shut down. He took another long drink. It was like coming home.

# 32

Before her face started appearing on the television screen, the receptionist alerted security every time she set foot in the CBS building. But since the chunked-murderer story had been picked up by the network, the door guards feigned a kind of delight when they saw her, as if she were a plumber making a midnight house call. Their efforts were even more pronounced, Kate noticed, when one of the television legends walked by. Early one morning, Kate spotted Dan Rather walking in a few paces ahead of her. The door guards straightened up as if the brick CBS building had become Buckingham Palace, and reverent echoes of "Hello, Mr. Rather" could be heard through the hallway. They all watched television, and in their minds, seeing his face was like having a movie star move into their neighborhood. It made them look at their own house with a little more pride. Dan Rather was thinner than Kate had imagined, a frail body supporting that large head and famous face. He moved slowly and with a surprising weariness, as if he were the last living brontosaurus, a serious journalist in a world where *Hard Copy* was considered good television.

She sipped her cappuccino on the elevator up, wondering how much caffeine was in each swallow. She squared her shoulders and walked into the morning meeting. As usual, Bartlett and Landis were relishing the day when heads would roll. Kate listened to them for a while, then blocked out their voices and simply watched them. Both men looked haunted. Not uneasy or nervous, but scared to the bottom of their paper-thin souls. Unlike her colleagues in the newspaper business who scraped along on modest salaries, contented by being outside and ever so slightly above the base human behavior around them, television executives were not observers. They were information suckers. They lived in terror that someone would know something and not tell them. She hugged her elbows, feeling desolate. She had been hard on Finn last night. She hoped he would be all right.

"Excuse me?" Landis was directing a question at her. She was aware that Landis's voice was propelled through his vocal chords without a trace of warmth or kindness. "You want me to do what?"

Landis and Bartlett exchanged an impatient look. "We want to repackage the father-looking-for-his-missing-foster-daughter story. Then we got a severe thunderstorm watch that the weather service thinks might turn into a hurricane. In the late afternoon, we want you to go camp out at the Jersey shore."

"I'm not sure I can get to the Jersey shore. I've got a bad feeling from that foster-daughter segment, and I wanted to do some real reporting, dig around the father's story. See if I can come up with anything."

The look of contempt that passed over Landis's face made Kate feel like Oliver Twist holding out his plate for more.

"Don't go Woodward and Bernstein on us again," smirked Landis. "Next we'll be hearing about your mobbed-up judge in Ozone Park. We're a city of weather wimps. Do you know what happens when the weather gets bad?" She suspected he was humiliating her for Bartlett's benefit. "Anxious citizens turn on their televisions. They want to see clouds on maps and windchill factors and rainfall estimates." His voice was building. "They want to see big waves crashing on the beach and water flooding into other people's basements." He was caught up by his excitement. "If we supply those pictures, do you know what that means for us?"

"Ratings!" shouted Bartlett, and the two men moved on to another producer.

# 33

Finn awoke to a grinding sound and an unfamiliar pain in his head. He had passed out with his head on the steering wheel, and his rearview mirror confirmed that he had a red indentation running across his forehead like a parallel eyebrow. A team of construction workers had begun to jackhammer the street twenty feet behind the spot where his car had stalled sometime last night. He stared at the block. He guessed from the tiny front yards he was in Gravesend, but he was unsure how and why he had ended up here. His hand moved to his holster, and for a panicky minute he thought that his gun was gone. Then he remembered he had locked his valuables safely in the glove compartment. He quietly pocketed them again with relief. He thought about Kate and misery began to grow like a wild vine up his back. He opened the car door hesitantly, half expecting that his legs might not hold up his weight. He needed to get a can of soda or some coffee, he thought, rubbing his head. He needed to take a piss. He walked around to the front of the car, wondering at the way his car was angled, nose first, to the curb. When he saw the grillwork, his breath stuck in his throat as if he had swallowed a spoon, and the backed-up urine evaporated. The front of his car was splashed with blood, some of it thin and drying and some of it thick and clotted. Finn leaned on the car and grabbed his temples and vomited. Oh God, oh God, oh God. He had finally plunged over the cliff. The jackhammer crew had stopped for a moment and Finn was aware that the workmen were watching him. He tried to stop his knees from shaking and licked the bile from his lips. The moment he had feared all his life was upon him. The tragic event that he had run from every day had finally caught up to him. As unobtrusively as he could, he bent down to see if whomever he'd hit was still under his car. The pavement was blotched with more blood and some old black oil stains, but Finn found nothing, alive or dead. He walked unsteadily into a bodega and bought a can of soda. He passed a pay phone whose receiver was already warm from the morning sunlight. He pushed in a quarter and then stopped. Whom should he call? The police? A hit-and-run was all IAB needed to get him off the force. Kate? He could never let her see him like this. He was so damn tired he could hardly push thoughts through his brain. He noticed a sticker for Alcoholics Anonymous on the side of the Plexiglas telephone hood. Numbly, he dialed the number, his fingers shaking and his throat parched. A kind-voiced man answered and gave him the address and times of the meetings nearest his apartment.

"I'm sick and I'm tired and I think I've done something terrible," said Finn weakly.

"AA meetings are for people who want to make a change," answered the man amiably.

"What happens at the meeting?"

The man gave a low laugh that sounded as if he had smoked his way through a pickup truck of unfiltered cigarettes. "Can't really say what will happen when you go. My first time, I'd say a miracle took place."

"I could use a miracle," Finn replied, feeling too overwhelmed to cry.

"If you want a miracle badly enough, you'll get it," the man said, and Finn hung up. He staggered back to his car. His training told him he should call the nearest precinct and let them pull what they could from the crime scene. His sense of self-preservation wouldn't let him do it. He opened the trunk of his car and pulled out a rag. He walked to the front of the car, sucked in a breath, and prepared to commit a crime. As he bent down to wipe off the blood, he noticed a length of rope-colored cloth in the bloody mess. He reached over to flick it off and found that it was some kind of hide, a chunk of tough animal flesh. He saw another piece, and another. He held the largest piece up to the light. Then he began to laugh. It was deer skin. Somewhere, somehow, he had mowed down a deer in the streets of Brooklyn.

He wiped off the rest of the blood, laughing and shaking his head. When he got behind the wheel, he thought of the kind-voiced man from AA. "If you want a miracle badly enough, you'll get it."

Finn checked his watch and drove to the AA meeting.

The gathering in the church basement had all the ambience of a PTA meeting except that everyone chain-smoked and drank coffee. To Finn's right, an enormous man with a scrawny goatee unwrapped one Hershey's kiss after another and stuffed them into his mouth. In front of him a youngish girl wearing a nose ring and some kind of net shirt over a black bra gave him a quick, nervous smile that signaled to Finn that she was ready to jump up and run out of the room. Aside from the kisses man and nose-ring girl, people greeted each other with the exaggerated good spirits that Finn associated with barrooms. A fat man with a flat, sloping forehead, who looked to Finn like a Hell's Angel on disability, took a seat near the front of the room. Finn decided then and there that if the nose-ring girl ran out, he'd run after her. To hide his growing discomfort, he read the wide-lettered chart on the wall. It was the twelve steps of Alcoholics Anonymous.

"We admit we are powerless over alcohol—that our lives have become unmanageable." They had his number. He had an apartment full of soot, a girlfriend who never wanted to see him drunk again, and a car covered in blood.

"We have come to believe that a Power greater than ourselves could restore us to sanity." Finn looked around and wondered if there were separate AA meetings for Catholics.

Finn skipped a few.

"We have made a searching and fearless moral inventory of ourselves." The meeting was being called to order. The floor was turned over to a scrawny boy in a big baseball hat. "My name is Philip and with the grace of God, I'm here to tell you I'm an alcoholic." The heavy emphasis on religion grated on Finn right away. He wondered if he was in the right place. "I used to be the toughest guy on the block," the boy began, and Finn immediately decided he was a liar. No way he was a tough guy. "I started drinking forty-ounce bottles and smoking blunts when I was like twelve years old. I was always very good at manipulating people, and I learned to be a master at it after I was transferred to special-ed classes in ninth grade. I got other kids to do my homework while I got drunk. I got my teachers to give me passing grades even though I was too stoned to come to class. That's when my alcoholism began to control my life." Finn figured a little skell like him would be good at manipulation. It was a trait he had noticed in a lot of people he arrested: they were always using people who tried to help them. An uncomfortable thought pushed its way from the back of his mind. He had hidden the tapes at Kate's house. He was manipulating the only person who had tried to help him.

The skinny young man launched into a tale of his life as an outlaw, shooting up movie theaters, robbing bodegas, getting into a gunfight with the owners of a Dominican restaurant after he and his friends hoovered a three-course meal and wouldn't pay. Finn wondered if he should excuse himself, go to a pay phone, and call the warrants squad. There had to be some charges outstanding on this kid. But the boy was continuing.

"I was so drunk that when my friends pulled the gun on the Dominican chef and I saw the three

Dominican waiters pull the shotguns out of a broom closet, I freaked." The boy was warming to his story. "I dropped to my knees and I grabbed the barrel of the head waiter's gun and I put it up to my face and said, 'Please don't shoot my friend.'" The boy paused. "And the waiter just looked at me"—he looked around at the people almost obscured by cigarette smoke—"just like you are looking at me now, like, 'You are so stu-pid.'" The people at the meeting dissolved into laughter, not mocking him, just happy to know him in a better time. Finn laughed, too. Then he remembered the look of contempt the Chinese henchman had given him. Finn stopped smiling and put his face in his hands. The girl with the scared smile looked at him for a minute, then looked away as if he might hurt her. The Hispanic guy stopped eating Hershey's kisses long enough to smile at Finn. "But here I am, sober for more than eighteen months. If I wasn't sober, I know I would be dead. Instead, I got a wife and a child in sobriety. And I thank God. Just this evening, I was walking on the street with a little time to kill and a kid from the neighborhood offered me a can of Coke. I took it, but before I drank it, I said, 'What's in it?' and he said, 'Bacardi,' and I said, 'It's just not enough for me now.'" The members of the audience clapped.

The next person to talk was a beautifully coiffed woman with long fingernails painted with clear varnish. "I can really relate when you said if you weren't sober, you'd be dead."

Finn stared at the woman in amazement. He picked her for a Junior League committee member, probably the wife of an investment banker. She continued, her voice clear and unwavering, "Four months after I got out of detox, I drank again and I ended up living on the street. I ate out of the Dumpster outside the Kew Gardens Dunkin' Donuts." She ran her fingers over her mouth lightly, as if recalling the taste, and touched the thick silk scarf at her neck. "I've been sober now for eight months, but I'm still taking it day by day."

A few more people spoke, including a rambling tale by a crusty-looking fellow who lived in the subway, and then the meeting was over. Finn was almost bursting. "I noticed you didn't say anything. Is this your first time here?" A small man with twinkling blue eyes was addressing him. Finn knew he had seen him before, but where? It was Paul Mackay, the usher at St. Augustine's in Bay Ridge. "Paul, it's me, John Finn, Mary Finn's boy."

"Oh, Johnny, forgive me, I didn't recognize you all grown-up. I'm so glad to see you here, and your mother, God rest her soul, would be so relieved."

"What do you mean? Mom never saw me take a drink."

Paul Mackay gave Finn a long look. "Maybe so," he said finally. Finn was embarrassed that someone from the old neighborhood had discovered him here.

"Anyway, I don't know why I came. Payback for a miracle, I guess." He was talking too fast. He tried to slow down. "This is the first time I've been to anything like this." His thoughts jumped to the society woman and the young speaker's list of felony crimes. "Do you think everyone tells the truth?"

Pauly Mackay pointed to one of the commandments on the wall, but he recited it by heart. "'We admit to God, to ourselves, and to another human being the exact nature of our wrongs.'" Then he paused. "By the time you get here, there isn't much point in lying. Let's get a cup of coffee." He lead Finn over to an urn on a wooden table to the left of the podium. "You read the twelve steps, what did you think?"

Finn was frustrated. He was expecting something a little more official, not to be sitting around with minor-league criminals and family friends. "It a fine set of rules, but what does it mean?" His throat hurt. "That boy talked about alcohol like it is the only thing wrong in his life. No one is talking about their maxed-out credit cards or their divorce." He was thinking of his days studying Greek drama at St. Sebastian. "It's like those old Greek plays. The hero has a single fatal flaw, alcohol. I happen to think that's a little simplistic. That life is a bit more complicated."

"I agree. And you can't know life if you're constantly battling yourself. If you wake up drunk and go to sleep drunk. The whole point of AA is to embrace life."

"It's just not for me," said Finn, turning to pour milk in his coffee. He didn't notice the mirror over the coffeepot until he saw his reflection in it. Maybe seeing Pauly Mackay was playing with his head, but for a second he looked just like his father. The congenial din of the meeting faded away. His features, which had emerged as he lost weight, looked haggard, and his eyes were too large. And here was something new. Sometime in the last few weeks, two capillaries had broken and blossomed to the right of his nose, like blood-sucking spiders. It was a drinker's face. He was thrown back in time. He was a child again, watching his inebriated father jam the star on the top of their six-foot Christmas tree. His father had stood on the top of the ladder, swaying from side to side while seven-year-old John watched in horror from below. While Bing Crosby carried on about a white Christmas, Finn was sure his father was going to fall off the ladder and out their second-story window to his death. Finn remembered the hot tears that ran down his cheeks. His father, drunk and uncomprehending, looked down at his crying son with exactly the same face that Finn now saw in the mirror, shouting, "Merry Christmas, Johnny-boy. Merry Christmas."

He became aware of the meeting again and Pauly Mackay standing patiently nearby. He ran his hand over his brow, shut his eyes, and tried to block out the memory. But it persisted. Even his father, for all his excesses, had his mother. Although Finn didn't know if Kate would stand by him in the long run, she'd already done the math for him. She'd laid it out clearly. She would not stand by him if he kept drinking. Finn opened his eyes and turned to face Mackay. "What else do you learn here?"

# 34

Driving to the Sunset Park bar, Kate wished she were meeting Finn. She hadn't heard from him since she'd kicked him out last night. The worry compounded with the slow news day made her feel depleted. The foster-father segment was too easy. Landis's storm went out to sea without menacing the metropolitan area. After a full day of disappointments, she would've liked to feel Finn's arms around her. If she couldn't be meeting Finn, she wished it were at least a friend instead of the man who had nearly got her mauled by a horde of angry off-duty policemen. She wrinkled her eyebrows dramatically, then consciously relaxed them, catching sight of herself in the rearview mirror. She was so surprised when Finn's supervisor called, she didn't think before she agreed to meet him. What she really wanted was a drink. Her hand unconsciously traveled to her tender breasts. She hadn't gotten up the nerve to buy one of those home pregnancy tests. She couldn't face it. Her desire for alcohol evaporated when she saw that the bar where Bigelow had arranged to meet her was a strip joint called Pure Gold.

NO COVER. LADIES DRINK FOR FREE boasted a neon sign topped with a set of neon legs that flickered open and closed.

She had interviewed enough prostitutes to know the strict hierarchy of skin bars in New York. Working in one of the midtown Manhattan clubs like Flash

Dance and Pure Platinum that catered to wolfish Wall
Streeters and drunk account executives was like working in a bank. They had standards. A girl couldn't get
hired there if she had obvious track marks or cottage-
cheese thighs. The employees were hired out as es-
corts but weren't expected to turn tricks for extra
money in the limousines with tinted windows. Most
of the dancers were pretty girls from Long Island, the
ones who'd had nose jobs at thirteen, charge cards at
sixteen, and silicone implants by the time they enrolled in junior college. Everyone told them they were
too pretty for the boy next door, and animal instincts
told them they wouldn't make it in Hollywood. After
a few bruising auditions for legitimate Broadway
musical shows, they became models-slash-dancers.
Once they started making $400 a night entertaining
men, they developed a spending jones that wouldn't
quit. After a few years, the women either married, left
town, or ended up in the smaller bars uptown or near
the tunnels. A few more years dancing on tables and
the really self-destructive ones ended up in the outer
boroughs at bars like Pure Gold.

As she walked in the door, Kate was overcome by
the fetid odor of air freshener, cleaning fluid, and
some animal smell that she decided not to identify.
She ignored the curious stare of the bouncer and
rounded a high divider. A well-built woman, devoid
of pubic hair, was flexing her knees while holding a
metal pole and throwing out her chin so that her hair
extensions rhythmically brushed the ground. The
dozen or so men in the bar appeared hypnotized. Kate
thought the performer looked uncomfortable.

She saw a big-jawed man at a back table beckon to
her and, feeling more naked than the dancer, made
her way to his table.

Bigelow stood and extended his hand. "Don't mind
the entertainment," he said, staring straight into her
eyes. She forced herself not to move away when he
moved his head closer. "I'm taking care of some
business. Police business."

"No problem," she said, taking a seat. Her fingers

touched the table. It was sticky. In spite of herself, she drew back her hand. Bigelow gestured for the waitress. A tired-looking woman in a transparent maid's apron over a bikini bottom sauntered over to wipe the table.

Kate ordered a seltzer, then faced him.

"It's nice to see you again," he said. Kate felt one of her eyebrows rocket upward and clenched her jaw to keep it steady. "I never got to say how sorry I was about that night at O'Brien's. I was just caught unaware." Kate said nothing. "It's nice to see you in person; I mean, I'm a big fan of Channel Seven news." She smiled again, wondering what he wanted. On the other side of the room, an athletic brunette dressed in a clear vinyl bodysuit took the stage and began an energetic workout that seemed fueled by panic or amphetamines. Kate stared at the woman's crotch, then smiled, recognizing the telltale bulge of a penis.

"It's a man," said Bigelow.

"I noticed," Kate said, glad Bigelow couldn't shock her so easily. He was, without a doubt, one of the most dangerous-looking men she'd ever met. He had a burly body under his thin shirt and raw, regular features. He spoke with the bravado of a man who had never lost a barroom fight. He reminded her of a gladiator. Kate tried to imagine how Finn could be friends with him.

"What did you want to tell me?"

Bigelow took a long sip of beer. "We've been watching you on the news and we thought you might be interested in a tip."

"Who's 'we'? You and your wife?" she taunted him.

"Nah, me and the guys from Brooklyn Narcotics." Kate nodded.

Bigelow sighed. "About an investigation."

"IAB?"

Bigelow nodded. "It's not much of a secret. You see, when the story breaks, it will fill airtime for you but it will hurt us. It hurts our standing in the community. We want you to be able to put it in perspective."

She gave him a polite smile. "And so?"

"And so, it falls to me, one of the supervisors, to make sure that you don't hurt a lot of people."

"You called me because you're afraid I'll hurt people?"

"Good, hardworking men."

"That's what you wanted to say?"

Bigelow's face darkened. "That may not mean much to you. When a drug dealer fires a gun, it's not pointed at a television producer, it's pointed at a cop." He was spitting every word out as an insult. "Men like me who put their lives on the line every day. Community support means everything to us."

His pointer finger hit the table in a righteous flourish. Kate watched him for a second, feeling real fear, trying to remind herself that every gesture he made was studied for effect. He was lying. Men who menace you in barrooms don't turn around and hand you a story. She might have believed he was worried about the department's perception in the press, but there was an entire bureaucracy to deal with exactly those concerns. More likely he was up for a promotion and didn't want a scandal getting him bumped to the barricade unit instead. He didn't know that after the feds got finished with Brooklyn Narcotics, no one would even remember IAB was involved. Now it was her turn. She looked at him. "You've been in Brooklyn Narcotics for a few years?"

"A little under two."

"And you're a popular supervisor. You must know a lot of men on the job."

"I know a lot of guys."

"You know anyone who works for Chinese gangs?"

Bigelow half stood in his chair.

"That's just the kind of disgraceful thing I'm talking about," he yelled. Kate was shocked by the sheer force of the man when he stood. It was like watching a calf grow into a bull before your eyes. She signaled for the waitress in the maid's costume, hoping that another woman within earshot would keep him from throwing his drink.

"A seltzer please, and another for my friend here."

Kate put the emphasis on *friend* and was glad her voice didn't shake. She imagined herself running away into the ladies' room until Bigelow cooled off. She wondered if Pure Gold even had a ladies' room.

"Sit down, Doug. My point is this. I believe you are a good cop." As she said it, she realized she believed the opposite. She wondered for a dizzy second what she was doing in this bar with this man. "And I know as I am sitting here that good cops don't like bad cops. So as hard as it may be to admit it to someone outside of the department, I'd like you to give me a tip I could use. Help me help the department get rid of the bad cops." What a load of bullshit, Kate thought. Bigelow was looking as if he might explode. Kate pressed on. "Because, face it, some flimsy news story wedged between a murder and a ASPCA appeal doesn't hurt the police department. Bad cops hurt the department. And that's who erodes your respect in the community."

She expected Bigelow to throw two twenties on the table and stalk away, but to her surprise, he silently sipped his Scotch.

She let her eyes travel to the floor show, which consisted of a woman dressed only in fishnet stockings with her back to the audience. She was bent over at the waist and was addressing members of the audience from between her shapely thighs. Kate hoped she had a fulfilling home life or a pet or something to take her mind off her work at the end of the evening.

Bigelow let his empty tumbler fall against the table. "Maybe you're right."

Kate couldn't believe her ears.

"Maybe."

She watched him tear a napkin into small strips.

"Well, let me ask you something. If I were to tell you something, for the sake of the good cops in the department, you couldn't ever say to anyone where it was coming from?"

"Right."

"Maybe I do know something."

"Go on."

As Bigelow began to talk, a middle-aged woman wearing tap pants and tassles on both nipples stood center stage. The woman began stroking her stomach, reaching into her pants and moaning. Unlike the other acts, which were stagey or lackluster or simply ludicrous, the middle-aged woman seemed strangely focused and frankly sexual. Men in the audience began to grumble. Bigelow stared at the woman. Kate blushed to the roots of her hair.

"It started when our unit was investigating drug trafficking within Chinese gangs. We received some intelligence that our own people were involved with the Ghost Brigade. Then, IAB got involved. It looks like someone from inside the department is trying to set us up, reveal our undercovers, scare off our informants. The only person who would do something like that is someone who is being paid to protect the gang."

"You think the men working for the Ghost Brigade are in your unit?"

"I know it."

Kate leaned forward. She could hear the woman's breathing, amplified by a microphone, coming faster and faster.

"What's his name?"

"You don't know?"

A strangled scream was creeping into the woman's voice.

"I'm interested in what you have to say."

Bigelow paused, took a measured look at the masturbating woman, then looked full at Kate.

"His name is John Finn."

Kate steadied herself against the table. The woman began a wild moaning and her knees sagged, as if she might faint dead away on the stage.

"John Finn?"

"You know him?" asked Bigelow, watching her closely.

Kate ignored him. The woman was making contented purrs into the microphone.

"How solid is the information?" asked Kate quickly.

"Well, you can't attribute it to me."

"But you know it as a fact?"

Bigelow shrugged. "I'm his supervisor."

# 35

"Jesus Christ, how could I have been so stupid? Oh my God."

The entire drive home, Kate surfed through the FM radio stations and cursed herself.

What had he said? These things aren't black-and-white. Ha! No wonder Finn wanted to handle it for himself. He was a drunk and a dirty cop. And she had gone along with it because she thought he was a good man trying to get out of a bad situation.

"Good in bed," she shouted as a nun driving a beat-up Chevy pulled past her and gave her a strange look.

"Where were my brains? What if I'm pregnant by a man who's going to end up dead or in jail?" she screamed, turning up the volume so she wouldn't be overheard. "I've ruined my life."

She pushed a Patsy Cline tape into the machine and braked for a stoplight. She leaned her head on the steering wheel. "John Finn. Oh, why?"

The car behind her laid on his horn and Kate looked up at a green light. The car next to her was filled with acne-scarred young boys who made inviting gestures and smacking sounds through the rolled-down window.

"Go harass someone your own age," she said sourly, and hit the gas.

Patsy swooped her way through "I Fall to Pieces" and Kate found herself nodding. Patsy was a romantic, a terminal romantic. That was her problem. She stayed with the wrong man too long. Kate parked the car and then sat in her front seat looking blankly out at her block.

There must be some mistake. Bigelow was talking about John Finn. A man she loved. A man who loved her. Had he said he loved her? Not since that day two years ago, but she could tell he did. Couldn't she? Wasn't it love when a man came to you in his darkest hour? Or was she the only one who would take him in? He had disintegrated in the last two years. But could the old John Finn be lost forever? The father of her child, she thought bleakly. She wound up the windows and locked the doors. Then she trudged off to the drugstore to buy a pregnancy test. It was hard to imagine Kate Hepburn grappling with an unexpected pregnancy. She banished her image from her mind. It was time to deal with reality.

# 36

Ignoring the soap operas on the three television consoles overhead, Kate angrily flipped through the news section of *New York Newsday*. One of their reporters, David Otto, had gotten a page-one story out of the missing foster daughter by doing the legwork on what Kate had feared all along. Otto had checked out the dad and found that he was questioned in connection with a missing child five years before. Otto's police sources stopped short of calling the dad the killer, but that was only because the cops hadn't found the child's body yet.

Kate thought of the rehash she'd aired last week and felt her cheeks burn. She didn't want to think about the news business now. She had taken the at-home pregnancy test last night and again this morning. The result was the same. Kate was definitely pregnant.

"Great news, Kate." It was Landis. He had dropped his usual jittery mannerisms but still spoke with the undiluted energy of a Super Bowl promotion. Kate looked at him. He had cut his hair close to his head on the sides, and the new haircut made him look younger and more attractive. Then she remembered how he had forced her to air the foster-dad segment. Too bad he was such an asshole.

"Yeah? What's great?" she asked sourly, holding up the front page of *New York Newsday*.

"I saw that. We'll have to do an update on the dad." He waved his hand dismissively. "But listen, early

ratings results have us in second place." He smiled
like a game-show host. Kate waited for him to continue. "Do you know what that means?"

"It means we can't attract viewers away from the
serial-killer series on Channel Four," she said, longing
for the newspaper business. It was true she'd had
some bad days at the *Herald*. But it wasn't until she
got to Channel 7 that her life had begun to spin out of
control.

"Sure, yeah. That's right," he said, missing her
irony. "I'm thinking about doing something about
David Berkowitz for next fall." Then he smiled again.
"But you see, if nothing changes, and we stay in the
number two slot instead of dropping to three, then
. . . then . . ."

"You get to keep your job," they both said at the
same time.

"Isn't that great?" asked Landis enthusiastically.

She threw the paper onto her desk in disgust.

"What's the matter? Don't you like working here?"
he asked, sounding worried.

Kate felt her emotions flipping around like a ball in
a spinning roulette wheel.

"You know, I can't figure you out. After work
you're telling me what a great guy you are, and the
next day you're counting the days until my contract is
up. Maybe I do like it here, but if I don't, are you
really concerned?"

Landis picked up her last word as if he were unused
to listening to a full sentence. "Of course I'm concerned." He looked flustered, aware that they were
experiencing something less than clear communication. "We want you to be happy. I told you, we have
great things in store for you here."

She blinked. There it was again. Just when she
thought Landis was a despicable worm, he said something nice and she realized he was a handsome guy.
She wondered if he liked kids, then was shocked that
she had even allowed that thought to burble into her
consciousness.

"Well, thanks," she said, a little confused as to

which incarnation of Steve Landis she was addressing. She tried to pick up on what he was saying.

"Yeah, Bartlett told me this morning that he'd finally got the word from network. He wants to talk to you."

Kate's heart sank. The network feelers would be withdrawn if they got wind of the fact that she was pregnant. Nobody wants to get the news from the Goodyear blimp. Why now? she wanted to howl.

"When?" she said, looking at her watch. After the pregnancy test came up positive this morning, she'd telephoned Finn and asked him to meet her on the Brooklyn Bridge at noon. She wasn't looking forward to seeing him. She couldn't decide whether to confront him with what Bigelow had told her or tell him he had gotten her pregnant. Her head throbbed.

"Don't go anywhere, I'll set up a time for the meeting."

She went back to the office and telephoned Finn. She told his machine that she wouldn't be able to meet him, but she knew he wouldn't get the message in time. She pushed a lead pencil around her notebook, doodling.

She brushed her hair back with her hand. How had she gotten herself into this mess? she chastised herself. It was clear to her after Finn showed up drunk at her house that he'd had a problem with alcohol all along. It was clear to her after meeting Bigelow that Finn was as corrupt as any of the other cops in Brooklyn Narcotics. That's why he couldn't come forward and work with investigators. Then why was he making tapes? Some kind of blackmail? She shut the door to her office and started to cry. How could she love someone who could do such evil things?

She looked down and saw she was drawing peanut-shaped fetuses, and the point broke off her pencil. Could she give birth to a baby whose father was in jail? Her mother and the ladies-who-lunch from Mamaroneck would never understand. She had to talk to him, she decided, dialing Landis's number in order to cancel the meeting. If the network wanted her today, they would want her in another year. She hoped so, anyway. Landis's secretary said he was too busy to take her call and she wouldn't take a message. Kate flashed on an interview she had done at Otisville prison. Ripe-looking pregnant women clogged the visiting room. A toddler spoke to his broken-looking father through Plexiglas. She tried to imagine herself among them and shuddered.

She checked her directory and dialed Andrew Fink. To her surprise, he picked up the telephone.

"Off to the network, are you?"

He caught her off guard. "How did you know?"

"I hear everything."

"Andrew, don't you think it's about time we met? I've worked here two months and only spoken to you by IFB."

"Sure, Kate, sure." He sounded vague. "But I'm taking in a big feed, sports special. Can't do it now."

"C'mon, Andrew. I need to talk to someone."

"So talk."

She sighed into the telephone. "I'll call you later," she said, resigned. She hung up and dialed J.J. No answer. She dialed Nina and decided not to leave a message.

As she replaced the telephone in the cradle, it began to bleat.

"It's Landis," said the voice, full of vibrato. "Could you come to Bartlett's office please?"

"Give me a minute." She dialed her gynecologist but hung up without a word when she heard the receptionist's voice.

A man with a full face and a yellow power tie stood up as Kate entered Bartlett's office, and Landis scrambled behind him.

"So nice to meet you," she said, accepting the hand of network news director Bob Baird. Even his handshake, which was warm and powdery, communicated a certain familiarity with power.

"Your work is very good," said Baird without preamble.

Kate smiled modestly, resisting the pleading looks of Landis and Bartlett, who were silently begging to be given credit in front of Baird like the zoo seals she had seen with Katieanne. "Thank you."

"Once you complete a reel, we're hoping you can fill an opening on our magazine show *Eye Alive*."

Kate wondered what Baird would do if her eyes rolled back in her head and she fainted dead away. "You mean with Dan Rather?"

"None other," said Baird, smiling.

She really did start to faint, but she caught herself on the corner of the table.

"So, when do I start?" she said, not even sure what she would be doing for the show.

Baird smiled. "You need to fill out a reel; maybe another long segment will do it. Then send it over. If the producers like it, and I'm sure they will, we'll be able to talk about a starting date." Baird looked at his watch, which looked like a piece of armor on his meaty wrist. "Got to go. Nice meeting you. We'll speak soon."

As soon as he was out of the room, Bartlett began to babble. He was pleased. Gratified. He loved to be a springboard for new talent. And she certainly had talent. He hoped she would remember him when she was working on foreign assignments, particularly London and Paris. He was all but handing her his résumé. Suddenly, Kate wanted to be alone. She pressed her temples and tried to smile.

"Thanks, guys. I've got to go. I've got a lot to think about."

"One more story to fill out your reel, Kate," said Landis, giving her a full, nearly steady smile. "If anyone can do it, we know it will be you."

Back in the office, Kate looked at her watch and imagined Finn standing alone on the Brooklyn Bridge. She imagined his expression turning from expectant to annoyed to desolate as the minutes ticked by and she failed to show up. She imagined their futures swimming together like two slick green bass in the deep, fast-moving water under the bridge.

As Finn waited vainly, Kate saw those fish swim away from each other, distracted by schools of silvery minnows and dangerous-looking boat hulls. The harbor was wide and once the fish lost sight of each other, they could sense each other's wake, and then that, too, disappeared. They swam in different directions, farther and farther away from each other, as they both headed out to sea.

She hit the redial on her telephone, then clutched the scars along the inside of her arm, feeling the old pain move through her in waves. She gave her name to the receptionist and her daytime telephone number.

"I'd like to schedule a termination," she said.

# 37

Finn spoke to no one as he walked into Albina's classroom, carrying his textbook, *Tools of Surveillance*. Even so, everyone's head turned as he crossed the threshold. He knew it was his last surveillance tactics class. Since Kate had left him standing on the Brooklyn Bridge, everything he did, saw, or heard was prefixed with *the last*. It was his first full day of sobriety, but he had no expectations for a rosy recovery. It wasn't giving in, he told himself. He was going out on his terms. He was glad when Albina, his eyes burning with strange energy, walked through the door and to the head of the class.

Albina cleared his throat. "I'm sorry to have to tell you this, but the department just received word. Mark Money was found dead this morning." He cleared his throat again. "Suicide."

Finn felt as if he had been kicked in the head. A phrase from the AA meeting came back to Finn and made him shiver: "If I didn't stop, I would be dead."

Everyone was falling away.

"How'd he do it?" called Stephen Lee, his voice sounding hollow from the back of the classroom.

"It's being investigated," said Albina, confirming everyone's suspicion that Money had overdosed on smack.

No one moved. They just waited for someone else to do something.

"Class is canceled," said Albina, and like sleepwalkers, the men stood and quietly began to file out.

"Mark Money was into some bad shit," said Bigelow loudly from ahead, and Johnson snickered.

Finn's eyes stung with outrage. Anything that Money put into his veins was a gift from Bigelow. They were in a dark stairway leading out of the Academy. Soft voices bounced off the walls. Knowing his life was over gave Finn a certain liberation. Nothing was holding him back.

"Yeah? Was he working for the Ghost Brigade, too?" Finn's voice was loud, but he directed his question to no one in particular.

There it was. Like the smooth prosthesis falling away from a festering stump. The stairway was suddenly silent, and the cluster of men stopped, frozen. Bigelow waved them forward and they obeyed. Finn walked carefully downstairs. By the time he got to Bigelow, the other men were a flight away, taking care not to look back. Finn felt fear but he pushed it away.

Bigelow put his arm around Finn and tenderly traversed the plane of Finn's back with his fingers, feeling for a wire. Finn wasn't wearing it.

"I didn't hear you. What did you say?" he asked with a thin smile. Finn could smell Bigelow's rancid breath. Finn spit on the ground to keep the smell from going into his mouth and up his nose. Then he leaned forward so his lips were close to Bigelow's ear. Intimate.

"I wondered if Money was as dirty as you," he murmured.

For a second, nothing happened. Then Bigelow put back his head and laughed. It was the kind of laugh that used to punctuate an evening of drinking. The kind of laugh that used to make Finn think he was in good hands. Now the sound curdled Finn's soul.

"What's the matter, John? Are you having trouble with your girl?"

Bigelow's hand slid up to Finn's head and pulled it close. He couldn't mask the evil in his voice when he whispered, "We have an understanding, that reporter and I. I met her and told her you were the dirtiest one of the bunch." Bigelow paused. "And she believed me."

Finn heard the roaring in his head. Of course. That's why she stood him up on the bridge. He had waited for her, holding two dozen red roses, practicing ways to tell her that in five years he wanted to be with her. He had murmured, "Will you marry me?" over and over like a mantra until the sun set and the first stars poked through the sky over the Twin Towers.

But Bigelow kept talking. "Funny thing about that reporter, Kate Murray. You never would think that such an uptight woman would be such a wild animal in bed. She said she loved doing it with cops."

Finn felt fury lift the top off his head like a hatch. Without receiving a conscious order, his fists began to punch Bigelow. His body was solidly behind his hands and he caught Bigelow unaware. Bigelow's head hit the railing and his feet started to slide. Finn was on him like a terrier on a rat. He grabbed Bigelow's shoulders and pushed him down again, throwing his weight into it.

"You think you're smarter than everyone, don't you? Don't you? You think you can play cops against criminals and get all the drugs and all the money and all the girls." Finn hit him on the face with his elbow and Bigelow's nose began to bleed. "You may call the shots for Group C, but you don't call the shots for me. Do you hear me? You can't have Kate and you can't have me." He hit Bigelow's face again, smearing the blood above his brow. Bigelow begin to shift slowly like continental plates. Then he erupted. In an instant, Finn was on his back pushing Bigelow's fingers out of his eyes. Bigelow jerked him forward, clearing the railing, then threw him down the stairs. From somewhere, a gun clattered down the stairs nearby. Finn blacked out. When he came to, he saw Bigelow's yellow teeth near his nose and felt Bigelow's warm blood flowing on his face. His yellow eyes were filled with hate. Bigelow held him by a handful of hair and was pounding his head against the metal tread of the step, punctuating his words.

"Who do you think is going to stop me?" Crash. "You? Just you?" Bigelow was panting as he smashed Finn's head. Crash. "It's too late. Everything is going to go off exactly as I planned it. You can't do a thing to stop me. You're weak." Crash. "You're nothing. You're a drunk." Crash. Every time Finn's head hit the floor, he heard birds chirping. His consciousness was like a kite in a gale and Finn was struggling to keep hold of the end of the string. "You think your girlfriend Kate Murray will stop me?" Finn drew his knee up to his chest and wedged it under Bigelow. The big man stopped pounding Finn's head. "Bad news, buddy. I fucked her. And she said she liked it. She said I was better than you."

*"Arrrggh,"* said Finn, kicking at Bigelow's groin, hitting him instead on his left thigh. Bigelow backed off. Finn pulled himself up and weaved unsteadily toward him, his hands covered with blood from Bigelow's nose. The side of Finn's head was already warm and pulpy. He lunged at Bigelow but Bigelow sidestepped him, laughing. Finn fell to one knee and tried to struggle up again. Bigelow leaned down, and for a second Finn thought his old friend was going to help him up. He could smell Bigelow's breath again. He heard a gravelly sound, like a car ignition failing to turn over, then felt Bigelow's spit in his face.

"She said she liked it," said Bigelow as he walked away.

Finn lay in the stairway listening to Bigelow's heavy footsteps. He heard the familiar, faraway voices of his friends. Then he heard nothing but the faint roar of a garbage truck and doors slamming somewhere in the Academy. When it was perfectly quiet, he began to cry.

# 38

It was a few minutes after dawn and Kate hadn't slept since two A.M. She had had dreams, terrible dreams about pushing a baby carriage with a television camera inside it instead of an infant. At the first squawk of the morning chorus she let herself out of her apartment and drove to Green-wood Cemetery. The caretakers were just arriving and, delighted to see anyone else up that early, waved her in. The sun was just beginning to roll back the heavy night sky. Kate knew it was a bad idea to walk alone, especially in such a desolate place. She'd covered half a dozen stories for the *Herald* about dog owners getting robbed or raped during Fido's morning constitutional. But she felt safe here. She reached into the pocket of her windbreaker for a Saltine—the only thing that would keep her from throwing up. She could hardly face work today, she was feeling so jumbled and confused.

She walked by the polished marble lady sitting on the edge of her polished marble tub. One of the caretakers had told her that a woman had committed suicide in a bathtub and her loving husband erected a monument to depict her tragic end. It must have been a very ladylike, Victorian end. Don't mind me, honey, I'm just going to take a long bath. Like for eternity.

She walked a bit farther, watching squirrels chase each other through the thick green leaves. She ticked off the time with her fingers. Five more days of pregnancy. It was Thursday and she'd scheduled the abortion for Tuesday morning at seven A.M. She sighed, low and sad. There didn't seem to be any other way. She had never looked after a cat before. She knew she'd be in over her head with a baby. She might be able to survive its infancy, but what would she tell the child when it got old enough to ask? Yes, I was in love with your father, but sorry, he won't be around until you're about to graduate from high school. He's in Attica.

She passed a mausoleum that looked like a small church. It belonged to the first Irish billionaire, a thickheaded man who founded the Southern Pacific railroad. In a fit of grandiosity, he had his mausoleum wired for heat and light. Despite the modern conveniences of his final resting place, all his relatives opted to be buried elsewhere. He must have been a real jerk.

She counted the monuments topped with veiled urns, the Victorian symbol for extreme and overwhelming grief. It was comforting to know that she was in a place so familiar with sadness. She wasn't sure exactly what she was mourning. She didn't agree with the pope—she wasn't a baby killer. But the thought of ending the potential for life didn't make her want to cheer.

She wandered down to Edith's grave and saw that her grandmother had a new neighbor. In the morning light, Kate considered the fresh grave. She couldn't think of a more peaceful place to be. She leaned her back against Edith's marker, pulling the heads off dandelions and throwing them into the new dirt.

"I've run out of options, Edith. I don't know what else to do," she said. "I never thought about a baby. I guess I would love her . . . um . . . him. But this isn't the right time. I'm sure I can't do it myself and I think Finn will be in jail before the year is out."

Edith, one of the real old-time feminists, railed against the Catholic Church's anti-abortion stand. She said abortion, like contraception, was a health issue and not a political one. But she was just as unequivocal about the value of being a mother. Whenever she spoke of giving birth to her three boisterous sons, her voice grew mossy and tender.

Kate would have loved Edith to meet her great-granddaughter. She imagined walking through the dappled graveyard, holding a little warm hand in hers. Even if her daughter didn't get a chance to meet Edith, she'd hear a lot about her. Kate imagined sweeping little Edie's wild hair out of her eyes, a gesture of tenderness that Kate would forever associate with her grandmother.

Kate caught herself suddenly, grabbed her elbows, and hugged herself tight. Something was changing inside her. In the last few minutes, her pregnancy had gone from a troubling conglomeration of cells the size of a rice grain to the precious blue-print of her beloved daughter. She felt a wild sense of hope and then a rush of protective love.

Finn said he didn't want her to get involved in his problems. But when he'd said it, he hadn't known what was at stake. Even docile circus elephants charge when their offspring are in danger. She wouldn't allow her daughter to slip from this life without a fight. And she squeezed her eyes tight and tried to make a plan. She wasn't even sure where to start. But what was it that Edith always said? Trust in love.

## 39

Finn woke up on the Friday before Labor Day and stared at the walls of his apartment. It was as simple as that. One eye opened, then the other. No rush of elation that faded out into blinding panic. No grappling for his gun and his shield. His eyes roamed around his room. This is what it was like for most people every day. They moved from sleep to wakefulness as you would step off a bus. But to Finn, the experience was like a gift. Tears of gratitude welled up in his eyes. They turned to tears of pain when he rolled over to pick up the ringing telephone. Every fiber of his connective tissue protested in pain. His fingers traveled up to his eye. Bigelow had given him the beating of his life.

It was Pauly Mackay on the telephone.

"How is it? You still with us?"

"My second day of sobriety," said Finn, sniffing.

"How do you feel?"

"I'm fine," Finn lied reflexively. Then he corrected himself. "Truthfully, in the first twenty-four hours of my new life of sobriety, I managed to get myself nearly beaten to death."

"You want me to pick you up and take you to a doctor?"

"No, I'll be okay."

"What happened?"

Finn rubbed his jaw. "It's complicated. But I'll tell you one thing. I used to be such a peaceful drunk. I had a few beers and a few brandies and I was the most peaceful guy you ever saw. Nothing bothered me until I woke up the next morning." He couldn't believe he had taken on Bigelow stone-cold sober and without a crowbar. "I'm finding that sobriety gets me pissed off."

"I can understand that."

Finn had a hard time imagining Pauly Mackay, St. Augustine's usher, rolling around on a barroom floor. But then again, he couldn't imagine that proper-looking woman at the AA meeting eating out of a garbage can.

"What do I do now, Pauly?" asked Finn as the morning hours loomed large and frightening before him. He had to get through the next two days somehow. "I can't stand being the man I was, and I don't think the man I am now has too much of a future." He was thinking about Kate. He'd asked her not to meddle in his problems, then he had dragged her down into the sewer of his life by leaving the tapes at her house. He felt weak and cowardly and he couldn't bear it.

"I want you to come to an AA meeting this morning in Brooklyn Heights."

"I don't think I need to go to any more meetings, Pauly."

"I guarantee you'll learn a few things. It's a lecture about making amends for the things you've done."

# 40

Kate was kneeling on the floor of the toilet on the third floor of the U.S. attorney's office throwing up her breakfast when the marshals started banging on the door.

"What's going on in there?"

"I'll be done in a minute." Kate's strangled voice didn't carry farther than the stall. She heard a spongy shoulder thump against the ladies' room door. She pushed against the cistern and tried to stand up, but was felled by another wave of nausea.

"What's your security clearance?" came another angry voice. "Open this door immediately." She heard another shoulder against the heavy door, then the sound of splintering wood. Two brush-headed marshals and a grandfatherly security guard crowded into the small ladies' room, the meatiest one rubbing his shoulder.

"Excuse me," said Kate, and then opened her mouth and vomited again.

The oldest man delicately plucked a towel out of the receptacle and handed it to her. "I saw this in my own wife nine times and in every one of my four daughters-in-law. What are you? About eight weeks?" Kate nodded and accepted the towel. The guard turned to the marshals, who suddenly seemed fascinated by the details of the plain yellow-tiled walls. "Well, I believe our report of a terrorist is unfounded. She's just a young *mamasita* in a family way." The bristle-headed marshals filed out, looking relieved.

"Sorry about the door, I couldn't get a word out," said Kate, flushing the toilet and splashing water on her face.

"It's nothing for you to worry about."

Kate looked at her watch. "Oh, God, I'm late."

"To where?"

"Mark DeMaris's office."

"The big man himself," said the guard, nodding to Kate approvingly. "You're a modern woman. Good luck to you. And get some Saltines, they always helped my wife."

By the time Kate entered DeMaris's wood-paneled office, her knees had gotten steadier and her gastric rebellion was momentarily quelled.

"How nice to see you again," said DeMaris, trying for charming and ending up looking predatory. "I thought I'd be seeing you when we were ready to wrap up our investigation."

Kate crossed her legs at the thigh and prepared to bluff her way through. "I understand your team is having some trouble bringing it down."

DeMaris gave her a practiced, blank, neither-confirm-nor-deny look. She had asked around about the investigation—none of her FBI sources could tell her how many people they expected to arrest or when. It sounded to Kate as if they weren't even sure of their targets.

"So what can I do for you?" asked DeMaris, and picked up a small stack of legal-looking papers.

"I know someone who can deliver the corrupt cops in Group C."

DeMaris pulled himself up like a judge facing a convicted prisoner. "If you know something about criminal wrongdoing, let me warn you that you could be subpoenaed to testify in front of a grand jury." DeMaris pressed a button on his multibutton telephone. "Agnes, please get me Fishbach." He was calling in his chief of staff. Once he got in the room, it would all be official. Kate would have no play at all.

"It's not me, it's a friend. He may want to make a deal," she said hurriedly.

"If your friend is interested in cooperating, I suggest to you that he needs a lawyer to represent him, not a television reporter."

There was a knock on the door. Fishbach must have left his office at a dead run, thought Kate. DeMaris turned to open the door.

"He has tapes," said Kate, trying not to let her desperation show.

DeMaris smiled in Fishbach's pale, hollow-eyed face.

"Give me a minute here, will you, Brian."

Kate stood up and walked to the back of the office and helped herself to a decanter of ice water sweating in the summer heat. It seemed like something Perry Mason would do.

DeMaris turned to face her. "How good are they?"

Kate had no idea if the tapes even existed. She shrugged. "I'm here, aren't I?" she said coolly.

"So give me a name. Who's going to play queen for a day?" The first meeting between a prosecutor and a potential informant is an uplifting event. The prosecutor is usually enthusiastic about the fresh information. The potential informant is having the experience, sometimes for the first time in his life, of going legitimate. DeMaris opened a file cabinet and picked up a blue folder marked NYPD—Kate guessed it was the case file.

"John Finn," she said.

DeMaris silently flipped through the file. "Divorced detective. Got a problem with the bottle." He looked up. "What if I tell you we were planning to indict him?"

"What if I tell you that would be a terrible mistake?"

"Tapes . . . homemade bootleg tapes," he mused. Kate could see DeMaris mentally preparing to present them to a jury. It would make a great case with which to spring into politics. She tasted bile on her molars and wondered what DeMaris would do if she vomited on his maroon, federal-issue rug.

"One condition. He doesn't do jail time."

"They're all going to do jail time," said DeMaris matter-of-factly.

Kate's head began to swim. Sorry, honey, your father won't be able to go to the ballet recital with the other dads. He's still serving his eight to twenty-two. Behind DeMaris was a wall calendar. She still had her appointment for Tuesday morning.

"Maybe I can sweeten the pot," said Kate. DeMaris's eyes swept over her, sizing her up. "You need television right now to launch your candidacy. I can get you onto the screen. I've got to cover the Caribbean Day parade Monday evening. But what about spending tomorrow morning with my crew? We can do a Channel Seven special report—at home with the DeMaris family—you know, up close and personal."

DeMaris licked his lips. He shot a glance out the wide window, and Kate could see that his office faced City Hall. "I see what you are saying."

"You, wearing a sweater with leather patches at the elbows, playing football with the little DeMarises." She wondered if she could go through with this and decided she could. If a mother could single-handedly lift a Volkswagen off her child, she could tape a puff piece on DeMaris.

"Tell your friend I'm ready to talk on two conditions. First, that he avail himself to federal agents within forty-eight hours. Tell him to pack an overnight bag."

"Why don't we say Tuesday? I mean, it's the Friday before the Labor Day weekend. Maybe he's gone away."

DeMaris looked as if he might snarl. "Yeah, he's probably in the Hamptons already." Then he paused. "Okay, Tuesday." She smiled. She was starting to feel like a player, a power broker, not simply a television reporter, a TV personality. "But there's another thing, a more important thing." Kate looked at him. He walked up to her and put his face too close to hers.

"This is not a game. If a word about our conversation leaks to anyone, John Finn goes to jail." He spread his hands out as if he were playing cat's cradle. He looked more sinister than any mob enforcer Kate had ever seen. "It boils down to this. You fuck me, I'll fuck you."

Kate forced a smile to cover a reflex to gag. But DeMaris wasn't finished.

"And after the series about my campaign is done, I never want you to come to my office again." She felt her newfound clout evaporate like steam. "Never."

# 41

Finn drove from the AA lecture in Brooklyn Heights to the Eighty-third Precinct, where he still had a desk and a pile of dead-end homicide folders. The last time I'll see the squad room, he said to himself. He felt light-headed, as if he were breathing pure oxygen, and wondered if Bigelow had knocked something loose in his brain. He was thinking about the eighth step. *Make a list of all the people you have harmed and be willing to make amends to them all.* Pauly was on the money. The lecture was worth the effort. He waved his hand through the cubes of gray sunlight coming through the window grate in the drab linoleum squad room. It was eleven A.M. but the squad room was empty of older detectives who usually worked a straight day shift. Finn was relieved not to have anyone from the squad see him banged up like this. They'd ask too many questions. He rummaged around in his desk, trying to find his copy of the paperwork from the arrest of the boys in the bodega. It'd been a crazy life. Finn rubbed his forehead. Three months ago, two kids had pointed a gun at him during a stickup, and now Finn couldn't remember their names. He found the file, then flipped through to find the kid's name, noting that only one had gone to prison. He jotted down the prisoner identification number.

Three hours later, his sense of determination fled as he stared at the razor wire strung up around the

Spofford Detention Center. He parked his car in the near-empty lot, then flashed his badge at the armed corrections guard at the door. Automatic doors slid open, admitting him.

He sat in the hard molded chair in the visiting room for almost thirty minutes, not listening to the blaring television, waiting for Vinnie Minor to be delivered to him. He wasn't sure now what he wanted to say to the little mongrel. He looked up when he heard the inner door slam. Vinnie Minor, a vision of adolescent misery, stood before him. At any age, Minor wouldn't have been good-looking. But the erratic spurts of hormones pumping through Minor's system had left him looking as if his body were made up of cast-off parts. His feet, which were clad in scuffed black sneakers, were enormous. His skinny arms, which were a good three inches longer than his sleeves, grew from an underdeveloped chest. His head was too large for his slender torso, and his pasty face was pitted with acne. The boy looked so lost and unloved, Finn almost smiled. Then the boy turned his head and Finn saw where Bigelow had bitten him. A fiery, mottled-red scar ran from the corner of Minor's eye to the edge of his nostril. It was a wound so deep that the flesh had congealed upon itself, puckering and turning his skin as it scabbed over.

"Sit down, Vinnie," Finn said, not letting his voice betray the shock he felt.

"I don't know anything about robberies," said Vinnie. Finn had told the corrections administrators he was investigating a string of robberies. "I've had enough police in my life. I'm going home soon. I don't want any more hassles."

Finn moved a chair back with his toe. "Sit down." The boy sat. "Look at me. Look hard. Do you know who I am?"

Vinnie looked at him intently, then his mouth opened in an O of surprise.

"You're the cop, but you all messed up," he answered, looking around as if he needed witnesses. Then he stuck out his chin, taunting, "If you came to give me a beating, you're out of luck. They don't allow hitting here."

Finn exhaled. "I didn't come for that. I've given all the beatings I'm going to give out for a while."

Vinnie looked at Finn's split lip and smiled.

"What then? I told you, I don't know about any . . ."

"Robberies," Finn finished. "Okay. Okay. No robberies."

They sat in silence for a while.

"I looked at your folder this morning. Says you took the first plea you were offered. Didn't anyone tell you not to do that?"

Vinnie shrugged his shoulders. "My friend, Billie Jackson—you remember, the tall guy in the bodega. He got there first. He told the prosecutor that I'd convinced him to do the robbery. Said I was hoping a police officer would come in. Says I was bragging about wanting to kill a cop."

Finn remembered how the boy trembled.

"It makes more sense than what really happened," said Vinnie, reminiscing sadly.

"What really happened?"

The boy just shrugged.

"No, tell me. I really want to know."

"I'd just bought that gun off the big cop with the mustache. The one who walked into the bodega and did this." Vinnie's hand brushed his mottled cheek. "It's the truth, but what judge is going to believe me when I say that?"

"So you jumped at the deal."

With as much weariness as he could muster in his skinny shoulders, Vinnie shrugged.

Finn let his attention drift. This was not the conversation he thought he would be having with the best buddy of a kid who'd pointed a gun at him.

"Why did you buy the gun?"

Vinnie looked at him. "What difference does it make?"

"I'm curious."

"Billie is a cokehead. Almost since elementary

school. He'd steal your lunch money so he could get high. The last few years, he'd do anything for money. Walk into any store, pretend he has a gun, get some money, do some drugs."

"You do any drugs?"

"Not me, I'm scared of my uncle. I've lived with him since my mother died, and he graduated from Daytop Village. He said it takes a junkie to know a junkie. Said if I got high, he could spot me in a minute. And he would kill me."

"But he doesn't mind you doing robberies?"

"He minded," Vinnie said quietly, and Finn could hear the heartbreak in his voice.

"So why'd you buy the gun?"

"This cop, you know, your boss, offers to sell us a gun. And he says, not says, kind of suggests, that if we did the deal with him, he would try and keep my friend Billie out of the reach of the law. And you know, Billie needed some help with the police. He was my friend and he was bound to get caught."

"Your friend?"

Vinnie looked off at the television. "Nah. He's not my friend no more."

Finn watched the boy, remembering how it felt to be caught in the anguished web of adolescence, suspended midway between childhood dreams and adult repercussions, unable to be comforted by one or guided by the other. He'd already said his mother was dead and his guardian was some kind of half-assed junkie. No doubt about it, Vinnie Minor needed someone to watch over him.

Finn tried again. "You've been here a while, right? Anyone visit you?"

"Nah."

Finn was quiet again. His head was pounding. His body was craving a drink. He remembered the tall guy at his first AA meeting nervously unwrapping the silver chocolate kisses.

He walked over to the candy machine and fed in a handful of change. He handed the kid a Snickers bar and opened one for himself.

"Look, it's not easy what you're going through."

Vinnie was silent.

"I mean, Spofford. And your, you know, your age. It's hard." It wasn't anywhere near what Finn wanted to say.

"Hmmm." Vinnie had stuffed the whole candy bar in his mouth like a toddler.

Finn looked at him. "You want another?"

"Sure," Vinnie said happily.

Finn handed him four quarters for the machine. He waited until the kid took his seat again.

"Look, kid, you're too young to know this so you just have to remember what I say. You got to think for yourself. Even people you think are really great friends can turn out to be bad. You got to watch out for yourself, no matter what."

"I know that now," said Vinnie bitterly. "Why don't you tell me something I don't know?"

Finn was silent and Vinnie's attention was drawn back to the television.

Finn tried again. "I'll tell you another thing. You gotta be careful what you do because you never know who you are fucking with. You thought because that guy Bigelow was a cop, he would help you. He's the most dangerous guy I have ever met." The boy touched his scarred face again. Finn wanted to give him some protection. A safety net. Maybe even the advice of one caring adult to hold on to. "But that's behind you. You got to look ahead. Say you're out of Spofford and on the subway and are about to rob a target you think is a nearsighted middle-aged accountant. But he could be an accountant with a black belt in karate or a psycho with a Luger tucked into his belt."

For the first time, Vinnie smiled. "Yeah. Then it's like revenge of the nerds. Bam, bam. Your taxes are *late.*"

Finn smiled. They both turned their heads away from each other self-consciously and pretended to be absorbed in the television. It was a stupid show called "The New Dating Game," full of bosomy women and

guys with capped teeth and full manes of hair. Finn
calculated. Vinnie was just seventeen. Unless someone gave him a leg up in the world, he'd enter
manhood thinking all guys are like the superheroes in
cartoons or contestants on "The New Dating Game."
Nobody ever told Vinnie about the real pleasures of
being a man—getting a paycheck, loving a woman,
smelling a brand-new car. Finn looked at his watch. It
was time for him to go. He noticed Vinnie's fingernails were bitten down to the ragged skin.

"What are you gonna be when you grow up?" Finn
asked, stalling. "Let me guess. You want to be the only
white guy playing for the Knicks."

"Forget the Knicks. I want to work for *Eyewitness
News.*"

Finn smiled, surprised. "You do?"

The boy placed his fist in front of his jaw and
recited a story about a water-main break.

"A water-main break?"

"Yeah. It happened outside my uncle's house. It
was great."

Finn smiled. "When are you getting out?"

"I got accepted into a Youth Division program. I'll
get remanded to them pretty soon. Maybe tomorrow.
Maybe Monday. Maybe next week," said Vinnie, and
Finn felt momentarily outraged. Vinnie was a juvenile, but he was doing less than six months for
robbing a store with a kid who coolly pulled a gun on
a cop. He would probably have gotten time served if
he hadn't accepted the first plea. Finn shrugged. He
was here to make amends. He reached into his pocket
and took out his card. He wrote Kate's name on the
back.

"When you get out, I probably won't be around. So,
wait until Tuesday and then go to Channel Seven and
find this lady." He pointed to the card. "See, that's
her name. Kate Murray." He thought of Bigelow's
coarse face against her lips and felt a chill.

But Vinnie was getting excited. "Yeah, I seen her on
the news. I seen her."

Finn nodded. "Can you remember all this? Listen

carefully now. On Tuesday, tell her I said she was the only one that tried to help me. The only one. Tell her that there are tapes in her flour canister."

The boy looked at Finn without comprehension.

"You got that? Flour canister."

"Flour canister," Vinnie said obediently.

"That will explain everything. And tell her I loved her." Finn closed his eyes, suddenly feeling weak. "Tell her you're going to finish your term at the Youth Division and ask her to help you get started in television."

# 42

She had left so many messages for John Finn since Friday night that late Monday afternoon his tape had run out. "You know what to do and when to do it," said the gruff voice, then all she heard was static.

Frustrated, she surveyed the giant chrysanthemums that nearly obscured a stack of newspapers and her scribbled yellow legal pads. The flowers were a congratulatory bouquet from Andrew Fink. The newsroom was buzzing with the gossip that she was being pulled up to network. Only Andrew had sent her the flowers and written her an encouraging note.

"Yeah, I'll leave a message if you don't mind," she was saying to Andrew's technical aide, checking her watch. It was Labor Day and she was supposed to cover the tail end of the Caribbean Day parade on Eastern Parkway, a pageant known for its elaborate costumes and throbbing crowds that milled about in the streets until almost midnight. "Tell him thanks for the flowers. Tell him I want him to be my second husband." Despite the fact that he worked brutally long hours, he seemed to Kate to be the most well-adjusted man working in television. He was sensitive. Smart. Always willing to listen and offer her good advice. She imagined that unlike DeMaris, who put on a good show this morning for the cameras, Fink was the kind of guy who really would kick a soccer ball around with his daughters. "Tell him when we finally sit down for coffee, I'll tell him how much he means to me."

"You never met him face-to-face?" asked his technician.

"It's the modern age," said Kate dryly. "We've only spoken by telephone and IFB."

"Oh, wow," said the technician. Kate, distracted by a tentative knock on her door, let it pass.

"Hang on a minute," she said, holding up her hands as a pimply adolescent with a gruesome scar on his face stood at her threshold.

She dialed Finn again. Damn. Damn. DeMaris wasn't going to let his deal stay on the table. Finn wouldn't have much time to think it over. It was already Monday evening and she hadn't even gotten a chance to tell him what she had done.

She turned to face the young man in her office and tried not to stare at his horrendous scar. He was shifting his weight from foot to foot, staring at the photographs of mobsters hung above her desk.

"What can I do for you?" she asked without letting him answer. "How did you get past security?" She took a breath and her hand traveled to her navel. She thought she felt something move, but she knew from all she had read in the last two days that the growing baby was no bigger than a lentil.

The youth's awed look was replaced by a wolfish smile. "I didn't think you'd be here on a holiday, but I took a chance." He showed her a canvas bag of tools he was carrying. "I told 'em I was fixing the cable wire."

She narrowed her eyes. "What cable wire?"

"They didn't ask," he said, showing the boyish gap in his front teeth. Kate smiled involuntarily.

"What can I do for you?" she said, eyeing her pocketbook. This kid definitely had larceny in his past.

"So this is where you guys put together the news?"

"Not exactly. This is my office."

"But this is where you sit when you get your information?" He gestured to her desk.

She suppressed her irritation. "No, I get most of my

information on the street. But tell me, what can I do for you?"

He looked at her as if he expected her to pull a rabbit from a hat. When she didn't move, he looked disappointed.

"Yes?" she prompted.

"This may sound weird to you, but I think a friend of yours might be in trouble."

She smiled indulgently. "Oh, really? Someone you know?"

"Well, he came to visit me at Spofford. A detective named John Finn." In an instant, he had her full attention. "I stuck up a bodega he was in about three months ago."

Quite an introduction. "What makes you think he's in trouble?"

"He came to Spofford to visit me." He said it proudly, as if Finn were a successful relation. "His face was all messed up like he'd been fighting. He told me to get in touch with you when I got out of jail and promised you'd help me get started in television news." Kate was looking irritated and Vinnie became more animated. "He gave me your number because he said he didn't think he'd be around."

"It's a holiday weekend," Kate said dryly. "Most people leave the city."

"Nah, it wasn't like that. He was—what's the word?—desperate. And I know desperate because my uncle graduated from Daytop Village."

Juvenile offender and freelance psychologist, thought Kate. "What exactly did he tell you?"

"He said to call you at this number." The kid pulled out a wrinkled white square. Kate took it and saw that Finn had written her number on the back of his card. She felt a chill. "He said something else."

"Yes?" she asked eagerly.

He changed up. "You need an assistant?" Kate felt as if she might explode. "What's your name?"

"Vinnie Minor. Vincent."

"Listen, Vincent, you help me now and I promise, I

won't forget it." The boy nodded. "But you got to tell me what he said."

"He said there are tapes in your flower garden."

"What are you talking about? I don't have a flower garden."

Vinnie looked deflated. "What do you mean?"

"I don't have a flower garden."

"Maybe he didn't say garden. He said flower, em, flower, containers, canisters. You have flour canisters?" Kate looked uncertain. "He said he put some tapes in them."

"Tapes?" Kate almost yelled. "What else?"

"He said you were the only one that tried to help."

She quickly dialed his number. She got the same message.

"Why did he tell this to you?"

"Like I said, he seemed desperate. I guess he thought I wouldn't call you until Tuesday."

She eyed the tools again. "How did you get out?"

He shook his head. "Nothing like that. I'm remanded to Youth Division. I got to work for them from nine to five, doing job corps, you know, picking up Nathan's bags in the park."

"Where are you going now?" asked Kate, already calculating how quickly she could get back to her apartment.

Vinnie was thinking along the same lines. "You got a big house?"

"No. I live in an apartment in Brooklyn," she answered, distracted.

"You got a spare room?"

"What?"

"I just got out of jail. I don't have anywhere to go," said Vinnie quietly. And for a second Kate realized how young and vulnerable he was. Then Vinnie shrugged. "Besides, if we're going to work together on television, we should get to know each other."

# 43

She skidded by security and jumped into the waiting van.

"It's eight o'clock and it's still too hot to hurry," said Manuel, stubbing out a cigarillo. He was right. In her few short minutes running from the CBS building to the van, she'd begun to perspire. "We don't go live until the ten-o'clock promo."

"I got worlds colliding, Manuel. I need to check something in my apartment. Could you please drive me there?" She paused. "Just as fast as you can."

Manuel brushed back his hair with his palm, gave a nod to Bernie in the back of the truck, and eased out into the traffic.

Two hours later, she was sitting in the oppressively stuffy van, brushing flour off her lapels, listening to Money tell Finn about Bigelow's drug shipment. Every word punctured her heart. The men in Group C sounded like any other drug ring. Except the dealers were cops. And one of those cops was Finn. She backed up the tape to listen to the start of Finn's conversation with Money. He started off by admitting that he was making good money working for Bigelow. He wanted more. "Why didn't you even let me in on it back then?" he asked Money.

Even as it was laid out for her, she couldn't make the two images of Finn come together. She tried to be rational. Maybe it was clear from the other tapes that

Finn was innocent. She didn't have time to listen to them all. By the end of the tape he made with Money, it was clear that Finn wasn't in on Versos's killing. And since he was the one making the tapes, he might have been lying to Money to get information about Bigelow. Or he might be a dirty cop. She was pregnant with his child, she thought, her hand creeping down to her belly. If it turned out he was a criminal, she prayed that one day she could stop loving him.

Outside, the parade had boiled down into a wild block party—the brutal heat and stifling humidity seemed to make the crowd more frantic. A pudgy brown woman wearing elaborate butterfly wings with an eleven-foot span waited outside the van to be the backdrop for Kate's ten-o'clock promo. A skinny man dressed in a gold loincloth and carrying a sun-topped scepter menaced other parade goers and laughed.

Kate was concentrating on the tapes. For the fifth time, she directed Bernie to stop, rewind, and replay the tape:

"He says solid gold is going to wash up on the Neponsit beach on Labor Day weekend and make him a rich man."

She gripped her elbows. Be a pragmatist, she instructed herself. She'd covered enough cases to know that federal informants didn't have to be clean. They just had to be quick to make a deal. She had to get Finn to bring these tapes to DeMaris. She punched Finn's number into the car phone. Instead of the usual snarl, she heard a different recording, this one calm, almost serene. "Kate, I didn't want to do this." It was Finn. Kate looked at her watch. He had changed his message sometime in the last forty minutes. "But when I took a hard look at the terrible things that have happened, I realized that it had to stop somewhere. I had to try and set some of them straight no matter what the cost. I had no choice. I hope you'll understand."

She hung up, frozen. She didn't know what to do. Then she put her head on her arms and began to cry.

Bernie gaped at her and Manuel patted her awkwardly on the shoulder.

She looked up at her techs, feeling tears carrying flakes of her mascara down her check. "How many more minutes until the broadcast?"

"Four."

"Oh, God." She sniffed and swiped her tears off her cheek. She took the IFB that Bernie offered her and climbed out of the van. Opening the door of the van was like opening an oven. She stood in front of the camera while Manuel framed the parade crowd behind her. She knew she looked, as Edith would have said, like something the cat dragged in.

"How's our network star today?" It was Fink talking to her through the IFB. She looked into the camera and smiled lamely. "Whoa!" He must have taken a look at Manuel's feed coming into the microwave room. "Are you okay?"

"I'm not doing too well," she sniffed. A cheer resounded from the crowd.

"I can see that," Andrew said smoothly. "You have about three minutes until your first live feed. Brush your hair off your cheek. It's sticking to the tears. Now, blow your nose and then put some foundation on the end, it's all red. . . . Great. You got blush? Put it high on your cheeks and right under your eyebrow. It will make that splotchiness seem like you spent the day on the beach."

Dazed, Kate did as she was told. It was like talking to a girlfriend. She spoke to Andrew through the camera. "Andrew, don't ever leave me."

His voice, coming through the IFB, sounded strangled. "Kate, I assure you, you'll be the one to leave me."

She put down her brush. "There."

"That's fine then. Now you look like the future network star. You have thirty seconds."

Another cheer went up. Kate plastered a smile on her face, put her arm around the woman with the butterfly wings, and began to read the promo.

\* \* \*

"Now sit tight. You'll be the fourth story at eleven," boomed Landis's voice after the promo was through. Kate thought of Katharine Hepburn. She thought of Edith and J.J. and all the women who weren't afraid to fight. She was going to Rockaway.

"I can't do it, Steve," said Kate, staring directly into the camera. "Something has come up."

His voice returned quickly, full of vibrato. "Let me remind you that you're not at the network yet."

"It's not that, Steve. I have an emergency. A personal emergency."

"Yeah. Well, I have an eleven-o'clock show and you're my fourth story."

Her mind was blank. She could come up with a snappy retort, but what was the use. "Look, the parade is over, it's just a block party now."

"Yeah, but I want the local color," Landis said, his voice nasty. "At four minutes after eleven I want you to deliver costumes and drumming and ethnic diversity. You're in Brooklyn for God's sake. I want a parade!"

"It could turn out to be a better story," she said lamely.

Landis sounded as if he were about to explode. "I'm the assigning editor. I'll tell you where I want you and when."

She started to respond, but Manuel, sensing she was losing the argument, cut the signal.

Five Haitian women, none under 165 pounds, undulated down the street to the thunder of bass drums. Kate climbed into the van. If she was fired from the station, she'd be out of a job for the second time in less than three months. She'd blow her chances of getting to the network. Of being someone famous. Of bringing home the big stories, like war and famine and international intrigue. But somewhere, on the beach at Rockaway, Finn, tarnished and confused, was courting redemption. Her daughter's one and only father was facing Bigelow alone.

"Manuel, Bernie, are you paid up on your union dues?" They both nodded. "I've got to pull out of here and find my boyfriend. He's in terrible trouble. I guess I'll get fired for it, but I can't stay away."

Bernie shrugged. "We're union. We don't get fired. But what about the network?"

Kate bit her lip. "I don't know. Maybe I should ask Andrew Fink. He's the most sane and normal guy at the newsroom."

Manuel looked at her curiously. "Do you know why he avoids you?"

"What do you mean?"

"I mean, a face-to-face meeting?"

"What are you talking about, we talk all the time."

"He doesn't want you to see him."

She was getting exasperated. "Why not?"

"He doesn't have any legs."

"What?"

"That's right," said Bernie. "He doesn't have anything below the waist. He got CBS to adapt the microwave room for wheelchairs, and he stays there most of the time. On the IFB, he's a god. On the street, he's a freak."

Kate pulled the IFB out of her ear and placed it on the dashboard. Then she rooted around under the passenger seat for a map.

"C'mon. We have to get to Rockaway."

# 44

Rain had already begun to slash at the windshield by the time the microwave van crossed the bridge to Rockaway. The rain had driven most of the beach-combers off the dunes, and the glare from their headlights as they headed back to the city made Manuel slow down. They pulled into a traffic circle. On one side was Jacob Riis Park; on the other, the well-groomed seaside neighborhood of Neponsit.

Manuel was trying his best to break the tension, singing along with the radio, patting the dashboard as if it were a snare drum, and rocking his head from side to side.

"I'm gonna wait till the midnight hour," he sang—then in falsetto, "In the midnight hour," adding his own backup like a singer in a third-rate bar band. Manuel paused for a breath. "For an old song, it ain't bad. Where now, boss?" he asked as they eased around the circle again.

Kate caught a glimpse of the swelling waves beyond the tall, salt-stung trees. "Where would I go if I were Finn?" she asked herself out loud. Manuel went around the traffic circle again. "We need to get to the beach," she said, stalling.

Bernie whistled. "Any idea which beach? Rockaway is a pretty long island," said Manuel.

"If we get near Neponsit, maybe I'll be able to see a boat."

"I thought we were looking for your boyfriend," said Manuel, pulling into Jacob Riis Park.

"Yeah, we are. He's trying to stop a friend of his from getting a shipment of heroin tonight."

Her techs sat in stunned silence. The parking lot was still busy. Manuel pulled the van into neutral.

"You planning to get it on video?" said Manuel, half-joking.

"We've got to find them first."

Cars were draining from the parking lot when Kate stepped into the rain. She jogged down the concrete boardwalk. She saw a couple of intertwined teenagers, but no one who resembled Finn. In the shallow water she saw dozens of surfers chest high in the angry-looking waves. She looked beyond them. At the horizon, clouds were stacking up like poker chips. She could see the lights from a school of pleasure boats and a few fishing trawlers disappearing in the mist. Her panic was growing. She wasn't even sure what she was looking for.

She ran past the concession stand and the handball courts, then doubled back. The private Neponsit beach was separated from the public beach by a long stone jetty topped with a twenty-foot chain-link fence. In the no-man's-land between the public and the private beach was the Neponsit geriatric center, an ugly, modern seven-story building with windows that faced the surf. Kate stared past it. A gust of cool, wet air blew in with the crash of a wave, and Kate turned her head away. Facing the geriatric center she saw that each window framed a frail silhouette. The residents of the old folks home were staring out toward the jetty, pointing and nodding at the private beach. Kate began to run toward the jetty, leaping over slippery rocks and climbing sand cliffs that gave way as she clawed at the dune grass. She finally made it to the top of the jetty and leaned against the fence. She could see what had captured the eyes of the old folks. Two dozen flares were sputtering on the damp beach. She saw John Finn pull another flare from a large satchel, stick it in the sand, and light it.

* * *

Finn felt the flame of the flare singe his hand. In a strange way the pain was a relief. When he was a rookie, he'd arrested a Palestinian livery-cab driver who had driven up the West Side Highway randomly firing a .380 out the driver's-side window. Finn had always believed there were good people and bad people. The livery driver was Finn's first glimpse of random evil. He had walked out of Spofford after seeing Vinnie Minor with the sickening realization that Bigelow had victimized people whose faces he would never recall. Finn knew he had not behaved much better. Yesterday, after he'd visited Spofford, he'd woken up stone-cold sober and decided not to take any of Pauly MacKay's calls. He lay in bed, counting the dust webs on his ceiling, listening to Kate's persistent messages, trying to remember the twelve steps. He couldn't call her back. There was nothing she could say. She was the best thing that had ever happened to him, but she had left him alone on the bridge. She had walked away again, and in his heart he knew she was right to leave him now. For a brief flicker in time, he imagined a future for them. But without her, he couldn't imagine a future for himself.

A stoned-looking teenager in a rubber shirt and longish floral shorts stumbled by carrying a surfboard.

"Whew, man, is this some kind of satanic ritual?" he asked Finn, his jaw slack.

Finn straightened. "What are you doing here?"

"Everyone is coming down, man, all the big boards," the boy drawled with a Brooklyn accent inflected by California sun culture. "Radio says we got the biggest storm of the summer roaring in. That means the *surf is up*."

"You got to get people to stay away from here," said Finn urgently.

"Why, are you gonna, like, slaughter a chicken?"

"No, this is police business. You need to get out of here."

The boy's jaw bobbed up and down. "It's cool, I'm amblin'" And he walked off. Finn bent down.

If there was a higher power, like the people in AA talked about, he knew his higher power was giving him one last chance to even up the score. Finn stuck another flare in the sand. It was his last chance to do one good thing. Then he would end his life.

Kate was back in the van, frantically dialing the car phone and screaming at Manuel. "Just drive. Drive up to the jetty."

"The truck'll get stuck in the sand," said Bernie without emotion.

"I'll pay for the tow," said Kate.

"No, we'll bill it to CBS," Bernie said as Manuel rolled over the dunes.

"I need to have DeMaris paged. . . . Yes, it's an emergency. I'll wait." Her eyes were bleary. "Fishbach? Yes, patch me through. . . . Brian? It's Kate Murray. Your best shot at having a cooperating witness in the police corruption case is about to get killed by a dirty cop. . . . Yeah. John Finn. And I got a television crew ready to record the whole thing. If this goes down, DeMaris will never set foot in City Hall." She paused. "No, Finn didn't sign a cooperation agreement." She roundly cursed Fishbach's precise legal mind. She thought fast. "But nobody knows that but you and me and DeMaris. Remember Rodney King. Nobody remembered that he was clocked driving at one hundred fourteen miles an hour. Details like that tend to get lost on television. . . . Yeah, I'll hold, but not too long." Prosecutors never acted spontaneously. "Yeah. Neponsit beach, right near Jacob Riis Park. Now. Right now."

Through the windshield she saw Finn's outline straighten. She crashed out of the door and ran up to the fence. "John Finn, John Finn." The rain blew against her face and the ocean was roaring. The full force of the storm was coming on. Then the wind switched and she screamed again. Seeing him, she was struck with a powerful beam of understanding. It was the thing that old people celebrated when they held hands. As they held each other's wrinkled fingers, they were telling the world that they'd made peace with their destiny. Finn would never be an easy choice, but he was her choice. She thought of the phrase *until death do us part*. In all the years ahead of her, she would never have a deeper appreciation of those words.

Finn looked at her without recognition, then trudged two paces through the sand and stopped. He started to shout, but the wind was fierce and his words were scattered across the sand. He lifted a hand and made a weary gesture. Go home. Kate put the toe of her pump into the chain-link fence.

"I made a deal for you," she screamed. "The U.S. attorney said no jail time."

The storm was whipping sandwich wrappers and dried kelp off the beach. She couldn't tell if her voice had reached him.

"I did it because I love you."

Kate put the other toe of her pump in the fence. "John, don't do anything stupid." The wind was making her eyes stream. "I'm going to have your baby."

Finn cocked, listening as the wind brought her words, faint but clear, to his ear. He stood stock-still. Then he leaped up, punching the air with his fist in joy. He collapsed as his feet came down on the uneven beach, and he struggled to one knee. Ignoring the grit and the garbage blowing around him, he kept his face on Kate. Kate felt as if he were absorbing her, memorizing her, tucking this moment away in some deep, hidden pocket. She began to sob. He put his fist over his heart, stretched out his arms, and unclenched his fingers. Then he waved to her again. Go home.

Kate's words had traveled across the sand as clearly as if she had spoken them in his ear. "I'm going to have your baby." He felt his own life force, which had dwindled to a tiny ember, come roaring back. She wasn't walking away. She'd proved that to him now.

And he wanted to live forever. Suddenly, he was aware of how much danger he was in. He had to protect himself, protect her, and most of all, his son. He touched the holster under his arm. He turned sharply away from her. She would have to understand. He reached down to light a flare, still smiling. His baby. His little boy. He was putting another taper in the sand when he heard Bigelow's singing close behind him. "And the cat's in the cradle and the silver moon, da da da da and de dah."

"What's this, hombre?" Bigelow said, hearty. His face was pale and he was sweating. His eyes had sunk deeper into his skull, as if his face were collapsing around his enormous jaw. Finn was frantic to see if Kate had hidden herself, but he didn't dare look in her direction. He pulled out another taper.

"Money told me about the drug shipment," he said, speaking loudly over the wind. "I'm here to arrest you."

Bigelow started to laugh. "You don't know the first thing about it. If you follow the rules all your life, you'll never do anything. You've got to treat drug dealers like the scum they are. Use whatever means possible. Take their drugs, their money, whatever."

Finn straightened up, his face illuminated by the light of the flares dancing in the wind. They heard a small-craft horn sound from a nearby cruiser and the stupid surfers crying "Far out." A boat had been drawn to the light. He looked Bigelow full in the face.

"I've heard you say all that. But you're not supposed to keep the drugs and money for yourself," Finn said quietly. "That makes you a drug dealer, too."

Bigelow hooted. "I should suffer while some mid-level mutt is making millions? You must be drunk."

"I'm not."

Bigelow shrugged. "Then you're just stupid." Then he reached into his Operation Drug Free jacket, pulling a gun out of his underarm holster. "It doesn't matter. You can't stop me."

"Don't be so sure about that," Finn said quietly.

Kate ran back to the van to find Manuel and Bernie wearing big, dopey smiles.

"How come you didn't tell us you were pregnant?" said Manuel.

"I just found out. But forget that, run the wires out on the beach. See if you can frame a shot with those flares."

Manuel scrambled from the van and shouldered his camera.

"The water is full of surfers," said Manuel with his eye on the lens. "Are you sure there's some kind of drug deal happening here?"

Kate said nothing.

"Another guy just showed up. He looks Chinese," he informed Kate as if he were announcing for the Mets.

"What? What do you mean?" She was about to jump out of the sliding door when Landis's voice filled the van.

"Kate Murray, where the hell are you?" Kate exchanged guilty looks with Bernie, who shrugged. "If you guys can't give me a feed from the Caribbean Day parade, Kate is fired as of eleven-twenty. And you two techs are going to be fetching Geraldo's coffee until you retire at fifty."

Bernie hooted and slapped his knee. "I love the Geraldo show."

But Landis couldn't hear. Bernie hadn't depressed the receiver on the mike.

Kate shouted to Manuel, "Get the film rolling. We'll give him a feed if he wants one."

Manuel purposefully moved in for the shot.

Kate watched as the three men on the beach turned to face a small powerboat that was about one hundred yards off the shore. "You getting this?" she called to Manuel, who remained silent. She could see that the camera's red light was on. For a second, the three men stood frozen, then Bigelow lifted his arm and sparks leaped out of it. The Chinese man fell on the sand, his head in shadows.

"Sweet Jesus," Bernie said.

Kate dialed 911 on the van's phone. "I'd like to report that a police officer has been shot. On Neponsit beach in Rockaway."

"Is the Chinese guy a cop?" asked Bernie when she had hung up.

"No, he's probably a member of the Ghost Brigade. But a cop is about to get shot."

She picked up the microphone to speak to the studio.

"Listen, Steve, we just taped a corrupt cop killing a guy in cold blood. It's in the can. Now we're going to tape a cop collecting kilos of heroin on the beach at Rockaway. We'll give it to you for the top of the eleven o'clock."

Landis's voice came booming back. "Goddamn it, I want the parade. You're fired."

She turned down the volume. "Listen, Steve. This is going to make the bombs over Baghdad look like Oprah."

Landis paused.

"I want the parade," he said petulantly.

Finn, reeling from shock at the brutal assassination, had just drawn his gun when both men heard the splash and turned toward the surf. Bigelow raised his hands over his head in rage. "Not yet," he screamed. Then he began kicking the flares. "It's those goddamn flares and those idiot surfers. They probably think they're Navy SEALs or Coast Guard divers. They're throwing the kilos overboard."

Just then a huge wave sucked a deep trench about thirty feet from the shore, grew, and crashed down into it with a roar. Three surfers were tossed into the air like confetti. The wave pushed tidal debris higher on the shore, leaving behind a loose surfboard with a large dent, a brown bottle, a Burger King bag, and a slick, unworn tire. About twenty feet away from the tire, a crumpled surfer lay stunned on the sand.

Bigelow ran down to the tire like a fast-footed tern. He crouched over it, and for a second Finn thought Bigelow might throw his body on it, protecting it, holding it for his own. Instead he pulled a well-wrapped package out of the recess between the rubber sidewalls. The surfer lifted his head, then saw the dead Chinese man on the beach. Bigelow pointed a gun at the surfer. The boy dropped his head back in the sand and lay motionless.

Finn stepped forward and Bigelow straightened and pointed his gun at Finn's head, then swiveled to face the dry-docked surfer.

Finn crouched in a shooter's stance. Bigelow was a decent-size target with his hair plastered to his head with sweat and a dash of sand stuck to his cheek. The pupils of his bloodshot eyes were enormous, and his lips twitched. Finn couldn't pull the trigger.

He was afraid Bigelow would shoot the groggy kid in the same offhand way he had shot the Chinese gangster. "I'm not afraid of you," he said to distract Bigelow, realizing he was mouthing a line from a bad John Wayne movie. It was a lie. He had never been more afraid in his life. Bigelow turned his gun back to Finn. Godzilla would be afraid if he were looking down the barrel of a gun. What Finn meant to say was that fear wasn't going to stop him from doing what he had to do. But Bigelow began talking.

"You never suffered," said Bigelow. "You enjoyed the high life—all the money and the booze and the drugs." Finn could see bits of foam at the corner of his boss's mouth. "If it wasn't for me, you would never have picked yourself up out of your slump. I gave you back your life."

"You took away my future," screamed Finn.

"Fuck you." Bigelow squeezed off a shot, but his hand was shaking. The shot went wild. From far away, Finn heard a lone siren.

It took a minute for Kate to realize that a bullet had shattered the windshield of the van. Bernie, pale and sweating, gave a little wave and began to elevate the golden rods. Kate jumped out of the van, holding the mobile telephone. She stood dialing as Manuel framed a shot of the shattered glass as her backdrop.

She dialed Fink's number in the microwave room. As he picked up, she could hear the opening notes of the intro.

"Andrew, we're in the middle of filming a shoot-out in Rockaway. Can you preempt the first three stories?"

Fink was silent. "Landis hasn't given the okay."

"I know that, Andrew. We're transmitting. Can we preempt it?"

There was a long pause.

She strained to hear a sound. She hated television with all her heart. She hated not being in control of her story, the fact that technology inevitably had the last word on what was reported and how. She wanted to go back to newspapers where it was just you and the paper and your own rancid soul. She didn't know if Fink was listening to her or busy taking another feed. "You know, Andrew, you didn't have to hide from me," she said, more to herself than to him. "I don't care if you're in a wheelchair. I'm not interested in running the marathon with you. You still would have been my best friend at the station." She could hear the steady *chunka chunka* sound of a police helicopter nearby.

Andrew Fink coughed. "I'm not getting your signal." That meant he was trying to bring in their feed. She gave Manuel the thumbs-up.

"Help me, Andrew," she pleaded. "Tell me what you need Bernie to do."

"Scan in the direction of the newsroom."

Kate looked at the black sky and tried to figure out which direction was west. She made a circle in the air with her finger, and Bernie slowly rotated the heads of the golden rods.

He shook his head.

"No good," she said into the telephone.

She shook her head. "Go west, go north."

The receptor spun. Nothing.

"Andrew, I've got to make this work," Kate said desperately.

"Look around you." Andrew's voice was calm and clear. "Look for any vertical surface."

"It's the beach, Andrew. There is nothing here."

"A billboard, a building, we can try to bounce the signal off of almost anything."

At the far end of the parking lot, almost obscured by fog, an eighteen-wheeler appeared to have been abandoned.

She gestured to Bernie.

He shook his head, no way.

She nodded more vigorously. Slowly Bernie turned the receptor.

"You are received in transmission," said Andrew, unperturbed, as if he were pulling in the weekly feature on cute dogs up for adoption at the ASPCA. "Lock it down."

Kate stuck her hair behind her ears and tried to muster a friendly but concerned look.

"This is Kate Murray reporting from Rockaway, where we believe a corrupt police officer, the target of a federal probe, is engaged in a major drug transaction. He has already killed one man"—she signaled for Manuel to cue the tape—"and is holding a hostage, another, honest police officer who tried to stop him."

As Kate's broadcast of the shooting leaped into living rooms all over the tristate area, porch lights in houses all up and down Neponsit flicked on like a string of Christmas lights. It was Kate's own private Nielsen survey as jaded television watchers recognized a murder taking place in their own backyards.

Finn aimed his revolver at Bigelow's chest, but his finger would not flex. "I didn't take away a thing from you," Bigelow taunted him.

"You killed Versos and you pushed Money so hard he killed himself," Finn screamed back. His lungs were hurting now with the effort. "They were my friends."

His supervisor pointed his gun haphazardly at Finn and squeezed off another round. It went wild again. Bigelow's hand was still quivering from the shot when the white lights from the helicopter hit his face.

"What the fuck?"

The sirens were getting louder. The surfers who had managed to stay on their boards waved cheerfully at the helicopter overhead.

Finn was shouting above the sound of the surf and the helicopter. "And now you want me dead. Anyone. Anyone who stands in your way. I can see you clearly. You think you're such a man, but I'll tell you, you're the biggest criminal of them all."

Bigelow squinted at the surf, fired off another shot, then waded into the water to retrieve another tire.

Kate heard the high whine of bullets, but she just kept talking. "The gun battle continues here," she said, and took a few steps closer to the fence. Manuel followed. The helicopter searchlight illuminated seven or eight men crouched over machine guns.

"The federal SWAT team has arrived, but their apprehension of the shooter is handicapped by the presence of quite a few bystanders. They appear to be . . . surfing."

She couldn't see Finn. Her heart pounding, she took a few steps closer. Aside from the dead gangster and the quaking surfer, the beach was empty now. She felt a scream building in her chest. Then she spotted Bigelow and Finn bobbing in the water.

Bigelow was chest high in water, his gun held over his head. "I tried to help you," Finn's boss said. "I would have done anything for you." Bigelow took one more step and seemed to fall off a sandbar. He was in over his head. He paddled past a surfer and was engulfed in a wave. When it drew back, Finn couldn't see Bigelow's gun. He waded out after him, but immediately found himself fighting the water. He could hardly keep his footing against the undertow. It was pulling at his sodden pant leg, pulling him down.

"I loved you," Bigelow called out over the water. And then repeated it more quietly, as if he were talking to the churning waves.

Another large wave washed up to Bigelow's chest and a tiré thumped into him. Bigelow's head disappeared, resurfaced, and disappeared again.

Finn waded out a few more steps and reached out his hand. His supervisor resurfaced and grabbed Finn, pulling him deeper into the waves. Bigelow was pushing him under, and Finn realized he was drowning. He swallowed water, then more, then coughed before his face broke the surface. He tried to push Bigelow away, but the big man wouldn't let him go. He was vomiting but the water was pushing the fluid deeper inside him. Bigelow's hands were around Finn's throat, pushing him under the waves. He thought of his unborn son. Finn's face hit something and his mouth was full of silt. His fingernails dug deep into the sand. He broke the surface and sucked in a breath. Bigelow was standing about seven feet away. He was laughing. "I loved you," he said, ignoring a large tubular wave roaring toward him. Two surfers were riding its crest, yelping for joy. He waded toward Finn. Abruptly, the wave broke, and the surfers seemed to be tossed off a ledge. Finn saw the leg line on one of the surfer's boards snap, and the piece was carried along by the powerful tail of the wave. As the water crested with a roar over Bigelow, Finn heard a thunk. The Fiberglas board caught Bigelow solidly in the back of the head. Finn watched the wave exhaust itself against the shore and grow flat. He scanned the water but couldn't see Bigelow.

# Epilogue

Kate sat at her desk at the *Daily Herald,* grimly choking down a half quart of skim milk. She was past the point in her pregnancy when everyone thought she was fat—but she still didn't see any fecund glow in her face when she looked in the mirror. She was absently editing a 450-word story about an armored car robbery written by one of the *Herald*'s most promising reporters. The guard refused to hand over the money, she reported, and chased the armed robbers across a three-lane highway.

She picked up the telephone. "Your story is great, Gail, but you forgot one detail. Put in how much the guard makes a year. He saved the company three million dollars and he probably makes minimum wage."

She hung up the telephone and smiled. Gail Mazur, a demure City College grad, was turning the police department on its ear. Three detectives had called Kate to complain that they couldn't keep her away from a crime scene. They had already dubbed her Rocket Socks.

Kate tried to be diplomatic. She didn't want to lose another job this year. Less than twelve hours after the shoot-out on the beach at Rockaway, Bartlett had left a message on her answering machine telling her she was fired. Bob Baird from network loved aspects of the broadcast from Rockaway, she was told. He thought it was the kind of spontaneity they needed for *Eye Alive.* Unfortunately, he hated Kate's part of it.

She had to agree with him. She reviewed the tape over and over, and even a sympathetic viewer would have to admit that she looked like an escapee from a mental hospital. Her eyes were wild, her nose was running. At one point, with a chopper overhead and the sound of gunfire from the beach, Kate nervously wiped her nose on the back of her jacket sleeve. On live television. What Baird loved was how quickly Fink acted to shore up the technical side of what he proudly described to Fink as Channel 7's "television event." Baird ordered the microwave rooms for *Eye Alive* to be renovated to accommodate a wheelchair, and Andrew Fink wheeled himself out of Channel 7 forever.

The day after Kate got fired and Fink was hired for network, J.J. showed up with a gift-wrapped present. It was a photograph made from a still of Kate wiping her nose on her jacket. It was mounted and framed in oak. Kate hung the picture over her couch. Four weeks later, Solomon Randall offered her a job at the *Herald* editing crime stories, making about 20 percent less than she had made as a crime reporter there four months before. Kate, glad to be able to pay the rent, accepted the job. She didn't intend to make the *Herald* her life, but somehow BIG FOOT COMES TO BROOKLYN was a cheerier sight than the unemployment line. Finn would be out of detox in a few months, and DeMaris would have to decide if he needed Finn to testify against Bigelow. EMS had found Bigelow, unconscious but alive, about twenty yards down the beach. Most lawyers Kate talked to said they thought Bigelow would take a plea. The tapes Finn had made were just too damning.

She tightened up the lead on Mazur's story. She wasn't sure what was going to happen when Finn got out. She rubbed her stomach, resisting the urge to pull up her shirt and scratch like some kind of surly ape. On the days that he called, he seemed optimistic but he never spoke with any certainty about the future. Lately, he had begun peppering all their conversations with AA jargon about serenity and the higher power until Kate wanted to scream. Maybe the new Finn wouldn't get along with the old Kate, she thought to herself. Maybe after all that, he won't even like me. She looked down at her belly hidden under her smocky shirt. Maybe he won't like us, she corrected herself. Because ready or not, their daughter was on the way.

Fall Victim to Pulse-Pounding Thrillers
by *The New York Times*
Bestselling Author

# JOY FIELDING

## SEE JANE RUN
71152-4/$6.50 US

Her world suddenly shrouded by amnesia, Jane Whittaker wanders dazedly through Boston, her clothes blood-soaked and her pocket stuffed with $10,000. Where did she get it? And can she trust the charming man claiming to be her husband to help her untangle this murderous mystery?

## TELL ME NO SECRETS
72122-8/$5.99 US

Following the puzzling disappearance of a brutalized rape victim, prosecutor Jess Koster is lined up as the next target of an unknown stalker with murder on his mind.

## DON'T CRY NOW
71153-2/$6.99 US

Happily married Bonnie Wheeler is living the ideal life—until her husband's ex-wife turns up horribly murdered. And it looks to Bonnie as if she—and her innocent, beautiful daughter—may be next on the killer's list.

Buy these books at your local bookstore or use this coupon for ordering:

Mail to: Avon Books, Dept BP, Box 767, Rte 2, Dresden, TN 38225          E
Please send me the book(s) I have checked above.
❏ My check or money order—no cash or CODs please—for $_____is enclosed (please add $1.50 per order to cover postage and handling—Canadian residents add 7% GST).
❏ Charge my VISA/MC Acct#_____Exp Date_____
Minimum credit card order is two books or $7.50 (please add postage and handling charge of $1.50 per order—Canadian residents add 7% GST). For faster service, call 1-800-762-0779. Residents of Tennessee, please call 1-800-633-1607. Prices and numbers are subject to change without notice. Please allow six to eight weeks for delivery.

Name_____
Address_____
City_____State/Zip_____
Telephone No._____                    JOY 0396